LORD CALDWELL'S KISS

"You may feel you know me quite well by this time, my lord, but you see I have come to know you, too. During our acquaintance you have generally manifested one of two moods toward me: either angry or amorous. And as I wish to avoid any expression of the latter, I think it better to encourage the former."

A reluctant, answering smile spread over Lord Caldwell's face. "You do know me," he said. "But I don't think your plan is working, Catherine."

He took a step toward her. Catherine, retreating a step, stumbled over a tree root. Lord Caldwell hurried forward in time to catch her in his arms. Catherine laughed weakly.

"Now you are in truth my defender," she said. Lord Caldwell said nothing, but the expression on his face made Catherine catch her breath. "You can let go of me now, my lord," she said in a small voice. "It is not necessary to hold me any longer."

"Yes, it is. I'm afraid you'll slip away if I don't." Lord Caldwell looked down at her searchingly. "You won't slip away from me, will you, Catherine?"

Catherine did not answer the question directly. Instead she rolled her eyes heavenward and sighed. "What a fool I am," she said.

"And I am another," said Lord Caldwell. "But I mean to mend my foolish ways from now on, Catherine. And though it might not appear that way on the surface, I am convinced this is the best way to go about it."

Catherine arched an incredulous brow, but any reply she might have made was effectively stopped by Lord Caldwell's mouth. "Oh, Catherine," he whispered, as his arms tightened around her. "I've dreamed about doing this ever since I did it the first time. . . ."

Books by Joy Reed

AN INCONVENIENT ENGAGEMENT

TWELFTH NIGHT

THE SEDUCTION OF LADY CARROLL

MIDSUMMER MOON

LORD WYLAND TAKES A WIFE

THE DUKE AND MISS DENNY

A HOME FOR THE HOLIDAYS

LORD CALDWELL AND THE CAT

Published by Zebra Books

LORD CALDWELL AND THE CAT

Joy Reed

Zebra Books
Kensington Publishing Corp.
http://www.zebrabooks.com

For John Scognamiglio, with thanks

One

"I cannot tell you, Victor, how glad I am to have you back home again." Smiling, the Dowager Lady Caldwell stretched out her hand to her son across the breakfast table. "The house always seems so dull and empty when you are away."

Victor Caldwell, Fifth Baron Caldwell and Baronet Waterford, laughed indulgently as he kissed his mother's hand. "You can't be happier to see me back than I am to be here, Mama," he said. "London is confoundedly dull this time of year. Not that it's much better during the Season! Almost I am persuaded to give over visiting the Metropolis entirely and settle myself to becoming a proper, dull, stay-at-home country gentleman."

"I wish you would," said Lady Caldwell with a sigh. "You will think it very foolish of me, Victor, but I cannot think London at all a healthy place to live. The country is so much—safer."

Her son regarded her with a knowing smile. "Is it my physical health or my moral health that concerns you, Mama?" he said. "You needn't fear I've taken up with any more highfliers, if that's what you're worried about. I'd be afraid to do so again, knowing the neighbors' tendency to tell tales out of school!"

Lady Caldwell flushed and gave her son a reproachful look. "Now, Victor, you know Mr. Fawcett was not telling tales out of school. He merely thought I ought to be concerned—and so I was concerned. That woman had a dreadful reputation. If you had done yourself an injury on her account, I never would have gotten over it."

Victor laughed. "Just what injury did you expect me to do myself, Mama? I wasn't so mad as to marry Thérèse, if that's what you mean. Nor did I ever consider putting a period to my existence, even when her fancy passed on to someone else. I merely accepted it as a lesson in feminine nature and went on my way, slightly damaged as to pride and pocketbook, but otherwise unscathed."

Lady Caldwell gave him another reproving look. "All that's very well," she said. "But you know, Victor, a mother dislikes to see her son involved in that kind of—of entanglement."

Victor regarded her with affection. "I know it, Mama. You would much rather I married some nice girl and settled down to live at Queen's Close like you and Papa did."

"Yes, I would," said Lady Caldwell with spirit. There was a trace of wistfulness in her eyes as she regarded her son. "Is there no lady who appeals to you in that light, Victor? You have spent every Season in London for the last eight or nine years. I would have thought in that time you would have been bound to meet *someone.*"

"Oh, yes, dozens of someones," said Victor, laughing. "It was the difficulty of choosing between them that perplexed me! But I think perhaps I'm narrowing the field a bit. There's one candidate in particular who strikes me as a fit successor to you, Mama. I was within an ame's ace of proposing to her when I was in London last week, but at the last moment I got cold feet. So I decided to come home and let you buoy up my courage for the ordeal."

"Oh, Victor, have you in truth found someone?" In her excitement, Lady Caldwell dropped the roll she was buttering and caught her son's hand in hers. "Who is she, Victor? Shall I like her?"

"She is very beautiful, very accomplished, and very well bred, Mama. And I certainly hope you shall like her. Seeing that you've been after me to marry for these past six or seven years, I should think you would welcome any lady who showed herself willing to have me."

Lady Caldwell shook her head firmly. "Ah, no! I want more for you than that, Victor. If you truly mean to marry, you must be sure to choose the right lady, not just any lady willing to have you. But of course, I know how you like to joke." She regarded her son with affection. "And the truth is, I suppose, that almost any lady would be willing to have you. Sometimes, Victor, I think you're altogether too good-looking for your own good."

"You flatter me, Mama," said Victor, grinning.

"No, it's the truth." Lady Caldwell surveyed her son with pride, from the top of his dark head to the toes of his well-polished boots. "You *are* a handsome creature, and I have no doubt you have been spoilt abominably by all the admiration you have received ever since you began to appear in society. I only hope your paragon is willing to put up with you."

"Oh, I think so, Mama." Victor smiled complacently as he helped himself to cold beef. "I have no doubt we shall come to an understanding, assuming the dibs are in tune. Lady Anne comes of an expensive family, and her mama has hinted that I shall be expected to do something pretty handsome in the way of marriage settlements if I am to have the privilege of taking her daughter to wife."

"Indeed?" said Lady Caldwell, giving him a searching look. "Who exactly is this Lady Anne, Victor? If her family is expecting you to pay for the privilege of marrying her, they must consider themselves something out of the ordinary way."

"Oh, they do—assuredly they do! Lady Anne is a Stoddard, you see, and all that family fancy themselves a little too fine to mingle freely with the rest of us. Just between you and me, I'm not so sure the masculine Stoddards are anything special, but Lady Anne is certainly all that one could desire. She is a paragon in truth, just as you described her." Victor smiled at his mother. "You see I am mindful of what is due you, Mama. I would not bring home an inferior bride on any account."

Lady Caldwell nodded, but there was concern in her eyes as she regarded her son. "Of course I should try to love any girl you brought home as a bride, Victor, if only for your sake," she said. "But I hope—I hope you are not marrying out of a mistaken sense of concern for me. It may sound contradictory when I have been encouraging you for so many years to marry and settle down, but in truth I would rather you waited until you had found a lady you could really love and esteem."

Victor gave a vexed laugh. "Indeed, you are very hard to satisfy, Mama! Here I have gone to great pains to choose a bride whom I thought you must approve, and now you begin to find fault with me. I assure you, I esteem Lady Anne most truly."

"But do you love her?" asked Lady Caldwell anxiously.

Her son hesitated a moment, then responded reluctantly, trying to smile as he spoke. "Upon my word, Mama, you press me hard! If you will have it—no, I suppose I am not what would commonly be called 'in love' with Lady Anne. But I do not see that that makes a marriage between us any less eligible. The truth is, I suspect, that I am not a man capable of that particular romantic flight of fancy. I have the greatest admiration and respect for your sex, ma'am, but I am too much a realist to be swept off my feet by any lady, no matter how lovely, charming, or accomplished she might be."

Seeing that his mother was looking troubled by these words, he gave her an encouraging smile. "Please don't fret, Mama. You know all this discussion is entirely premature. I have not even proposed to Lady Anne yet—and if you don't like the idea of my doing so, then I shall give her up without a murmur. But I had supposed you would be more enthusiastic at the prospect of my marrying. Only think, Mama: My being wed to Lady Anne would mean you had a full-time companion here at Queen's Close—someone who would be here to keep you company when I was obliged to be away."

"That would be pleasant, of course," agreed Lady Caldwell. "Assuming the young lady was congenial, of course."

"I am sure you would find Lady Anne congenial," said Victor firmly. "She seems to me to embody every feminine grace and virtue. Of course she has not much in the way of a marriage portion—but fortunately I am not obliged to hang out for a rich wife. I can please myself in the matter of whom I marry, and the fact is that I have seen no other lady who pleases me so much as Lady Anne. And if I continue of the same mind for the next six months or so, I intend to make her an offer when I go up to London this spring."

Lady Caldwell merely shook her head at these words. "If you really loved her, Victor, you would not wait six months to propose to her," she said.

"Perhaps not, but that is my intention, Mama. I cannot help it if I have an unromantic soul. Now if you will kindly give over lecturing me, I would like to get on with my breakfast."

Recognizing the futility of arguing with her son while he was in this mood, Lady Caldwell meekly passed him the butter and jam and sat watching as he consumed his toast and eggs. "It's a beautiful day," she said. "Are you very busy this morning, Victor? I know you had mentioned meeting with your bailiff."

"Yes, but I told him I could not see him until tomorrow. I had thought to spend this first day with you, Mama, doing whatever you would like. I think I owe you that much, seeing that I have been away from you for the last few weeks."

"Oh, Victor, you *are* a good son!" said Lady Caldwell. In a burst of contrition, she added, "I'm sure I didn't mean to tease you about Lady Anne. It's only that I want you to be happy—"

"And I want you to be happy, too," said Victor, circumventing this subject with great firmness. "So you must tell me what you would like to do today, and we will do it. Shall I wind wool or play at backgammon—or would you prefer to go for a walk in the gardens? I would be happy to call the footmen to bring out your wheelchair."

"Oh, Victor, I am sure it is very noble of you to give up your whole day to entertain an invalid like me. But it happens there is something you can do for me that I would like even better than playing at backgammon or walking in the gardens. Do you remember my writing to you about my cousin, Martha Everhart?"

Victor frowned in an effort at recollection. "I think so. She was recently widowed, was she not?"

"Yes, and in great need of a home, poor dear. Apparently her husband made some unlucky speculations just before he died, so she and her little girl were left practically penniless. I wrote to ask if you were willing they should have Crossroads Cottage to live in. You know it has been standing empty since Will Sturges and his wife went to live with his mother in Winchelsea."

"Of course," said Victor with a smile. "I remember the matter very well now. You know I am always glad to assist any protégés of yours, Mama. And these Everharts sound most worthy people."

"Oh, they are, my dear. At least Martha is, though I believe her daughter is no more than a child." Lady Caldwell's face took on a reminiscent look. "Martha and I were very close growing up, more like sisters than cousins. We both made our bows the same Season, and she was bridesmaid at my wedding. But we drifted apart soon after that. And of course, now that I am such a sad invalid, it has prevented me from seeing most of my friends and relations as regularly as I would like." Lady Caldwell looked down at her withered limbs with a grimace. "But even if we have not seen each other in twenty years or so, Martha and I have always kept up a correspondence. And when I learned she was in difficulties, I was very glad to offer her Crossroads Cottage."

"Yes, it is a comfort to be in a position to offer charity to worthy objects," agreed Victor. "Does your cousin plan to move here very soon?"

"Today, dearest. In fact, I believe she is already moved in, for she sent a servant over last night to ask for the key and to find out what rent we were asking for the cottage. Of course I sent a message back saying no rent was necessary among such close relations. And I also took the liberty of sending over a few dozen eggs and some garden produce."

"Very proper, Mama," said Victor with a smile. "Now I suppose you wish me to call on your cousin in person and make her welcome?"

"If you would be so kind, dearest. You know I would go myself, but it's such a fuss getting in and out of the carriage when one must be carried every step of the way." Again Lady Caldwell looked ruefully at her useless limbs. "I would be so grateful if you would act as my emissary."

"Of course," said Victor. "I would be very happy to call on your cousin."

Saying happily that she possessed the best of all possible sons, Lady Caldwell settled down to give more specific instructions. "Give Martha my warmest compliments, if you please, and apologize that I was unable to pay them in person. Tell her I will invite her and her daughter to dine with us as soon as they are settled. And find out if she needs anything besides eggs and garden produce. It must be so uncomfortable for her, for she is scarcely out of deep mourning, besides being a stranger in the neighborhood. And with a child to attend to, too! I would not like to leave any attention undone."

"Certainly not," agreed Victor, rising from the table. He dropped an affectionate kiss on his mother's brow. "I'll see to everything, Mama. Just you leave it all to me."

Two

As Victor prepared to set off for Crossroads Cottage, it occurred to him that there was nothing to prevent him from combining his mother's business with a certain amount of personal pleasure. The day was a fine one, and the home woods, through which he must pass to reach the cottage, were temptingly full of grouse, wood pigeons, and other small game. Accordingly, he provided himself with his gun, his shot belt, and his favorite dog; then he set off through the woods toward Crossroads Cottage.

It was certainly a very fine day. The woods were bright with dappled sunlight and alive with the music of birdsong. Victor strode along, taking deep breaths of the woods-scented air and noting that the trees were just beginning to change their summer foliage for the richer tints of autumn. Beau, his dog, trotted beside him, stopping now and then to nose some particularly enticing scent. Occasionally he would break into an ecstatic frisk as though he, too, were rejoicing in the beauty of the day.

"It is a lovely day, isn't it, old fellow?" said Victor, smiling at the dog's capers. "I don't even mind that we haven't seen any game so far. It's enough just to be outside on a day like this."

So lovely was the day, indeed, that Victor was tempted to declare with the poet:

> God's in his heaven,
> All's right with the world.

He looked about him with content. It did seem at that moment as though all the world was right with him. Here he was, on his own well-managed estate, free to enjoy the beauty of an exceptionally fine September day. He had an old and respected name, excellent health, and (though it ill became him to boast of it) a degree of good looks well beyond the average. And he had riches enough not only to allow him and his family to live a most comfortable existence, but to enjoy the additional pleasure of indulging their charitable impulses.

His mind dwelt with pleasure upon his present errand. It was true that Mrs. Everhart and her daughter held little interest for him personally; a man in his position could scarcely have much personal interest in an indigent widow and a little girl. But as objects of charity they must be both interesting and satisfactory. Victor smiled to himself, anticipating the widow's grateful thanks and the orphan's tearful smiles as he welcomed them to their new home. Truly, he was a magnanimous man to be bestowing a cottage rent free upon such individuals!

These enjoyable reflections occupied him all the way through the woods. At last, after about a half hour's walk, the trees began to thin, and the heavy growth of beech and fir was replaced by scrub pine and underbrush. Crossroads Cottage lay only a little farther on, its front windows overlooking the crossroads from which it had taken its name. Through the trees, Victor could glimpse the cottage's vine-covered chimney and a gable or two. He paused to shoulder his gun and straighten his hat upon his head before opening the gate that led into the cottage grounds.

At that moment, Beau let out an excited bark. He had been running along with his nose to the ground, but now he began to circle the ground, snuffling closely and uttering periodic yelps. Suddenly he lifted his head, let out an ecstatic *woof* and broke into a run, disappearing around the corner of the cottage.

"Must have scented a rabbit," muttered Victor to himself. He could hear Beau barking in a staccato manner somewhere ahead of him. Gradually the barks escalated to a positive frenzy of canine delight.

He's cornered it, thought Victor. He began to hasten his own steps along the path. Hardly had he done so, however, when there came a yelp of surprise and pain, and Beau came hurtling back along the path. Victor, observing him with surprise, saw there was a set of deep, bloody scratches across his nose.

"Good God!" said Victor. "Must have been a badger, not a rabbit, eh, old fellow? Let's go and see."

He set off down the path with Beau following him at a cautious distance. It was clear that the dog was not eager to reengage his late adversary. Indeed, as they approached the cottage, Beau hung back, whining, and refused to go any farther.

"Come on, old fellow," said Victor encouragingly. "We'll not let old Brock take another swipe at you." Beau whined and consented to go a few steps farther, but it was evident he was reluctant. "Stay there then," said Victor in exasperation, and strode round the corner of the cottage. Beau followed after him, still whining, at a distance of some twenty paces.

"Get that dog out of here!"

Victor halted in surprise. The words, spoken in a furious voice, had seemed to come out of nowhere. "Get that dog out of here!" repeated the voice, and Victor, turning with surprise, found himself face-to-face with a young woman. She was a tall young woman with red hair and green eyes, and in her arms she clutched a large ginger cat, whose eyes were as green as her own. "Are you deaf, sir?" she said, her eyes snapping with ire. "I said to get that dog out of here!"

"I beg your pardon," said Victor, recovering from his first surprise. He had thought at first he was being assailed by an avenging fury. Now he saw that the girl was merely some kind of maidservant. There was a mobcap atop her red-gold curls, and an apron streaked with grime covered her rather shabby gown of blue cambric. "I beg your pardon," he repeated, lifting his hat and giving her the smile that had never failed to charm women of both high and low station. "I have come to call upon your mistress. Is she—"

"I have asked you three times to get your dog out of here,"

said the girl, speaking with cold precision. "If you do not do so this minute, I shall take the broom to him."

Surprised and mortified by the failure of his much vaunted charm, Victor turned to look at Beau. The dog had retreated some paces and stood hovering anxiously near the corner of the house. "He is doing no harm," said Victor.

"No harm *now*," said the girl. "But only a few minutes ago he attacked my cat most savagely, right here in the yard. I saw the whole thing from the porch. Poor Ginger!" She cuddled the cat in her arms. "I am sure he was frightened out of at least eight of his nine lives."

Now it happened that Victor disliked cats. He especially disliked the look of this particular cat, an overgrown creature who (he fancied) was regarding him smugly from its refuge in the girl's arms. However, he sought to be conciliating. "I'm sorry, ma'am," he told the girl. "I did not know there was a cat living here. I thought Beau had merely cornered a rabbit or something of the sort."

"Well, you ought to have made sure before you allowed him on other people's property," said the girl, not in the least conciliated by Victor's words. "I should think you would be ashamed of yourself, encouraging your dog to attack a defenseless creature so much smaller than himself!"

Victor looked with distaste at the cat. "If you're talking about that beast, ma'am, he's about as defenseless as Boney's armies," he retorted. "Let me remind you that it is my pet who sustained the injuries in this encounter."

"And so it should be, seeing that he was the aggressor," returned the girl with unanswerable logic. "Now will you take him off my property, sir, or must I get my broom?"

Victor regarded her incredulously. "Your property!" he said. "My dear, ma'am, I'll have you know that this is *my* property."

"Your property?" exclaimed the girl, looking as incredulous as he. "But you cannot be—are you—?"

"Victor Caldwell, at your service," said Victor, sweeping her an ironic bow. "I have come to call upon Mrs. Everhart and her daughter."

He observed with satisfaction that these words seemed to have rendered the girl speechless. But when she finally did speak again, her voice and attitude were quite as belligerent as before. "I must say, my lord, that I think it very bad of you not to have declared yourself sooner. You should have told me immediately that you were Lord Caldwell."

"You gave me no chance to tell you who I was!" exclaimed Victor. "I was attacked as soon as I came into sight! And thereafter I was too busy defending myself to make any declaration at all."

Something that might have been a grudging smile flickered across the girl's face. "Perhaps I was rather hasty," she conceded. "But you must see that I was upset about my cat being attacked. Poor Ginger is no longer so young as he once was, and I am afraid the business of moving has been hard on him." She ran a caressing hand over the cat's fur. "He would not leave my room at all last night. Today was the first time he has ventured outside since we arrived here. And then, almost as soon as he did, he was attacked by your dog!"

"He seems to be able to defend himself quite well in spite of being a valetudinarian," said Victor encouragingly. "Poor Beau was put to the rout most decisively. And you can see he is very reluctant to reenter the fray."

The girl glanced to where Beau stood nervously hovering near the corner of the house, looking as though the slightest move would suffice to put him to flight. "He does seem to have learned his lesson," she agreed. "Very well, my lord. I shall suffer your dog to remain so long as he behaves himself."

Victor was amazed by this assumption of authority on the girl's part. He supposed it must be an eccentricity of Mrs. Everhart's to allow her maidservants such freedom of action and expression. But in mitigation of this eccentricity, the girl did seem to be unusually well spoken for a servant, and it was easy to see that she possessed a forceful personality. Victor was not eager to cross swords with her again and so decided to let her rather arrogant statement pass unchallenged. He merely smiled and said, "I am glad we have that matter settled, ma'am. Now if you would show me into the house, I would appreciate it very much. I am most eager to make the acquaintance of Mrs. Everhart and her daughter."

The girl laughed. "You have already made the acquaintance of her daughter," she said. "I am Catherine Everhart."

Victor was staggered. He stood with his mouth open, regarding the girl with doubt and astonishment. "You are Mrs. Everhart's daughter?" he said.

"Yes, I am," said the girl. She lifted her chin and fixed him with a gaze that held a strong flavor of her former hostility. "Is there any reason why I should not be?"

"None whatever, ma'am," said Victor hastily. "It is only that I was told that Mrs. Everhart's daughter was a little girl."

Catherine smiled in an incredulous manner. "You can see for yourself that I am not a little girl, my lord," she said.

Victor, running an eye over her figure, was obliged to admit the truth of this statement. There could be no doubt that Catherine was fully grown—and rather nicely grown, too, if one were to judge the matter impartially. But Victor was no impartial judge, and any admiration he might have felt was lost in a growing sense of resentment. He felt once more that Catherine had put him at a disadvantage. Already he had taken a dislike to her, seeing her as a quarrelsome female, and now he was obliged to own that same quarrelsome female as a relation!

With an effort, Victor summoned up a smile. "Yes, of course I can see you are not a child," he told Catherine. "I have my mother to blame for my falling into such an error. She said distinctly that her cousin's daughter was only a child, and I took her statement at face value. I should have remembered that Mama, like many older people, does occasionally lose track of the passage of time. Why, she still insists on referring to me as a boy now and then!"

He followed up this speech with another would-be ingratiating smile. After a moment, Catherine returned it. "Of course, my lord," she said. "My mother, too, is prone to such errors. I only hope Lady Caldwell will not be disappointed to find me so different from her expectations."

Victor thought to himself that her disappointment could be nothing compared to his. But he was too polite to voice such sentiments. He merely said, "I am sure my mother will be delighted to make your acquaintance, Miss Everhart. Or should I say rather Cousin Catherine? We *are* cousins, you know, if only second cousins—or would it be cousins once removed? I never can keep those distinctions clear in my mind."

Catherine said that she never could either, but that she had no objection to his calling her Catherine. Victor thought he detected a slight mellowing in her manner as she made this speech. Perhaps she was, after all, willing to act the role of the grateful orphan, and he might now reap some of the gratification he had anticipated earlier. He put on his best lord-of-the-manor air.

"I hope you and your mother will be very comfortable here, Cousin. My mother has charged me to give you her compliments and to ask if there is anything we can do to assist you in getting settled. Have you need of fruit or game or garden produce?"

"No, thank you, my lord," said Catherine, shaking her ginger-colored curls with a decided air. "You and your mother have already been most generous in that direction. But that reminds me: We have not yet settled the matter of the rent on the cottage. Mother and I sent a servant over last night to inquire about it, but she seems not to have made herself understood."

"On the contrary, Cousin," said Victor with his most magnanimous smile. "It is she who failed to make *you* understand. There is no rent to be paid on Crossroads Cottage. I am happy to be able to provide a home for you and your mother as long as you need it."

Catherine's brows drew together. "That is very kind of you, my lord, but my mother and I could not think of accepting such a gift," she said coldly. "I must insist that we pay for the use of the cottage. If you will tell me what is the amount of the rent,

I will give it to you now. I assure you we have funds enough for the purpose."

Victor felt his ire rising once again. His magnanimous gesture had been rejected—without hesitation and with hardly a word of thanks! His own brows drew together. "I don't doubt you have the funds, Cousin, but I must beg you to save them for some other purpose," he retorted. "I will accept no rent on this cottage."

Catherine's eyes flashed fire. "Then I am afraid my mother and I shall have to find some other dwelling," she said. "We are certainly not so rich as we once were, but we are not so poor that we must accept charity."

"Don't be ridiculous," said Victor angrily. "It is not charity I am offering, but merely a friendly arrangement between relations. The fact is that my income is quite equal to my needs without taking your money—"

"And ours is quite equal to paying a reasonable rent," returned Catherine. "Therefore, I must insist upon your accepting payment for the cottage, my lord. If you will not name a fair price for its use, then Mother and I will be forced to go elsewhere."

Victor, surveying her with dislike, thought he had never met with a more cross-grained female. It was obvious that she intended to give not a single inch on this or any other issue. Catherine's eyes were bright with defiance, and she stared at him belligerently, one hand still absently stroking the cat in her arms.

As Victor was meditating whether or not to accept her ultimatum, the door of the cottage opened, and a middle-aged woman came onto the porch. "Catherine dear, are you done with those—" she began, then caught sight of Catherine and Victor standing together. "Oh, there you are, my dear!" she said. "I did not know you had company."

"Yes, Mother," said Catherine, reluctantly shifting her gaze from Victor to the woman on the porch. "This is Lord Caldwell, the owner of our property. He has come to call on us."

"Indeed!" said the woman. A broad smile spread across her face. She came hurrying down the steps to where Victor was standing. "I need not tell you what a pleasure this is, my lord," she said, curtsying. "My daughter and I are delighted to make your acquaintance."

Victor, politely returning her salutation, felt himself to be on solid ground once more. He had liked this sweet-faced, gray-haired lady on sight, and her manner toward him was warmly grateful—just what one would desire in a distant cousin and prospective tenant. It was certainly very different from what her daughter's had been! As Victor relayed his mother's greetings a second time, a Machiavellian idea popped into his mind. Catherine might have refused to accept the cottage rent free, but in actual fact she was in no position to refuse it. The offer had been tendered to her mother, not to her, and he felt confident he could overcome any scruples Mrs. Everhart might feel. Smiling inwardly, he settled himself to outwit his adversary.

"My dear ma'am, I find there has been some question as to the terms of your occupancy here," he told Mrs. Everhart. "I was just talking to your daughter, and she seems to have the idea that you were to pay something in the way of rent. I beg you will relieve your mind of such an apprehension. It is my pleasure to bestow the use of the cottage upon you rent free, for as long as you care to inhabit it."

Mrs. Everhart's eyes grew wide with surprise and pleasure. "Why, that is very kind of you, my lord," she said. "I do appreciate your generosity, and so does Catherine, I know. But of course, we would not dream of accepting the cottage without paying something for its use."

"You wouldn't?" said Victor stupidly.

"No, it is quite out of the question." Mrs. Everhart spoke pleasantly, but there was a finality in her voice that did not admit of further argument. Victor, stealing a look at Catherine, surprised a triumphant grin on her face. His feeling of dislike increased. Really, she was the most cross-grained girl!

Mrs. Everhart, meanwhile, had gone on speaking. "If you will tell us what rent you ask for the cottage, my lord, we would be very happy to pay it to you now. Please do not be offended that we must decline your most generous offer." She gave him a smile that did much to ease the sting of her refusal. "You have been very generous already, you know, sending us eggs and all that lovely garden produce. I should be ashamed to take any more from you."

Victor made one last effort. "But you should not be ashamed, ma'am," he said. "We are relations, you know."

"Yes, we are relations, and that is why I was happy to accept your mother's offer to come and live here in the first place. But I think Catherine and I would both be more comfortable if we kept this particular matter on a business footing."

"Of course," said Victor, accepting defeat with good grace. He named a small figure for the cottage's rent, and though Mrs. Everhart shook her head and declared that it was too small by half, she was eventually brought to agree to it. This was some balm for Victor's wounded feelings.

"You are just like your mother," said Mrs. Everhart, smiling as she paid over the agreed sum. "Sophronia always was the most generous creature. You favor her in looks, too, though perhaps you resemble your father more." She surveyed Victor with reminiscent eyes. "Indeed, you have a great look of him, my lord. He was always accounted a most handsome man."

This speech elicited a noise from Catherine that sounded suspiciously like a snort. When Victor looked in her direction, however, he found her face bland and innocent. "I thank you for the compliment, ma'am," he said, bowing to Mrs. Everhart. "It has been a pleasure to make your acquaintance. And yours, too, Cousin," he added, forcing himself to smile at Catherine.

Catherine smiled frigidly in return and gave him the smallest of possible bows. Victor eyed her with dislike and turned away. Having assured Mrs. Everhart that he would convey her thanks to his mother, he whistled to the chastened Beau and set off through the woods in a thoroughly disgruntled mood.

Three

Having bade Victor farewell and accompanied him as far as the cottage gate, Mrs. Everhart returned to where her daughter still stood beside the porch.

"What a delightful man is Lord Caldwell," she said happily. "I thought him most pleasant, did not you, Catherine dear? Such amiable manners, without the least height or condescension."

"I thought him *very* condescending," said Catherine. She stooped to set Ginger on his feet, then straightened up and fixed her mother with a stern gaze. "To my mind, Lord Caldwell is a rude, conceited, overbearing beast."

"Oh, Catherine, how can you say so?" said Mrs. Everhart, regarding her daughter with pained surprise. "When he was so generous, too! Why, he wanted to *give* us the use of the cottage—give it to us without our paying a penny of rent."

"To be sure he did. His generosity is part and parcel of his conceit." Catherine picked up a rug that was lying nearby and began to shake it out with more energy than was strictly necessary. "It makes our noble cousin feel even more noble when he thinks he can treat us as paupers," she said angrily, between shakes. "I was glad you told him plainly that we wanted none of his charity, Mother."

"Yes, to be sure, I did. But you know, I cannot help feeling you wrong Lord Caldwell, Catherine. I am sure he had no motive beyond being kind."

"Rubbish," said Catherine, putting down the rug she had been shaking and picking up another. "I took his measure at a glance, Mother. He's one of those men who fancies himself a Lord Bountiful, distributing his largesse among the poor. I simply can't bear that kind of condescension."

Mrs. Everhart sighed. "I know you cannot, dear," she said sadly. "But I do wish you would try not to take offense when people make what are meant to be kind gestures. I am quite sure Lord Caldwell had no thought of offending you. Indeed, he has behaved very generously toward us both. And even if we cannot accept the cottage on the terms he suggested, we can still be grateful that we have such a pleasant and economical place to live. I do not know where we would have gone if he had not offered us this cottage."

Mrs. Everhart's eyes filled with tears as she spoke these words. Catherine saw them, and her heart was filled with contrition. Putting down the rug she was beating, she came over and put her arm around her mother.

"Don't cry, Mother," she said gently. "We *are* here, and that's the chief thing. And I am sure that if your cousin had not written and offered us this cottage, something else would have turned up. Why, if worse came to worst, we might have bought a horse and a wagon and lived like the Gypsies!"

This sally produced a wan smile from Mrs. Everhart. "I am glad it did not come to that, my dear," she said, wiping her eyes. "Of course this place is a good deal smaller than our old home." She cast a deprecating look at the cottage behind them. "But I have no doubt we shall be very happy here, once we are settled in."

"Of course we shall," said Catherine firmly. "I haven't the least doubt of it."

"I am glad to hear you say so, my dear." There was concern in Mrs. Everhart's eyes as she regarded her daughter. "Of course these next few weeks cannot help but be a little strange and difficult for us. Especially since we have been through so many difficulties already. First your father dying so suddenly as he did—and then to learn we must give up our house and most of our things and relocate to a little out-of-the-way place like this! I feel it most on your account, Catherine dear. Anything will do for me, for now that your father is gone, I have no wish to figure in society. But for you, who are young and just beginning your life, it seems almost a tragedy."

"Nonsense," said Catherine, giving her mother another hug. "You know I never cared for Bath society above half, Mother. And though this has certainly been a painful experience, it's not been without its educational aspects as well."

"Educational?" repeated Mrs. Everhart, giving her daughter a worried look. "Whatever do you mean, Catherine?"

"Why, only what philosophers have been saying for centuries. There's nothing like a touch of adversity to show you who your friends really are."

Catherine smiled as she spoke, but there was an undertone of bitterness in her voice. Her mother gave her another worried look. "You are talking about your engagement, I suppose," she said. "Indeed, Catherine, I do feel badly about that. Are you sure—quite, quite sure—that everything is over?"

"Quite sure," said Catherine. She spoke shortly, but there was a touch of rueful amusement in her eyes as she turned to her mother. "Never mind, Mother. I am sure things are better as they are. Truly, I ought to be rejoicing that I found out my prospective bridegroom was worthless before the wedding—rather than waiting till afterward like most women!"

"Oh, Catherine, I do not like to hear you talk that way," protested Mrs. Everhart. "It sounds quite cynical and ill natured."

Catherine resisted the urge to say, *I feel cynical and ill natured.* Instead she gave a little laugh. "Oh, it's not so bad as that, Mother. I am merely in a foul mood today. I'm afraid heavy housework does not agree with me." She looked ruefully down at her apron. "It's very lowering to have to do one's own scrubbing and sweeping and scouring. I think Lord Caldwell took me for a maidservant when he first arrived!"

"Well, I am sure you have no one to blame but yourself for

that, dearest. You know I told you to leave those rugs for Mary Ann and Emily to do. Indeed, there is not the least reason why you need do more than unpack your own personal things."

"There is if I want anywhere clean to unpack them to," said Catherine. "You know we have not a dozen servants to tend to us anymore, Mother. I thought it more important that Mary Ann and Emily should concentrate on getting the kitchen in order so we might have a hot meal tonight instead of another round of bread and cheese."

Mrs. Everhart agreed to this statement, but in a slightly absent voice. It was clear that her daughter's words had suggested another train of thought to her. The nature of that train of thought was made clear by her next words. "I suppose we shall soon be invited to dine at Queen's Close. Lord Caldwell said Sophronia intends to ask us as soon as we are settled."

"More Lord Bountiful," said Catherine in an acid voice.

Her mother regarded her with exasperation. "I thought it a very kind, neighborly thing to do! Why have you taken such a dislike to that young man, Catherine? I am sure you are being quite unjust."

"It is merely that I have no use for men of Lord Caldwell's stamp," said Catherine. "Particularly ones who have such a very good opinion of themselves!"

"Well, I am sure that if anyone has a right to have a good opinion of himself, it must be Lord Caldwell," said Mrs. Everhart stoutly. "By all Sophronia tells me, he is a model son and an excellent landlord. We know firsthand his generosity to those in need. And of course he is remarkably handsome, too."

"Yes, and how well he knows it!" said Catherine. But Mrs. Everhart looked so distressed by this statement that she swallowed the rest of her criticism and gave her mother another hug. "There, Mother, I shan't abuse Lord Caldwell if you don't like it. I suppose we *are* indebted to him for giving us a place to live. And I daresay I won't be obliged to bear with his condescension very often, for it stands to reason that the owner of Queen's

Close will have little to do with a couple of indigent females living in a cottage."

"No, though we *are* cousins," agreed Mrs. Everhart. "But whatever you may say about Lord Caldwell's conceit, dearest, you must at least admit that he was not too proud to acknowledge the connection!"

"I think in my case, he would have been glad to disavow it if he could," said Catherine ruefully. She recalled once more her initial encounter with her noble cousin: the opening confrontation over the dog, leading into the argument about the cottage rent and his attempts to bully her into submission. Truly, he was a most pigheaded, infuriating man. And the fact he had taken her for a maidservant at first glance did not tend to make her like him better.

Of course she cared nothing for Lord Caldwell's good opinion. He was welcome to think her anything he chose, but she could not help feeling resentful when she remembered how his eyes had glanced over her and then quickly dismissed her. "As though I were a menial," Catherine told herself with scorn. "Does the man suppose a woman wears her best dress to unpack and sweep floors?"

Such thoughts were clearly unprofitable, however. Catherine stooped to pick up the rugs she had beaten. "Come, Mother," she said cheerfully. "Our rooms are all swept now, and I have these rugs ready to put down. And if we hurry, we may have our bedchambers in order by tonight."

Victor, as he retraced his steps through the woods, was oblivious alike to birdsong, dappled sunlight, and Beau's frolickings. He stalked along, his earlier happy mood gone as if it had never existed. When a flock of grouse flew up practically in his face, he regarded them blankly and never raised his gun. When Beau startled a plump rabbit from a nearby covert, Victor ordered the dog back to his side with a curt command. He had no thought for sport at that moment. He was thinking of his cousin Catherine.

Truly, she was the most vexatious, cross-grained girl. On that opinion Victor was quite decided. He fumed as he recalled the brusque way she had rejected his efforts to waive the rent on the cottage. Even worse was the way she had openly jeered at him when her mother had endorsed her refusal. He bore no ill will toward Mrs. Everhart, for she had refused his offer gently and with suitable expressions of gratitude. But Catherine had behaved as if he had offered her a mortal insult rather than a rent-free house to live in!

This injustice continued to rankle in Victor's mind all the way home. He was still in a bad mood as he entered the house and divested himself of his hat, gun, and shotbelt. Having entrusted these articles to a footman, he went to the drawing room, where his mother was eagerly awaiting him.

"Have you been to the cottage, Victor? Are Martha and her daughter there yet? And did you find out if there is anything we might do to assist them?"

Victor gave a disagreeable laugh. "Yes, I have been to Crossroads Cottage, Mama," he said. "I saw both Mrs. Everhart and her daughter. And speaking of her daughter, I take it very ill that you should have misled me on that subject. Cousin Catherine is not a little girl at all, but rather a young woman of at least one- or two-and-twenty."

"Is she indeed!" exclaimed Lady Caldwell. "I might have known it, I suppose, for I remember now that she was born the year you went off to Eton. And that would have been just over twenty years ago. Catherine is her name, you say? To be sure, I ought to have remembered that from Martha's letters, but my memory is so poor nowadays. Is she a good-looking girl?"

"No," said Victor in an uncompromising voice. "She is exceedingly plain."

"Indeed!" said Lady Caldwell in surprise. "Well, I should never have suspected *that*. Martha was one of the prettiest girls I ever knew. What does Catherine look like?"

"She has red hair, green eyes, and a most disagreeable countenance. I'm fairly sure she has freckles, too." Thinking back, Victor could clearly recall a sprinkling of freckles across the bridge of Catherine's nose. "Yes, freckles," he said with satisfaction. "In fact, she is a positive antidote."

"Poor girl, that is very unfortunate," said Lady Caldwell with sympathy. "But I daresay she is nonetheless agreeable for that. I have often observed that very pretty girls do not cultivate their powers of conversation so assiduously as plainer ones."

"You are quite out in your reckoning there, Mama," said Victor with a mirthless laugh. "Cousin Catherine's personality is as disagreeable as her appearance. I never met a less prepossessing girl."

"Well, that is very bad, Victor. But are you sure you are being entirely fair to your cousin? You could scarcely have had the opportunity to discover how agreeable she is in the short time you were at the cottage today."

Victor had no desire to go into the details of his encounter with Catherine. He sought to change the subject. "At any rate, I found Mrs. Everhart very agreeable," he said. "We talked a bit, and she begged me to send you her compliments, along with her thanks for the eggs and garden stuff. She seems a very pleasant, well-bred lady."

"Yes, I always liked Martha," said Lady Caldwell with satisfaction. "It will be delightful to have her where I can see her often. I must start planning a party so 1 can introduce her to the neighborhood. It has been over a year now since Mr. Everhart died, so there can be no objection to her and Catherine attending a party."

Victor gave an unenthusiastic assent to this proposition. He had no objection to inviting Mrs. Everhart to his home, but it went against the grain to think of entertaining her spitfire daughter.

"I shall be ashamed to acknowledge her as a relation before the neighbors," he told himself. "A haughty, ill-favored, disagreeable girl—and a very dowdy dresser, too. I'm no authority on lady's clothes, but even I know that dress she was wearing was years out-of-date." He did not express these sentiments to his mother, however. Lady Caldwell spent the rest of the day very happily occupied in planning a party to introduce the Everharts to the neighborhood.

Four

Victor's feelings about his cousin underwent no change in the weeks that followed. He was very busy during this time, attending to business about his estate and taking advantage of the newly opened partridge season. Even so, however, he found his thoughts turning frequently to the occupants of Crossroads Cottage. Once he even made an excuse to ride past the cottage, but he caught no glimpse of Catherine. He found himself actually sorry for this circumstance. It was not that he really wished to see his cousin, of course, but his pride still smarted from the blow it had sustained during their last encounter.

Victor told himself that he must have been in a very weak and spiritless mood that day to allow a girl like Catherine to ride over him roughshod. He resolved that such a thing should never happen again. Now that he knew his cousin's nature and had recovered from his initial defeat at her hands, he was eager to engage her in combat again and perhaps this time succeed in besting her.

Lady Caldwell's party for the Everharts had been fixed for a date about two weeks after their arrival at the cottage. It was to be a dinner party, with some two dozen of their neighbors invited to meet these newcomers to the area.

Early on the day of the party, Victor ordered an extravagant quantity of fish, fruit, and fowl to be delivered to Crossroads Cottage. Remembering Catherine's earlier strictures on charity, he felt sure this generous gift would raise her ire, and he mentally rubbed his hands together at the thought of their coming encounter. He counted on her mother's presence and that of the other guests to keep Catherine from making any outward reproach for his gift. She would be forced to accept it with a semblance of gratitude, all the while fuming inwardly at her helpless position. Since he himself had been fuming inwardly ever since their previous encounter, he felt this to be only justice.

As he dressed for the party that evening, he indulged himself in the fancy that he was girding his loins for combat. To be sure, heroes of old had commonly worn armor more substantial than black evening coats, stockinette pantaloons, and pearl-tinted waistcoats, but then, their combat had been of a more active kind.

"This will be a battle of wits," Victor told himself with a smile, as he tied his neckcloth and set a single pristine pearl in the center of its precise arrangement of knots and folds. Having assumed his coat with the assistance of his valet, he hurried downstairs so as to be on hand whenever the enemy should make her appearance.

Most of the other guests had already arrived by the time this event took place. Victor found himself growing impatient as the clock drew nearer to seven and still no Catherine had appeared. "The Everharts are not here yet," he whispered to his mother as she sat in her wheelchair near the door greeting guests. "I see it is twenty minutes to seven now. Ought I to call the carriage and go after them?"

His mother smiled serenely. "Oh, I already had the carriage sent to them, Victor. But it is very kind of you to think of doing so, all the same." She reached up to pat his face affectionately. "I am sure the Everharts will be here any minute. Why don't you go over and talk to old Mrs. Langley until they arrive? She has been trying to get your attention these fifteen minutes."

Victor reluctantly acceded to this suggestion. Mrs. Langley was growing deaf, and since she was too proud to use an ear trumpet, conversation with her tended to be an ordeal. He was shouting out the latest news from London when Mrs. Langley suddenly dug her elbow into his ribs.

"These must be your guests of honor," she bawled, nodding toward the door. "What a handsome gel! That would be Miss Everhart, of course. And that must be Mrs. Everhart beside her, in the widow's weeds. Ah, there goes that rascal Jack Banks over to greet them. He's always got an eye for a pretty girl."

Victor looked toward the door and experienced a shock. Could this be the same mobcapped termagant who had raked him over the coals in the garden of Crossroads Cottage? He had to look twice to make sure it was indeed the same girl. She had ginger hair like the girl at the cottage, but instead of being tucked carelessly beneath a cap, it was arranged in a wanton mass of curls and ringlets that gleamed copper gold in the candlelight. Her dress of dull green brocade was admirably calculated to set off both her vibrant hair and voluptuous figure.

And her face—Victor was obliged to admit that he had been altogether mistaken in calling Catherine plain. She was not a real or classical beauty, of course, but one might be tempted to forget that fact in surveying her heart-shaped face with its green eyes, tip-tilted nose, and laughing mouth. Laughing? Victor looked once again, unable to credit such a thing of his shrewish cousin. But there was no denying it. Catherine was laughing at the sallies of Mr. Jack Banks, who was gazing down at her with a most palpably smitten look on his face.

"Good God," said Victor weakly.

Mrs. Langley dug her elbow into his ribs a second time. "You'd best get over there, Caldwell. No telling what Jack'll be up to if you don't. But there, I don't suppose I need to urge you to do your duty by a pretty girl!" She cackled gaily, then shook her head. "My granddaughter Cordelia won't be best pleased. You know she fancies herself the belle of the neighborhood. This girl being so handsome is likely to put her nose out of joint. Aye, look at Cordelia now, scowling at Miss Everhart! That'll be because of Jack, I don't doubt. He used to be one of Cordelia's beaux, but it's plain he's switched camps now."

Victor gave only a brief glance at the young lady Mrs. Langley had indicated. Cordelia Langley, a pretty blonde in her late teens, had indeed enjoyed a position of superiority among the neighborhood girls, but she had always been too countrified a belle for Victor's taste. On this occasion he preferred rather to look at Catherine. But galvanized by another jab from Mrs. Langley's elbow, he finally went forward to greet his cousin, who was still engaged in laughing at Mr. Bank's gallantries.

"Good evening, Cousin Catherine," he said with a bow.

The smile on Catherine's lips did not fade when she saw Victor, but a slightly wary expression crept into her eyes. Still, she replied civilly enough, "Good evening, my lord. I am sorry we are so late arriving. Your carriage arrived in good time, but we had a little trouble at the last minute finding Mother's best shawl. I am afraid your coachman has but a poor opinion of us for having kept him waiting so long."

"I wish I had been there," said Mr. Banks gallantly. "I would have waited hours most willingly for the chance of driving *you*, Miss Everhart. And if I'd had my phaeton, I could have whisked you and your mother here in no time, shawl or no shawl."

"More likely you would have put them in a ditch somewhere along the way," said Victor with false affability. It annoyed him to see the fatuous way Mr. Banks was hovering over Catherine. He added with a tight-lipped smile, "You must not take Mr. Banks's professions at face value, Cousin. I am persuaded he would lead you astray, both concerning his abilities as a whip and in other things as well."

"I say, Caldwell, that's unkind," protested Mr. Banks.

Catherine merely laughed. "Never mind, Mr. Banks," she said. "Lord Caldwell and I differ on other issues, and it is possible we might differ on this one as well. If ever you and I should happen to go out driving together, I will be happy to judge your abilities for myself."

"It's a bargain, by Jove," said Mr. Banks happily, and he proceeded to set an appointment to take Catherine out driving under Victor's very nose.

Victor waited in irritation as they settled dates and times; then he took Catherine's arm. "My mother is most eager to make your acquaintance, Cousin," he said. "If Mr. Banks will excuse us for a minute, I would like to take you to her now. I see she and your mother are already renewing their acquaintance."

"To be sure they are," agreed Catherine, looking to where Mrs. Everhart stood talking animatedly to Lady Caldwell. Victor observed, with an added burst of irritation, that her voice and manner were perfectly composed. It nettled him that she seemed not at all shy or awkward about receiving Mr. Bank's gallantries, but rather accepted them as her due. It nettled him even more that she should be so perfectly justified in doing so. He had set his heart on her making a rude and gawky appearance, and instead here she was, setting up to be the belle of the evening. Other gentlemen besides Mr. Banks had been eyeing her with interest, even old Mr. Scott, who was verging on being an octogenarian. Victor decided to see if he could shake her out of her composure. He gave her a genial smile.

"Did you receive the fruit and things I sent this afternoon?" he said. "I ordered the servants to make sure they were brought around before you left for the party."

"Oh, yes, we received them, my lord." Catherine raised clear green eyes to Victor's face. He found himself marveling at how very green they were. "It was very kind of you to send so much," she added, with a quizzical look. "I am sure there was enough food there for a dozen people."

"I will be happy to send more whenever you like," said Victor. He still hoped to prod Catherine into a display of temper, and it seemed to him his chances of success were good. She looked as if she were struggling with some inward emotion. Finally she glanced up at him again, a faint, rueful smile on her lips.

"Indeed, that would be very kind of you, my lord. You cannot know what a boon your gift proved to be. Mother's appetite has been so little these last months that our cookmaid and I often despair of finding anything to tempt her. It was a pleasure to see her enjoy anything as much as she enjoyed those lovely grapes and figs you sent."

If Catherine had struck him, Victor could not have been more surprised. He had expected a scolding or a snub; instead he had been thanked with a gratitude no less real for being slightly grudging. And there had been such candor in the smile that accompanied Catherine's words that he was taken completely off his guard. He caught a glimpse of a proud spirit harried by care and circumstance, and he knew, with sudden intuition, what such a reply must have cost her.

Impulsively he grasped her hand. "I am glad," he said. "I shall send more figs and grapes as long as they continue in season. You need not bother to thank me," he added as Catherine opened her mouth to reply. "We are relations after all, so you are welcome to all we have, as much as if it had been your own. I would gladly do anything that would help your mother—and you."

Catherine gave him a surprised look, but any reply she might have made was cut off by Lady Caldwell's cry of joy on beholding their approach.

"Oh, and this must be Catherine! Bring her here at once, Victor dear. I am most anxious to meet her." Clasping Catherine's hand between her own, Lady Caldwell looked up into her face searchingly. "You must know how glad I am to finally make your acquaintance, my dear. Martha has told me so much about you in her letters through the years—and Victor has told me something, too, since meeting you the other day." She threw Victor a look of reproach. "I must say, however, that his description of you left something to be desired."

Victor felt himself coloring. Catherine gave him another quizzical look, then smiled at Lady Caldwell. "I have no doubt he described me as looking a perfect dowd, ma'am," she said. "Mother and I had been housecleaning that day, so naturally I was wearing my oldest dress and covered with dust and cobwebs. Our first meeting was a little awkward. Indeed, I am afraid that in the stress of the moment I did not behave toward him quite as I ought."

She gave Victor another look—this one distinctly saucy. More than ever he felt off balance. Catherine had done it to him again! He had prepared himself for one kind of battle, only to find his weapons rendered useless in his hands. When Jack Banks presently appeared and insisted on carrying Catherine off to a corner by himself, Victor was left feeling completely routed.

Nor was his mother inclined to let him recover from his defeat in peace. "Whatever do you mean, Victor, by describing that girl as plain?" she hissed. "She may be red haired, but her face and figure are altogether lovely. And I found her manners very charming, too."

"She does have freckles," said Victor weakly. He had been at pains to confirm Catherine's freckles when he had first approached her that evening. But somehow he could not derive much comfort from the existence of Catherine's freckles. Sprinkled across a charming retroussé nose, with a set of clear green eyes above and the sweet curve of a full-lipped mouth below, they seemed no disfigurement at all, but rather an additional charm.

It was clear that Mr. Banks had no objection to freckles. He continued to monopolize Catherine up till the moment the party went in to dinner. He even took it upon himself to introduce her to the other guests—a task that would more properly have been Victor's. Victor was left to perform the same office for Mrs. Everhart. He had barely finished the last of these introductions when his butler announced that dinner was ready.

As Victor took Mrs. Everhart's arm to lead her into the dining room, she gave him a grateful smile. "I must thank you, my lord, for the wonderful gift we received from you this afternoon. But perhaps Catherine has already told you how pleased we were with the fruit and poultry?"

"Yes, she did," said Victor morosely. Catherine had already made him feel small by thanking him for a gift given solely to annoy her. To have Mrs. Everhart's gratitude added to this burden was almost more than he could bear.

As he helped Mrs. Everhart into her seat, he shot a covert look in Catherine's direction. Mr. Banks, not content with taking her in to dinner, had also arranged to sit next to her—an arrangement quite at odds with the dictates of etiquette. As guest of honor, she ought to have been seated at Victor's right hand, while her mother took the slightly more exalted place to his left. The fact that Victor had been grumbling for days about the necessity of sitting next to Catherine did not prevent him from hotly resenting Mr. Bank's temerity now.

If he had been in an observant mood, he might have noticed that he was not the only one displeased by this change in the seating arrangement. Cordelia Langley, originally assigned to Mr. Banks, was now forced to go in on the arm of elderly Mr. Scott and take the vacant seat between him and Victor. But instead of being gratified by this elevation (which gave her precedence over her own mother and grandmother), she sat sulking throughout the meal, obviously irritated by Mr. Banks's attentions to Catherine. Victor, irritated himself and for much the same reason, scarcely noticed Cordelia's sulkiness. He left her to the mercies of Mr. Scott and grimly set about serving soup to the assembled company.

It was necessary, of course, that he make some attempt to converse with Mrs. Everhart during the meal. This proved not so irksome a task as it might have been. Mrs. Everhart was a mannerly, well-educated lady, and once her first shyness was past, she proved very ready to talk. Victor, asking polite questions to draw her out, soon became really interested in her replies. Mrs. Everhart seemed grateful for his interest. By the time the soup and fish courses had come and gone, and the roast of venison was being served, she was confiding to him the story of her and Catherine's recent difficulties.

"Everything came upon us so suddenly. One day we were living well, with a nice house and plenty of servants, and Matthew well and happy and talking about taking a trip to Brighton.

Then the next day he was gone—and almost everything we had went with him. Such a shock it was! Of course the loss of the money was nothing compared to the shock of losing Matthew, but losing our money at the same time made everything so much more difficult. We couldn't even mourn Matthew's death properly because we were forced to give our attention to selling the house, sorting through our possessions, and dealing with clerks and attorneys and agents."

Tears had come into Mrs. Everhart's eyes as she spoke these words. Victor murmured a few words of condolence, and she reached out to pat his hand. "You are very kind, my lord. I don't mean to complain, but it was certainly a difficult time for Catherine and me. I can't help but be a little resentful that we were denied a period of peace and privacy in which to come to terms with our loss." Wiping her eyes, she forced a brave smile to her lips. "However, it seems that business is as relentless a force as time and tide. One can only bow to its exigencies."

"Perhaps, but even so I should think it might have waited a few weeks," said Victor. "What was it about your husband's affairs that demanded such immediate attention? There wasn't a question of a bankruptcy or anything of that nature?"

"No, not exactly, my lord. I believe it was some sort of speculation gone wrong. Matthew was always a great speculator. In fact, he enjoyed risk taking of any kind. He was a dreadful gamester in his youth. My papa used to shake his head and warn me that no good would come of my marrying such a man, but I wouldn't heed him." A sad, reminiscent smile touched Mrs. Everhart's lips. "And to do Matthew justice, he was usually very fortunate in his speculations. In the last year he was alive, he did so well on 'Change that we were able to move into one of the best neighborhoods in Bath. I have no doubt that if he had lived, this speculation would have come out as well as the others. But his dying at such a time meant all his affairs were plunged into confusion."

"It must have been very difficult," said Victor with sympathy. Mrs. Everhart nodded, dabbing at her eyes.

"Yes, it was. But it could have been worse. I cannot be grateful enough to Mr. Carr. Mr. Carr was Matthew's partner, you must know. He was very helpful in telling me just what was due Matthew's creditors and how best I could go about realizing the necessary funds. He took care of paying the different creditors for me, too. I suspect he paid a good deal out of his own pocket to spare Catherine and me any further expense."

Victor regarded Mrs. Everhart with fixed attention. "You say your husband had a partner in his speculations?" he asked.

"Yes, in this instance he did, though that was not usually the case. In general Matthew preferred to act alone. But on this occasion, I believe the speculation was on such a scale that Matthew found it necessary to enlist the help of another investor."

"But in that case—" Victor hesitated. Mrs. Everhart looked at him inquiringly. "I do not wish to pry, or to annoy you with impertinent questions, ma'am," he said. "But you know, I have dabbled now and then in speculation myself, and what you have told me makes me rather curious to know what were the terms of your husband's partnership with this Mr. Carr."

Mrs. Everhart said warmly that she was sure she would never consider any inquiry from Lord Caldwell to be impertinent. She went on to give Victor such details as she could recall of her husband's dealings with Mr. Carr. These were very few, however, and it was evident that the widow had possessed little knowledge of her late husband's multifarious business affairs.

"I'm afraid I don't have a very good head for business, my lord," she said apologetically. "I do know that Matthew often said that if anything ever happened to him, Catherine and I would be provided for. I suppose we would have been if he had died at any other time, but his dying at such a critical moment meant we were obliged to use all our resources to discharge his obligations."

Victor shook his head vigorously. "Your own personal assets should have been protected, even so," he said. "Of course that would depend to some extent on the settlements made at the time of your marriage and on any subsequent settlements made in your and Catherine's names. But your husband sounds as though he was in general quite wide awake in his speculations. I tell you frankly, ma'am, that I don't like the sound of what you have told me concerning this Mr. Carr. He seems to have been altogether too busy on your behalf—and this attorney you employed to help you untangle your affairs seems to have worked more in his interests than in your own. Mr. Carr didn't suggest you employ that particular attorney, by any chance?"

"Why, yes, he did," said Mrs. Everhart, opening her eyes very wide. "Do you think he can have had a wrong motive for doing so?"

"It looks very like it. But of course I cannot be sure without a thorough investigation of the affair. Would you permit my own attorney to make a few inquiries? He could do so quite discreetly, you know, so that if by any chance Mr. Carr is innocent of wrong-doing, he would never know you had doubted him."

"That would be wonderful!" exclaimed Mrs. Everhart. With a sigh, she added, "I find it hard to believe that Mr. Carr would have tried to cheat me in such a way. He was so kind and helpful and such a support to Catherine and me during those first few weeks after Matthew's death. But of course, there's no denying that there are a great many wolves in sheep's clothing going about in the world. And most of them seem to regard widows and orphans as their lawful prey."

"It has been so ever since biblical days, I'm afraid," said Victor with a sympathetic smile. "We are fortunate nowadays in possessing legal means of redress. I'll write my attorney tomorrow and give him full particulars of the business. And with luck, perhaps we can find a few spars of your husband's fortune yet afloat."

"Perhaps," said Mrs. Everhart, with another sigh. "But I shall not depend on it, my lord. It would be wonderful to recover a little of our money, but I very much fear it was all swept away in the general wreck." Forcing a smile, she added, "Indeed, I should not complain. There are many much worse off than I am,

I know. I have a small income, at least, and since you have been good enough to provide me with a place to live, I want nothing more to be content. Nothing for myself, that is—but I confess I should like something more for Catherine's sake. It is very hard for her, at her time of life, to be reduced to penury."

"I should think it would be much harder for you than for her," said Victor, sweeping a jealous glance at Catherine. "Youth is commonly held to be resilient, you know."

"But you have not considered, my lord!" There was hesitation and also a touch of appeal in Mrs. Everhart's eyes as she regarded Victor. "Catherine is a young lady, you see. And like all young ladies, it is natural that she should desire a home and husband and family of her own."

"Yes, I suppose so," said Victor. He cast another glance at Catherine. She was laughing at something Mr. Banks had said, and the sight of her lovely, laughing face reawakened his old irritation. "I should not despair if I were you, Mrs. Everhart," he said dryly. "Your daughter appears to be going the right way about achieving her desires."

Mrs. Everhart also shot a quick glance at Catherine and her dinner partner. Observing Mr. Banks's smitten expression, she smiled, but shook her head. "Ah, you say that, but indeed you have not considered, my lord. I daresay many young men might admire my daughter, for I do not believe I am prejudiced in thinking her a very lovely girl. But admiring a girl and wishing to marry her are two different things. It is a sad fact, but most men nowadays expect their wives to bring something to their marriage besides themselves. And Catherine will be almost penniless."

Victor, who had indeed not considered this aspect of the case, floundered slightly as he attempted to reply to Mrs. Everhart's speech. "Yes, to be sure—but I see no need to take such a dark view of the situation, ma'am. If your daughter were to attract a well-to-do man—a man who was wealthy in his own right, you know—I daresay he would not care for the fact that she had not a large marriage portion."

He spoke these last words in a more confident tone, for it had occurred to him that his own courtship of Lady Anne exactly corresponded to this situation. Mrs. Everhart, however, merely shook her head once more. "I fear not," she said. "There *was* a young man of that sort interested in Catherine—a very well-off young man he was, and he seemed quite sincerely fond of her. He and Catherine were engaged to be married at the time Matthew was taken ill. But when Matthew died and all the business of his debts was brought to light, the engagement fell through."

"You don't mean to say that her fiancé cried off?" said Victor in amazement. "I should think any decent man would be ashamed to behave in such a manner!"

"No, he did not cry off exactly. I believe Catherine released him from the engagement." Mrs. Everhart heaved a deep sigh. "She is a very proud girl, you know. I daresay it went against the grain with her to know she would come to her wedding dowerless. But I cannot help believing that the young man might have overcome her scruples if he had really wanted to."

"I see," said Victor. He shot another look at Catherine. At that moment she looked up, and her eyes met his. She gave him a brief and slightly wary smile; then she turned again to Mr. Banks, who had leaned over to address some confidential remark to her.

Victor, returning his attention to his plate, felt Mrs. Everhart's summing up had probably been correct. Catherine was undoubtedly a proud girl, and he could easily imagine her breaking off an engagement in the circumstances her mother had described. "And a lucky escape her poor devil of a fiancé had of it, too, if you ask me," he told himself irreverently. Yet somehow, he could not help feeling a reluctant admiration for Catherine's behavior.

Mrs. Everhart, meanwhile, was still bemoaning the loss of her daughter's matrimonial hopes. "For months afterward I kept hoping the young man would write or come to call on us and explain there had been a misunderstanding," she said with a shake of her head. "But it has been just over a year since Matthew's death, and not one word have we heard from him. What a muddle it all is! Much as I should dislike to think ill of Mr. Carr, it would be a blessing if it were to turn out that he was keeping some part of Matthew's fortune from us. Then Catherine might patch up her engagement, and all be set to rights."

"Would she want to patch up her engagement?" inquired Victor in a voice of surprise. He had been acquainted with Catherine only a short time, but in that time she had shown herself a notably proud and independent spirit. It seemed impossible that such a girl could humbly welcome back a suitor who had shown himself unworthy of her affections.

Mrs. Everhart nodded, seeming to understand Victor's surprise. "I daresay you would wonder at her doing so, my lord. It does not seem much like Catherine, I confess. But I know the breaking of her engagement hurt her very much. Indeed, she has never been quite the same girl since. Not that I mean to imply she was an angel prior to that event." A smile of tender amusement appeared on Mrs. Everhart's face. "Catherine has always had her faults, but she used to be of such a happy, hopeful temperament. Having her around the house was like—oh, like sunshine if you will. Now and then there might be a storm, but it always passed quickly, and the sun seemed only to shine the brighter for it afterward."

"And that is no longer the case?" asked Victor as she paused.

Mrs. Everhart shook her head despondently. "No, I'm afraid not, my lord. Now it is as though the sun were always behind the clouds. It's not that Catherine is consciously cross or gloomy. She tries very hard to be cheerful for my sake, and sometimes she almost deceives me. But I can tell she is not happy as she was before. And that is one of the reasons why I am so grateful that you offered us Crossroads Cottage to live in. Here, in a new place, away from all the things that must remind her of her former engagement, perhaps she will be able to recover her spirits."

Victor, watching Catherine laugh and talk with Mr. Banks,

reflected that she did not seem to be suffering from any dearth of spirits tonight. On the whole, however, he felt that he could take very little personal credit for her recovery.

Five

For the rest of the meal, Victor found himself watching Catherine with a new interest.

Her mother's words had given him considerable food for thought. The fact that she had once been engaged and then had lost her fiancé owing solely to her father's financial reverses had inspired him with a grudging sympathy. Yet as he watched Catherine, it struck him that she showed no signs of wearing the willow tonight. He could not actually accuse her of flirting with Mr. Banks, but that gentleman's enamored behavior made it clear that she was doing little to discourage him.

And why should she discourage him? Victor asked himself. *Like other women, she desires her own establishment. Jack can give her a very fair one, certainly a better one than she possesses now. Why should she not exploit his attraction to her if she can?*

Victor could think of no good answer to this question. Yet he found himself vaguely dissatisfied as he watched Catherine laughing and talking with Mr. Banks. Her attitude might be the conventionally feminine one, but though he could accept Catherine's femininity easily enough (the green gown made it difficult to deny, forsooth), he felt it wrong that she should be in any sense conventional.

Nor was this his only cause for dissatisfaction. Bad as it was to suppose Catherine a mere marriage-minded maiden, it was better than supposing her to be pining for a lost lover. And yet Mrs. Everhart had seemed very sure of her facts. Victor supposed she ought to know, but he could not help feeling disappointed that Catherine should take her broken engagement in such a spirit.

Of course women were different from men. They seemed quite regularly to forgive offenses even worse than cowardice, greed, or infidelity. Victor supposed there was nobility in such conduct, but for his part he thought he would respect Catherine more if she greeted her errant lover with scorn and reviling rather than tears of joy.

"I would not have thought it of her," he told himself, regarding the proud tilt of Catherine's head as she conversed with Mr. Banks. "I certainly never would have thought it of her. I would have supposed that if ever a man tried to crawl back into her good graces after serving her in such a way, she would treat him to a tongue-lashing such as she gave me the other day!" And he found himself dwelling almost nostalgically on the terms of Catherine's abuse.

Catherine, for her part, soon became aware of Victor's surveillance. Several times during the meal she had discovered his eyes on her, and though she had responded the first time with a smile, she had become irritated when the scrutiny had continued.

"Does he think to put me to the blush by such conduct?" she demanded of herself with indignation. "Fine behavior from one's host! If we were alone, what pleasure I would take in telling him what I think of him. Odious, odious man! I begin to wonder if he sent all that fruit and game merely to vex me, because I was stiff with him the other day over that business of the cottage rent. Although he did seem quite nice about it when I thanked him for it earlier this evening. But that may have been just pretense. At any rate, I shan't give him the satisfaction of seeming to notice him now." And she took care to pointedly ignore Victor for the rest of the meal.

When the dessert had been cleared from the table, Lady Caldwell gave the signal to rise. One by one the ladies filed out of the dining room, preceded by Lady Caldwell in her wheel-hair. Catherine, stealing a glance at her host, found he was once more watching her with a pensive expression. Even as she indignantly abused him for his conduct, she found herself wondering what he was thinking.

"But there, it's probably something quite inconsequential," he told herself. "Perhaps he is thinking what a dowd I look in his ancient gown." She glanced ruefully down at her dress. Like all her clothing, her green evening dress was a couple of years old; she had had no new dresses except for black ones since her father's death. And though the green gown had always been a favorite of hers, it was extremely simple in its lines, with no lavish lace or embroidered trim to elevate it above the rank of common dinner dresses. Most of her real finery had been sold before coming to Crossroads Cottage, partly to appease her father's creditors and partly because she had no anticipation of needing it in the retired society in which she and her mother expected to live.

"And this dress is plenty good enough for a country dinner party," Catherine told herself defiantly. "I may be a Season or two behind the times, but so is nearly everyone else here tonight." Looking around at the other female guests, she was able to satisfy herself as to the truth of this statement. There was no fault to be found with Lady Caldwell's lilac crepe dinner dress, but the elderly dame beside her wore a full-skirted gown such as had not been in fashion since the previous century, and even the pretty blond girl who had been introduced to her as Cordelia Langley wore an ugly, old-fashioned diamond necklace with her dress of primrose spotted silk.

"Not that I should criticize," Catherine told herself. "At least she has diamonds to wear, which is more than I have." She gave the girl a friendly smile, but Cordelia merely stared at her coldly, then turned away under the pretext of examining the pianoforte that stood in one corner of the drawing room.

It did not occur to Catherine to connect this coolness with Mr. Banks. Although she was amused and flattered by his attentions, he had seemed to her too frivolous a character to be taken seriously. That Cordelia might cherish him as a suitor never entered Catherine's head. She supposed rather that the girl's snub was motivated by contempt for her own humble status as a cottager, and her heart swelled with indignation.

Nor was this the only snub she was obliged to bear during the ladies' interval alone in the drawing room. Two other young ladies, Miss Scott and her sister Miss Cleone Scott, found occasion not long after to approach Catherine and submit her to a long inquisition concerning her birth, education, and antecedents.

"Of course, *our* family have lived at Laurel Hall forever," said Miss Scott, shrugging her shoulders to show how tiresome was such long-term occupation. "It is the traditional seat of the Scotts, and Cleone and I are doomed to live there until we marry. I assure you, Miss Everhart, I would a thousand times rather live in a pretty little cottage like yours. Such a snug place it looks! I am sure it must be nicer than a great rambling house like Laurel Hall."

Catherine returned a civil reply to this speech, but she was pretty sure its intention was to elevate Miss Scott's pretensions while simultaneously depressing her own. Nor was she soothed when one of the dowagers of the party, by way of welcoming her to the neighborhood, made allusion to the change of fortunes that had brought her there.

"You must look on it as God's will, my dear," she said, patting Catherine's shoulder with condescending kindness. "I daresay it is hard for you and your mother to live in such a small way when you were brought up to luxury and ease. But alas, worldly wealth and position are but uncertain things, as the Scriptures say. You must humbly endeavor to do your duty where God has placed you, and then you may be sure of receiving your reward."

Catherine, surveying the dowager's jeweled aigrette and dog collar, wondered how humbly she would endure the loss of her own worldly wealth and position. It was evident from her smug face that she anticipated no such event. *How easy it is to counsel humility and resignation when your own life is going smoothly,* thought Catherine, and she returned a short answer to the dowager's homily. Altogether she was relieved when Victor entered the drawing room a short time later. He might be a rude, conceited, egotistical beast, but at the moment Catherine thought she would prefer rudeness, conceit, and egotism to the mixture of cattiness and condescension she had endured from the ladies.

She watched critically as Victor made his way across the room. "He *is* very handsome," Catherine admitted grudgingly to herself. "If only he weren't so extremely well aware of it! But I suppose he could hardly help being aware of it, when there are so many women willing to make fools of themselves." She watched with a contemptuous eye as the Miss Scotts swooped adoringly down on him, laughing shrilly at his every utterance and determinedly repulsing the advances of Cordelia Langley, who had abandoned her mama and grandmama in order to secure her own share of Victor's attention.

Determined to distance herself from this display of servility, Catherine turned her back on the party and pretended to be busy inspecting an embroidered firescreen that stood beside the hearth. To her surprise, she felt a touch on her arm a minute later. Turning, she discovered Victor standing at her side.

"You seem to find great interest in that firescreen, Cousin Catherine," he said with a smile. "May I ask if it is the design or the workmanship you find so fascinating?"

"Both," said Catherine in a firm voice. She returned her eyes to the screen, but not in time to avoid seeing Victor's smile. Try as she might, she could not help responding to that smile, though she resolutely refrained from returning it. She was annoyed to find herself susceptible to Lord Caldwell's charm, even in spite of knowing firsthand his many shortcomings. Consoling herself with the reflection that she need not betray her susceptibility, she said aloud in her most businesslike voice, "The design of the screen is charming, my lord, and the workmanship very fine. It is quite the most handsome screen I have ever beheld."

Victor's smile took on a tinge of mischief. "Well then, you must allow me to make you a present of it, Cousin," he said.

"I'll order the servants to place it in the carriage so you may take it with you when you and your mother leave tonight."

Catherine opened her mouth to protest, but she caught Victor's look of mischief just in time. This time she could not keep a reluctant smile from her lips. "Ah, you are quizzing me! Indeed, you shall not impose on me that way, my lord. I absolutely refuse to take your firescreen, and I must ask that you refrain from giving me anything else that I might happen to admire this evening. Otherwise I might take advantage of your generosity by saying that Queen's Close is the loveliest house I have ever beheld!"

Victor laughed. "That stratagem would not serve you, Cousin! Unfortunately the house is entailed along with the rest of the property. But I thank you for your compliment—assuming that you did really mean what you said. Perhaps you were only offering it as an example of the strategy you proposed to follow."

"No, I meant it," said Catherine. "This is a beautiful house, my lord. And your grounds and gardens are very lovely, too. Mother and I were admiring them on the way over this evening."

"Were you? Then you must come over some afternoon and see them properly," said Victor with a little bow. "I'd be happy to show you about if you like. Or if you prefer, you can explore them on your own. I'll inform my head gardener to be on the lookout for you."

It was on the tip of Catherine's tongue to refuse this offer, but on further reflection she determined to let it pass. It was not as though Victor were attempting to bestow a material benefit on her, as he had in the matter of the cottage. And of course she need not accept his offer unless she wanted to. So she merely curtsied slightly and said, "I thank you, my lord, but I beg you will not put yourself to so much trouble. Mother and I are so busy that I doubt either of us shall have time for visiting in the next few weeks."

Catherine thought Victor looked disappointed by this speech. But he made no reply to it—or perhaps it was rather that he had no chance to reply it. Mr. Banks had just entered the drawing room, and having observed Catherine standing beside the fireplace, he lost no time in making a beeline to her side.

"There you are, Miss Everhart," he said, smiling in an ingratiating manner. "I wondered where you had got to. You know you promised to sit with me while I was drinking my tea."

"I recall making no positive promise, Mr. Banks," said Catherine, but she suffered herself to be led away all the same. She thought it as well to quit the vicinity of Lord Caldwell as soon as possible. Not because he was behaving badly—on the contrary, he seemed to be in an unusually amiable mood tonight. But this only made it the more imperative to get away from him. Knowing him to be a rude, conceited, egotistical beast, it would be fatal if she actually found herself liking him!

Victor, watching her walk away with Mr. Banks, was seized with a feeling of irritation. For the first time in their acquaintance, he and Catherine had been having a pleasant, rational conversation together, and then Mr. Banks had had to come along and spoil it all with his impertinent demands. It really was most irritating, Victor reflected, as he watched Mr. Banks solicitously seat Catherine in the best chair in the room and then hurry away to fetch her some tea.

Even more irritating was the look of smug triumph on Mr. Banks's face as he returned with the tea and seated himself in the chair next to hers. He obviously felt that in securing Catherine's company he had secured a prize of inestimable value. Victor would have ridiculed any suggestion that he was jealous of Mr. Banks, but it was vexatious to be deprived in this manner of the lady he had been talking to. However, there were plenty of other ladies about. Looking around the room, Victor spied Cordelia Langley standing alone beside the pianoforte, leafing through some music that stood open on the rack. He strolled over to join her.

"Oh, my lord, you startled me! I beg you will forgive me for taking this liberty with your possessions." With a deprecating smile, Miss Langley indicated the music in her hand. "I could not resist the urge to see what you had here on your pianoforte."

"Yes, you are a musician yourself, are you not?" said Victor politely. Cordelia's reputation for music making was well established throughout the neighborhood of Queen's Close, though he himself had never seen much to admire in her performances. Being accustomed to the superior standards of London, he found her amateurish renderings of opera arias and concert pieces barely endurable. Nor did he care for her manner of pushing herself into the spotlight, all the while protesting her reluctance to perform.

True to form on this occasion, Cordelia responded to his remark with an affected laugh. "Oh, I do not consider myself a musician, my lord! The merest dilettante, I promise you. Indeed, I am quite ashamed to have been caught in such a position. I shall just restore your music to its place and remove myself from the scene of my indiscretion."

Cordelia seemed in no hurry to do either of these things, however, and Victor was not really surprised when her mother came hurrying up at that moment, a beaming smile on her face.

"Ah, Cordelia, has Lord Caldwell convinced you to play something for the company?" she said. "I knew it must be so, when I saw the music in your hand. What have you there? 'The Soldier's Adieu?' That will do famously. And you must be sure and give us also that new sonata you have been working on."

"Mama, I could not think of playing tonight!" protested Cordelia, affecting a maidenly timidity that Victor found nauseating. Her mother immediately set about overcoming her qualms, and to Mrs. Langley's exhortations were presently joined the coaxings of the elder Mrs. Langley and several of the other ladies. At last, with feigned reluctance, Cordelia consented to seat herself at the pianoforte.

The performance that followed was neither better nor worse than Victor had expected. He gave it only cursory attention in any case. From where he sat, he had a fine view of Catherine's profile, and he whiled away the time by counting the number of occasions she smiled and shook her head in response to Mr. Banks's whispered remarks.

When Cordelia had finished playing (a consummation that did not come to pass until her mother and grandmother had coaxed her into playing several songs besides those initially promised), the Miss Scotts were urged, in their turn, to give the company a little music.

"Impossible!" protested Miss Scott with a violent shake of her head.

"Antigone and I would feel quite ashamed to air our little talents after Cordelia's delightful performance," agreed her sister with a look of affected admiration at Cordelia. Nevertheless, after a good deal of coaxing and encouragement, they, too, mounted to the pianoforte and took their turn at playing for the guests. At the conclusion of their performance, Mrs. Langley looked around the room with an arch smile.

"Now perhaps someone else will play for us. What about you, Miss Everhart? Do you play or sing?"

Victor observed that Catherine looked discomposed by this question. But she replied with quiet civility, "Yes, I play a little, ma'am. But I assure you I am not at all a superior performer."

"I am sure you play delightfully, my dear. Give us a song, do, and let us be the judges."

Catherine hesitated a moment, then rose to her feet with a resigned smile. "Very well, ma'am," she said.

Mrs. Langley, who had obviously expected more of a struggle than this, looked taken aback by Catherine's easy capitulation. There were murmurs and looks of surprise from the other ladies, too. Cordelia Langley, who was seated near Victor, gave a vengeful titter. "Upon my word, she was not very difficult to persuade, was she, my lord?" she whispered. "I could wish I had her effrontery!"

"I would not call it effrontery because she plays to oblige your mother," said Victor, regarding Cordelia steadily. "Indeed, I think the better of her for acceding with so little parade or protest. There is nothing worse than a performer who claims to be unwilling to take the stage when it is obvious she is eager to display her talents."

Cordelia looked nettled by this speech, as well she might, considering its pointed reference to her own behavior. But she contented herself with replying, "Well, let us hope Miss Everhart has talents to display, my lord. Otherwise, this wonderful willingness to oblige must count for nothing."

"On the contrary, it would be in that case all the more commendable," returned Victor. "A superior performer loses nothing by displaying her talents, you know. But for a person of inferior talents to willingly expose her deficiencies must be counted an act of courage."

Cordelia gave another angry titter. "Perhaps so, my lord," she said. "But I would think such a person would better conceal her deficiencies if she could!"

"Miss Everhart has already disclaimed her powers of performance," said Victor gently. "It was another who insisted on their display." He did not name who that other was, but he let his eyes rest significantly on Mrs. Langley's corpulent figure. Cordelia understood him well enough. Biting her lip, she turned away and addressed no further remarks to him throughout the evening.

Pleased at the success of his set down, Victor now gave his attention to Catherine. He found himself hoping she would silence her critics by giving a performance superior to the ones that had gone before. But these hopes were doomed to disappointment. The single song Catherine played for the company was rendered adequately but not brilliantly, and the voice with which she accompanied her playing was remarkable neither for its power, range, nor flexibility.

All the same, Victor derived considerable enjoyment from Catherine's performance. It was always pleasant to look at a pretty girl, and there could be no denying that Catherine looked a very pretty girl tonight. But it was not only her looks that won Victor's admiration. Cordelia Langley was a pretty girl, too, and her playing had indisputably been better than Catherine's. Yet to Victor, Cordelia's performance had been spoilt by the airs and affectations that she considered necessary to her role as an accomplished musician.

Catherine had displayed no airs or affectations. She had played her single song in a quiet, ladylike manner, making no apology for her performance apart from her first modest disclaimer. Victor admired this conduct very much. It occurred to him, as he joined with the others in applauding her efforts, that his cousin's manners in company were as admirable and elegant as her appearance.

"Bravissima, Cousin," he called, applauding warmly as she resumed her place beside Mr. Banks.

Catherine gave him an incredulous look, then curtsied ironically. Mr. Banks, meanwhile, was lauding her performance in terms calculated to raise the ire of the other performers.

"That was dashed fine playing, Miss Everhart," he said enthusiastically. "Prettiest thing I ever heard, 'pon my soul. You've got a voice like a nightingale—or is it a lark I mean? At any rate, one of those birds everybody proses about."

"I daresay you mean a raven," suggested Catherine with a straight face.

Mr. Banks, however, declared it was not a raven he meant at all. "Ravens don't sing—they croak," he said with authority. "There's a couple of 'em nesting near my father's place, and I give you my word they make the most ungodly racket, Miss Everhart. Not at all like your singing. I tell you what, though. Your voice makes everyone else's sound like a raven's." Pleased with this compliment, he repeated it loudly for the benefit of the others in the room. "That's the dandy, all right. Your singing makes everybody else's sound like ravens croaking, Miss Everhart."

Naturally this comparison did not endear him to the other young ladies. The Miss Scotts threw him dark looks, and Cordelia Langley, smiling scornfully, addressed a low-voiced remark to her mother. The remark was inaudible, but the look that accompanied it was directed pointedly at Catherine. Catherine's color rose, but she gave no other sign of embarrassment or unease. She merely thanked Mr. Banks for his compliments with a composure that won Victor's admiration once more.

He would have liked to pay her a few compliments himself, but Mr. Banks blithely circumvented this desire by remaining at Catherine's side throughout the rest of the evening. He even insisted on taking the Everharts home in his own carriage, thus depriving Victor of his last opportunity to speak to his cousin in private. He had to content himself with addressing a few words to Catherine publicly as she was leaving the party with Mr. Banks and her mother.

"Well, Cousin, it has been a pleasure having you here this evening," he said, smiling as genially as he could. "You must come again soon. And as I mentioned earlier, you are welcome to drop by and explore the gardens anytime you like."

Catherine gave him an inscrutable look. "Perhaps I will," she said. Extending her hand, she added politely, "Thank you very much for your hospitality, my lord. It was a most delightful evening."

"I am glad you enjoyed yourself," said Victor, saluting her hand. She gave him a prim smile and drew her hand away rather hastily. Victor surveyed her with frustration. As she turned to go, he could not resist adding, "You are sure you will not allow me to drive you and your mother home, Cousin? I don't like to speak ill of Mr. Banks, but he has the reputation of being a somewhat reckless driver."

Catherine's face lit up with sudden laughter. "Oh, but he says the same of you, my lord! That was one of the reasons he gave for wishing to drive Mother and me home tonight. But of course I assured him that his worries in that direction were needless. It was not you but your coachman who drove us here this evening."

She spoke in dulcet tones, but Victor was too indignant to appreciate that she was joking. "It happens that I am an *excellent* driver," he said hotly. "Why, I've been a member of the Four-in-Hand Club for years!"

Catherine laughed. "Ah, but I have only your word for that, my lord! And since Mr. Banks is equally warm in his own praise, I have no way of knowing which of you is speaking the truth—if indeed either of you is. All things being equal, I think I will do best to abide by our original arrangement."

"In that case, you must let *me* drive you home," said Victor triumphantly. "For it was originally arranged that my carriage should bring you here and take you back to the cottage afterward."

Catherine gave him a look in which amusement and annoyance were about equally mixed. "Yes, but it would be silly to have your carriage brought out when Mr. Banks already has his waiting," she said in the voice of one explaining an obvious fact to a slow-witted child. "He has assured us that Crossroads Cottage is on his way home, so you see this plan will be much less trouble for everyone, my lord."

Victor could not argue with this statement. But he felt a surge of renewed irritation as he watched Catherine enter Mr. Banks's carriage and drive away.

Six

Mr. Banks proved a perfectly capable driver, delivering Catherine and her mother to their own doorstep in good time and excellent order. They thanked Mr. Banks for his courtesy, then went into the cottage together.

"That seems a very pleasant young man," observed Mrs. Everhart as she fastened the latch on the door and began to remove her cloak and gloves. "He is not, perhaps, very intellectual, but his manners are both amiable and obliging."

Catherine agreed, but rather absently. Her mother gave her a searching look. "Did you have a pleasant evening, my dear?" she asked. "I noticed you and Mr. Banks seemed to find a great deal to talk about."

Catherine made a face. "You mean Mr. Banks found a great deal to talk about! I could not convince him to stop talking even when the other young ladies were playing. I am afraid they thought us very rude."

"I am sure they did not," said Mrs. Everhart comfortably. "After all, old Mrs. Langley and some of the other ladies were talking during the performance, too."

"Yes, so they were, though not so loudly as Mr. Banks. Still, I do not mean to criticize. He is not, as you say, a very intellectual gentleman, but he is amusing enough for one's dinner partner. And that is all I should ever ask of him."

Catherine spoke in a decisive voice. Her mother sighed, but said nothing more on the subject of Mr. Banks. Instead she began to praise the beauty of Queen's Close. "Such a lovely house! Everything of the first elegance and no discordant element anywhere. But then Sophronia always has had exquisite taste."

"It is a lovely house," agreed Catherine, albeit with little enthusiasm. Her mother gave her another look.

"And I thought Lord Caldwell a most delightful host, did not you, my dear? On this occasion, at least, you can have found nothing to criticize in his manners."

"No," agreed Catherine grudgingly. "His manners were very well. Although I am persuaded he was quizzing me abominably when he was pretending to be so taken with my pianoforte playing!"

"I am sure he had no thought of quizzing you, my love," said her mother anxiously. "I was observing him as you were playing, and I thought he looked quite pleased and impressed."

Catherine laughed shortly. "Yes, he and Mr. Banks! I acquit Mr. Banks of hypocrisy, at least, for it's obvious he knows nothing about music. But you cannot tell me that a man like Lord Caldwell could honestly believe my performance was at all superior."

"I thought you played delightfully, dear," said Mrs. Everhart loyally.

Catherine laughed and kissed her on the brow. "Yes, you would, Mother. You firmly believe I am the most beautiful, intelligent, accomplished creature in the world, and no evidence to the contrary will ever change your mind. So let us be agreed that I played delightfully this evening and leave it at that. I for one am dropping with fatigue and quite ready to seek my bed."

Mrs. Everhart agreed that she, too, was ready for bed, and as soon as she and Catherine had extinguished the lights downstairs, they took up their candles and went upstairs to their bedchambers.

Catherine, in her own room, went briskly about the work of undressing and making herself ready for bed. But when she was finally lying between the cool, lavender-scented sheets, she found herself very far from sleep. It had been a long time since she had attended a social event of any kind, and the one she had attended that evening had served to agitate her feelings on several levels.

There had been Mr. Banks's attentions, for one thing. There could be no denying that they had been a notable feature of the evening. But in truth Catherine spared scarcely a thought for Mr. Banks. She had already classed him as an agreeable but not very bright gentleman who had chosen that evening to single her out for flirtation. Another time he would probably devote himself to some other lady. As far as Catherine was concerned, he was welcome to do so. It had been pleasant to have an admiring cavalier on hand, especially in a gathering where she was a stranger and feeling a little unsure of herself, but Mr. Banks's fatuous conversation had soon palled upon her. And though she knew nothing of his past courtship of Cordelia Langley, she was keen enough to have perceived that his attentions had won her no friends among the female members of the group.

That was important, for it was the ladies who would largely determine how enjoyable she found her residence in the neighborhood of Queen's Close. Catherine spent some time dwelling upon the various remarks that had been addressed to her that evening by the other lady guests. Very condescending remarks they had been for the most part, and Catherine gritted her teeth when she recalled the Miss Scotts' superior attitude and Cordelia Langley's contemptuous one. Not for the first time, she reflected that the hardest thing to bear about her changed circumstances was not the loss of gowns and carriages and other material objects, but rather the change in the way other people treated her.

This train of thought brought Catherine naturally to the subject of Lord Caldwell. And it was on this subject that her thoughts dwelt longest.

Catherine was at a loss to understand her cousin's behavior that evening. He had greeted her with seeming civility on one hand, yet he'd stared at her in the rudest way throughout much of the evening. He had sent a quantity of fruit and game to the cottage for reasons which she strongly suspected to be ignoble, yet when she had ventured to thank him for it he had dismissed her thanks with an air almost of embarrassment. And he had applauded her performance at the pianoforte as enthusiastically as though she had been a virtuoso of the first water when he must have realized she was nothing of the kind.

Try as she might, Catherine could not determine whether this behavior had been kindness, condescension, or mockery. Her earlier encounter with Victor led her to the view that it must be either condescension or mockery, but whenever she tried to make up her mind to this viewpoint, she would recall the way he had smiled at her when they had been talking together before and after dinner. These recollections tended to disturb the unfavorable picture she was attempting to form of Victor and sent her back to the beginning of her conjectures once again.

"Wretched, wretched man," Catherine told herself, pounding her pillow and twisting about among the bedclothes in a vain effort to make herself more comfortable. "I half suspect him of behaving in such a contradictory way merely in order to puzzle me to death! And ninny that I am, his strategy is succeeding."

A protesting mew from the vicinity of her feet informed Catherine that Ginger had been disturbed by her restless movements. She sat up and felt about in the darkness until her fingers touched his fur. "I'm sorry, Ginger," she said, stroking him affectionately. "How thoughtless of me to disturb your sleep! Now you shall have to nap twelve hours tomorrow instead of your usual ten to make up for it."

Ginger responded with a rumbling purr. Catherine continued to stroke the cat as she reflected aloud upon her predicament.

"It is quite intolerable that Lord Caldwell should intrude upon our sleep this way, isn't it, Ginger? Clearly it would be better if I had as few dealings with my noble cousin as possible. Indeed, there's something about that man that sets up my back in the most amazing way. I suppose it's much the same way his dog affects you, Ginger." She scratched the cat gently beneath the chin. "He seems invariably to provoke me to scratches and snarls!"

Ginger purred louder and rubbed his head against her hand, signifying his wish that her caresses should continue. Catherine obligingly resumed them, still musing aloud. "From now on, I shall make sure that Lord Caldwell has as few chances to vex me as possible. I shan't go near his gardens, though he did invite me to come see them. But I imagine he only did that to be polite. If I mistake not, he finds me quite as irksome as I find him and he would be glad to dispense with my company. It's odd how some personalities seem destined to conflict, Ginger. And it's unfortunate that such a conflict should happen here, where I am obliged to make my home for at least the next few years. But if I keep my meetings with Lord Caldwell to a minimum and practice great self-restraint when I am around him, I daresay we shall rub along reasonably well."

Having reached this conclusion, Catherine lay down and attempted once more to compose herself to sleep. Ginger, still purring, came up and resettled himself beside her pillow. Soothed by his familiar purr, Catherine found herself growing sleepy. Before long she dropped into a slumber as profound as her feline companion's.

Catherine woke early the next morning. For some time she lay in bed, surveying her room, with its low-beamed ceiling, chintz hangings, and modest oaken bedstead. It was an attractive room, though not as luxurious as the one she had left behind her in Bath. For a moment she felt low, reflecting on what she had lost; then she resolutely put these reflections away from her.

"Mother has a hard enough time keeping up her spirits without my giving way to that kind of nonsense," she told herself. "I live here now, and I may as well try to make the best of it." Rising, she began to make her toilette for the day.

Ginger also rose and performed a leisurely ablution while Catherine washed, dressed, and arranged her hair. When she went downstairs to the parlor, the cat trailed after her and sat watching expectantly as she and her mother took their places at the breakfast table.

"Yes, you may have your breakfast, too, sir," said Catherine and gave him some scrambled egg and a piece of cold ham. He sniffed these viands with disdain, but finally deigned to eat them when nothing better was forthcoming. Having daintily consumed everything but the rind of the ham, he then trotted off to the kitchen, where he could presently be heard begging a share of the new milk from the cookmaid.

"It seems not to have taken Ginger long to adapt to life at Crossroads Cottage," said Mrs. Everhart with a smile. "He quite won Emily's heart yesterday by catching that mouse that had been terrorizing her down in the cellar."

"Did he indeed? I call that quite intrepid behavior for such an elderly cat," said Catherine, buttering another piece of toast. "What can I do for you today, Mother? I know you spoke of changing the summer hangings for winter ones."

"Yes, I would like to accomplish that before the weather gets really cold. If you would look after the curtains, Catherine, I might see about preserving some of those plums Lord Caldwell sent over yesterday. He sent us such a quantity that we can never eat them before they spoil, and they will be very nice this winter as a change from apples and pears."

Catherine promised to attend to the curtains, and as soon as breakfast was over, she set to work. The heavy woolen hangings had to be lugged down from their trunk in the attic, shaken free of the camphor and bitter apples tucked among them to keep out the moths, and hung out to air. Then the light chintz and dimity summer hangings had to be taken down and put to soak in a washtub, preparatory to their being laundered and stored away for the winter.

All this kept Catherine busy until well past noon. When she was finally done, she bathed, changed her cambric work dress for a light muslin, took up a favorite novel, and went out on the porch to rest and recover a little from her labors.

"Ah, this is luxury indeed!" she said with a sigh, sinking into one of the wicker chairs that stood upon the porch. "I don't know about you, Ginger, but I am happy to sit down for a while. And it seems to me that the finest velvet sofa could not feel better at this moment than this rickety old rocker."

Ginger, who had accompanied her onto the porch, signified his agreement of this statement by jumping into her lap and settling himself for a nap. Catherine opened her book and leaned back to read, enjoying the light breeze that stirred her hair and the warmth of the sunlight filtering through the vines that shaded the porch. Every now and then a wagon or carriage rattled by on the high road, providing a new source of diversion. Bees hummed among the flowers of the garden, and the air was sweet with their perfume, slightly sharpened with the promise of autumn.

Catherine read on and on, enjoying this interval of leisure after the morning's exertions. She was just telling herself that she ought to go in and see if Emily needed help with the dinner preparations when she saw Ginger lift his head alertly. Catherine looked up, too, just in time to see Victor coming round the corner of the porch.

He was wearing a bottle-green frock coat whose well-cut lines emphasized the breadth of his chest and shoulders. A pair of close-fitting pantaloons and Hessian boots embellished his handsome legs, and his dark head was bare and slightly tousled by the wind. "Oh, but he is good-looking," thought Catherine, and she felt a certain satisfaction in reflecting that she was wearing her nicest afternoon dress. Then she chastised herself for the thought. What did it matter what she wore? She cared nothing for Lord Caldwell's opinion, after all. She summoned up a smile as he approached, but felt as though her lips were stretched into a most foolish and unnatural grimace.

Victor, for his part, felt a sudden embarrassment as he approached Catherine. He had gone to bed the night before in much the same frame of mind as she: piqued, provoked, and resolved to avoid her company as much as possible. He had awakened that morning still strong in his resolve, but as the day had worn on, he had found himself gradually weakening.

It was only right that he should call upon Catherine that day. Thanks to Mr. Banks's assiduity, he had had no opportunity to tell her how much he had enjoyed her playing the night before. Mr. Banks's intrusive presence had also prevented them from setting any date when she might come to tour the Queen's Close gardens. And it was most dissatisfying to recall how he had parted from Catherine, with that childish and quite unjustified thrust about Mr. Banks's driving.

How had he come to lower himself so far? He, who had always been famed in London society for his elegant manners and unshakable poise! Victor told himself that he had merely been annoyed because Mr. Banks had usurped the role he had assigned to himself—that of benefactor to the Everharts. But though this might be an explanation, it was no excuse for his behavior. It occurred to Victor for the first time that his attitude toward his cousins had from the beginning had a good deal of self-congratulation in it. Perhaps it had contained more self-congratulation than it had real generosity.

Well, that's another reason why I ought to call on Catherine, he told himself. *I can see about alleviating that bad impression my first call may have left on her. I'll make a simple neighborly visit, just to pay my respects—and I'll take along some of those partridges I shot the other day.*

This program Victor had followed, but when he had come within sight of the cottage and found Catherine sitting on the porch, he found himself suddenly abashed.

Catherine's reaction to his appearance did nothing to remove his embarrassment. She had smiled at him, true, but he thought her expression was wary—as wary as that of the cat who lay on her lap. Ginger stared at him with unblinking green eyes as he mounted the porch steps.

"Good afternoon, Cousin," he said, with a would-be hearty air. "I hope I find you well. I hope I find you well, too, Ginger," he added, addressing the animal with spurious friendliness. The

cat merely lay back his ears and regarded him more balefully
than ever.

Catherine, however, responded civilly enough, smiling and
extending a hand to him. "Good afternoon, my lord. Yes, both
Ginger and I are very well, thank you." There was a brief pause,
during which Victor had time to note what a pretty picture she
made in her white muslin gown, with her book in her lap and
the wind stirring her coppery curls. Finally, Catherine cleared
her throat and spoke again. "Did you come to see Mother, my
lord? I'm sorry, but she is out this afternoon. I would be happy
to give her a message, however."

"No, I have no message," said Victor, feeling more foolish
than ever. "I called merely to see if you were recovered after
your exertions last night. And I also brought you a couple of
partridges." He showed her the birds in his hand. "I noticed your
mother seemed to enjoy the ones we served at dinner last night,
so I thought they might be welcome."

"That is very kind of you, my lord," said Catherine. Victor
could not tell if she meant the words ironically or not, but he
thought she looked pleased. She rose to take the partridges from
his hand. This obliged Ginger to jump out of her lap. The cat
looked much affronted by his mistress's inconsiderate behavior.
He leaped up on the porch rail and deliberately turned his back
on both Catherine and Victor.

"Now I've done it. I do believe he's giving me the cut indi-
rect," said Victor, regarding the cat with amusement. "I never
saw so much offended dignity expressed in a creature's back!"

Catherine laughed. "Yes, Ginger is not shy about showing his
displeasure! Mother says he is dreadfully spoilt. But since he is
as open about showing pleasure and approval as their opposite,
I am able to forgive him his occasional crotchet."

Victor thought how pretty she looked with a smile on her lips
and her eyes bright with laughter. "On my honor, I didn't mean
to disturb either you or your cat," he said. "You made such a
comfortable picture sitting there with him on your lap. Do please
sit down again, Cousin. I'll take those partridges around to the

scullery in a minute. But there were some things I wished to say to you first."

This speech brought the wary expression back into Catherine's eyes. At Victor's urging, however, she consented to put down the partridges and reseat herself in the rocker. "However, I will agree to sit down only if you sit down, too, my lord," she said, indicating the other chairs on the porch. "Mother and I gave these chairs a good cleaning just the other day, so you need not fear to spoil your clothes."

Victor was not sorry to avail himself of this permission. He seated himself in the chair beside Catherine's, then turned his head to smile at her. "What a pleasant bower! You have a comfortable place for your reading, Cousin."

"Pretty comfortable," she agreed, still regarding him warily.

It occurred to Victor that his remark might be taken as patronage, seeing that he owned the cottage and had been instrumental in establishing the Everharts there. He sought for a less sensitive subject. "It's a lovely day today, isn't it? More like midsummer than September. The farmers will rejoice to have such favorable weather for sowing and setting their wheat."

"I suppose they will," said Catherine. "I'm afraid I am woefully ignorant about agricultural matters, my lord." In a formal voice, she added, "You spoke of having some things to say to me, my lord. May I beg you to tell me what they are?"

It was not the opening Victor would have liked, but he did his best. "Why, I wished merely to say how much I enjoyed your playing and singing last night, Cousin. 1 would have liked to say so at the time, but was prevented by the clamor of your other admirers." He purposely abstained from mentioning Mr. Banks by name, being still a little embarrassed at the way he had denigrated that gentleman the night before. He feared Catherine might refer to the subject even as it was, but she merely looked amused and a little incredulous.

"Indeed, you do me too much honor, my lord," she said. "Don't tell me you came all the way over here to praise my musical talents? I am persuaded they merit no such tribute."

"Indeed, they do," said Victor warmly, but Catherine merely arched a disbelieving eyebrow at him. Victor felt his anger rising. He did not wish to praise her in overblown superlatives as Mr. Banks had done, but he had sincerely enjoyed her performance, and it annoyed him that she seemed so reluctant to receive his praise.

"Perhaps I can explain my admiration better by saying it was not alone your musical talents I wished to praise," he said, choosing his words carefully. "It was your manner of performing as much as the performance itself that I found so admirable."

Catherine laughed. "What, because I did not make a piece of work about playing like Miss Langley? But you must know such airs are better suited to a real musician than a dabbler like myself, my lord. It has been my observation that reluctance on the part of the performer merely whets the audience's appetite. And then how disappointing to regale them with *my* little talent!"

"Ah, but a little talent may on occasion be more satisfying than a larger one," returned Victor. "It's all in how it is presented. To use your metaphor, Cousin, I would rather have a simple dish of fruit neatly and modestly served than any amount of elaborate and indigestible French pastry. And I much preferred your performance last night to anyone else's."

Catherine again looked incredulous. But all she said was, "Then I thank you for your compliment, my lord. I am glad my performance gave enjoyment to someone."

"Now you are being falsely modest, Cousin," said Victor, smiling at her. "You must know at least one other person enjoyed your performance last night. Heaven knows he was not backward about saying so!"

This speech brought a self-conscious smile to Catherine's lips. "Heaven knows," she agreed. "I believe the less said about that, the better, my lord. But it was altogether a pleasant gathering last night. I know Mother enjoyed it very much. She was so pleased to see Lady Caldwell again after so many years apart from her."

"Yes, so was Mama pleased. She could talk of nothing else at breakfast. You and your mother must come often to Queen's

Close, Cousin. It would mean a great deal to Mama, being such an invalid."

Catherine hesitated a moment before speaking. "I am sure my mother would be delighted to come, my lord," she said.

"And you must come, too, Cousin. Indeed, that is one of the other reasons I came to call today. I wondered if you had decided what day would be best for your visit to the Queen's Close gardens."

A shutter seemed to come down over Catherine's face. In a formal voice, she said, "I am rather busy this week, my lord. I believe it would be best to fix no particular day, but rather leave the matter to chance."

Victor was irritated by this speech. Even more irritating was the change in Catherine's manner, which seemed to imply he had made a faux pas in giving his invitation. Yet how could that be? He had worded his offer in the most gracious and deferential manner. Now here it was being thrown back in his face! "You scarcely look busy at the moment, Cousin," he retorted. "I should think you could spare a few minutes from your reading to pay a visit to our gardens."

Anger flashed in Catherine's eyes. "I have been working hard all the morning and most of the afternoon, my lord," she said in an icy voice. "I sat down with my book less than an hour ago."

"Did you indeed?" said Victor. "Then I have done you an injustice, Cousin."

He attempted a conciliatory smile, but Catherine was having none of it. She swept on with growing ire. "And let me tell you that I do not appreciate being lectured by you as to what I should and should not do, my lord!" she told Victor. "We may be cousins, but that gives you no right to interfere in my life. I shall order my leisure hours exactly as I see fit, and you shall have to make the best of it. I beg you will excuse me now, my lord. This particular interval of leisure is quite over."

Catherine rose to her feet as she spoke. Victor rose, too, alarmed by the finality in her manner. "Please don't go," he said. "You must know I had no intention of interfering in your life, Cousin. I was, perhaps, a little hurt that you seemed so reluctant to accept my invitation—but of course you are free to do as you like in that regard. Sit down again, and don't allow my foolish behavior to ruin your interval of leisure."

Catherine looked mollified by this speech, but she refused to sit down again. "Indeed, I must go in, my lord. To speak truth, my interval of leisure ought to have ended some time ago. Thank you for coming by—and for the partridges, too. Mother will appreciate them very much, I know."

Although she spoke pleasantly enough, it was evident that she was determined to be done with the interview. Seeing her determination, Victor felt he had no choice but to accede to it. He saluted Catherine's hand, then looked about for the partridges she had laid down. One still lay on the porch beside his chair, but the other was nowhere to be seen.

"That's odd," he said, looking about him with puzzlement.

"What's odd?" said Catherine. She stood in the doorway with her arms folded across her chest, obviously impatient for him to be gone. Victor felt a passing flash of resentment at her attitude, but at the moment he was more absorbed by the mystery of the missing partridge.

"One of the partridges I brought seems to be missing," he said, showing her the solitary bird in his hand. "Surely there *were* two to begin with?"

"Yes, there were two. Oh!" A look of comprehension appeared in Catherine's eyes. She began to look around the porch. "Ginger? Where are you, Ginger? I know you're here somewhere." Having searched every potential hiding place atop the porch, she went down the steps to peer under it. A gasp of laughter escaped her. "Oh, you naughty, naughty cat! How could you do such an abominable thing? And they were such nice partridges, too!"

Victor swung himself over the rail of the porch and joined her where she stood. There, beneath the porch, crouched Ginger with a look of intense self-satisfaction on his face. Beside him lay a heap of feathers, whose distinctive markings identified them only too clearly as those of the missing partridge.

"That damned cat!" swore Victor. "He ate it! He ate one of my partridges!"

Catherine had been laughing, but her face assumed a look of reproof at these words. "I would appreciate it if you would refrain from using such language in my presence, my lord," she said austerely. "And I would remind you also that you had already given me the partridge before Ginger ate it. Therefore, it was technically my partridge he ate rather than yours."

"That may be, Cousin, but I cannot see that that lightens the offense. I brought the partridges for you, not your cat, and it goes sorely against the grain to see a valuable game bird wasted in such a way!"

"Yes, it is a great shame. But I beg you won't be angry at Ginger, my lord. He was only following his natural instincts, and you can hardly fault him for that."

"Oh, yes, I can," said Victor under his breath. He threw a look of hostility at the cat beneath the porch. Ginger stared back at him smugly.

Meanwhile, Catherine went on speaking, her voice amused but also a little anxious. "Indeed, you must not feel so badly about this, my lord. It was beastly of Ginger to steal one of your partridges, but you know the fault was really mine more than his. I ought to have remembered how fond he is of birds. And since it was my fault, I'm willing to pay the penalty for his crime. The partridge he ate shall be my share of your gift, and I'll make sure Mother eats all the remaining one. That ought to square things nicely, oughtn't it, my lord?"

Victor recognized the justice of this speech, but his feelings were too wounded to make any acknowledgment. Bowing wordlessly, he turned on his heel and walked away.

Seven

Catherine was at first rather offended by Victor's abrupt departure. But when she had considered the matter at length, she was obliged to admit that he did perhaps have grounds for displeasure.

"Of course anyone would feel bad to have their gift spoilt almost as soon as it was given," she told Ginger, who merely twitched his tail in response. "It's true Lord Caldwell ought not to have visited his displeasure on me when it was you who were at fault, you naughty cat. But at that, I suppose I would rather he abused me than you. His displeasure doesn't do me any harm—and indeed, I ought to be growing used to it by now!"

But though Catherine assured herself that she could comfortably bear the brunt of her cousin's displeasure, she found that the idea of Victor being angry at her did give her a certain discomfort. There was no logic in it. She had already incurred his displeasure several times before now, and she ought indeed to be growing used to it, as she had humorously assured herself. But somehow, on this occasion, she could not shrug the idea of Victor's displeasure aside by telling herself he had got no more than he deserved.

This, too, was illogical. His manners had left as much to be desired on this occasion as on all the others. Indeed, when he had made that remark about her having plenty of leisure to read, his behavior had passed beyond thoughtless to become openly offensive. But somehow Catherine could not dwell on Victor's offenses. She found herself remembering instead how he had praised her manners and musical performance at the party, and the warmth of his smile when he had assured her he preferred her playing to everyone else's. And she reflected with gloom that the partridges that had been the chief cause of their falling out had been originally brought as a thoughtful gesture to tempt her mother's appetite.

All in all, it was enough to make Catherine very uncomfortable. She found herself hoping Victor would call again soon so that she might apologize. Of course she had already apologized once about the partridge, but it was possible that on that occasion she had treated the matter too lightly. It would do no harm to express her regrets more fully. And in fact she need not even wait for Victor to come to the cottage in order to do so, for she had a built-in pretext for calling at Queen's Close in the shape of his invitation to see the gardens. Nothing could be easier than to say she had found after all that she had some spare time and had decided to accept his invitation. And while he was showing her about the gardens, she could deliver her apology quite privately and conveniently.

Catherine toyed with this idea for some time, but in the end she decided against it. She felt it would be better to wait for Victor to come to the cottage rather than seek him out in his own home. Although she did not like to admit it, she had been impressed by the grandeur of Queen's Close the previous night. It had brought home to her her cousin's exalted rank and position, both so much superior to her own. Catherine felt it would be humbling enough to apologize to Victor without doing it in a setting calculated to magnify her humility. And what if she should tender her apology, only to have him reject it! That would be the most humbling experience of all.

No, I shall wait until he comes to call at the cottage, Catherine resolved mentally. *If he comes here again in the next week or two, I can take it that he is disposed to take a lenient view of the affair. Indeed, it may be that he has already forgotten it and no apology will be necessary. It was only a partridge, after all—and he had already given it to us when Ginger ate it. But oh, he did look most dreadfully angry when he left here yesterday! Well, never mind. If he comes again, all is well—and if he doesn't come, that will be very well, too. I would as lief not meet with a man who is so quarrelsome and quick to take offense.*

Catherine was obliged to sustain herself with this philosophy for the next few weeks, for Victor did not come to Crossroads Cottage. This did not mean that she saw nothing of him, of course. In the limited society of the country, it was inevitable that they should meet on occasion. She saw Victor at church on Sundays and in the village now and then when she was there making some purchase. Very frequently she caught glimpses of him driving or riding past the cottage on the high road. He always raised his hat politely when he saw her, and now and then he would stop to address a few words to her. But Catherine observed that this only happened on occasions when she was accompanied by her mother.

Nor did he cease to send gifts of fruit and game to the cottage, though he came not himself. Catherine supposed these gifts were sent out of respect for her mother, and she was grateful accordingly. But her pride was hurt that Victor should still be angry with her about the partridge episode. And so, whenever Lady Caldwell sent a groom to the cottage with a note inviting her and her mother to spend the afternoon or evening at Queen's Close, she made an excuse to stay behind. If Lord Caldwell found her presence objectionable, then she would not inflict it on him!

Victor, meanwhile, was doing his best to convince himself that he did find his cousin's presence objectionable. He had certainly been disgusted over the partridge episode, but not for the reasons Catherine supposed. Once his first anger had passed, it was his own behavior he found disgusting. The loss of a partridge was a small thing, and Catherine had already apologized for the incident, generously taking all the blame on herself. Yet he had stomped off like a child in a tantrum without vouchsafing her so much as a word in reply!

He supposed he must have still been irritated by her refusal to come to Queen's Close. But that was no excuse for such conduct. The fact was that he seemed incapable of behaving well around her. She piqued and provoked him as no woman had ever done before, and it was plainly essential that he should avoid her company in the future if he wished to maintain his own self-respect.

Thus had Victor resolved, and in the weeks that followed, he clung grimly to his resolution. Yet he found it a struggle in spite of his professed dislike for Catherine. He made excuses to ride or drive past the cottage, hoping to get a glimpse of her. He even took to attending church on Sundays—a thing he had not done in years—merely in order to have the excuse to see and speak to her for a few minutes afterward.

Victor recognized that he was becoming dangerously obsessed on the subject of his cousin. That was how he put it to himself: *dangerously obsessed.* It did not seem to him that his feelings for Catherine could be anything more, for was there not quite as much irritation as admiration in his attitude toward her? And even such admiration as he felt was tempered with a clear recognition of her faults. She might sing and play pianoforte in an elegant, ladylike manner, but her voice was mediocre and her playing indifferent. She undeniably possessed a handsome figure and an attractive smile, but she was also red haired, green eyed, and freckled. She might have a keen mind and a lively sense of humor, but she also had the very devil of a temper.

Clearly it was irrational that a red-haired, green-eyed termagant should obtrude herself so frequently on his thoughts. Victor told himself it was irrational, but this did nothing toward ridding him of his obsession. After he had spent a whole afternoon hanging about the village post office, merely because Mrs. Everhart had happened to mention that Catherine usually walked into the village each day to fetch the family mail, he made up his mind that drastic measures were necessary.

It's merely because I never see another tolerable-looking female from day to day that I am so obsessed with my cousin, he told himself, conveniently forgetting that he had passed as much as six months at a time in the neighborhood of Cordelia Langley without becoming obsessed by her. *I need something to divert myself—something besides sport and estate business. In fact, I begin to think it's time I took Mama's advice and thought about marrying and settling down. I've been talking about it long enough, heaven knows, and this business with Catherine is a sure sign that I've been a bachelor long enough.*

Feeling satisfied that he had hit on a proper solution to his difficulties, Victor lost no time in communicating his decision to his mother. "Mama, I think I'm ready to take the plunge," he announced at dinner that night. "Should you be willing to entertain a small party here at the Close for a month or two?"

Lady Caldwell looked up in amazement from her soup *à la Reine.* "A party?" she repeated. "To be sure, dearest, I would be very glad to entertain anyone you might invite to Queen's Close. But I did not know you contemplated inviting a party here."

"I only made up my mind to it this afternoon. As I said, I think I'm ready to take the plunge." Victor repeated the words with a slightly self-conscious air.

His mother merely looked puzzled. "But you have had parties here before, dearest," she said. "Hunting parties and shooting parties and that party you held for that queer Frenchman who was supposed to be so clever—"

"Yes, but this is different, Mama," said Victor impatiently. "By saying that I am ready to take the plunge, I mean that I am ready to get married."

"Oh," said Lady Caldwell, looking startled. "Are you indeed, dearest?"

Victor, who had expected more of congratulation than this, was irritated. "Aren't you going to ask whom I mean to marry,

Mama?" he said. "I should think you would like to know who your future daughter-in-law will be."

"To be sure, dearest. I confess I had not got quite so far along as that. I was still reeling in shock at your announcing so suddenly that you mean to get married."

"It is not sudden at all, Mama! I told you weeks and weeks ago how much I admire Lady Anne Stoddard."

"Yes, so you did," agreed Lady Caldwell. She paused a moment, then added, "It is Lady Anne you mean to marry?"

"Of course it is," said Victor, a bit testily. "Whom else should I marry, Mama?"

"No one, dearest. Only when you spoke of Lady Anne before, I did not sense that you had at all made up your mind to marry her."

"Well, I have made up my mind now," said Victor firmly. "Lady Anne is the most beautiful, accomplished girl I have ever met, and I cannot imagine anyone making me a better wife. I intend to invite her and her family to Queen's Close and to make her an offer as soon as possible."

"Very well, dearest," said Lady Caldwell, though she still looked doubtful. "Did you mean to invite anyone besides the Stoddards?"

"Yes, we may as well make a regular party of it as long as we are having guests. I give you carte blanche as to that, Mama. Invite anyone you think agreeable, but make sure invitations are sent out as soon as possible. I don't want any delay in getting this business settled."

Lady Caldwell refrained from remarking that he himself had already delayed proceedings by more than a month and that assembling a party of guests on such short notice might prove a difficult venture. She merely said, "I will write out the invitations this evening, my love," and let it go at that.

Satisfied, Victor devoted himself to his dinner, reflecting that he was now well on his way to recovering from his foolish obsession with his cousin. With the excitement of a house party and an incipient betrothal, there would be no time for thoughts of a red-haired termagant.

The invitations were sent out, and a surprising number of the invitees wrote back saying they would be delighted to come to Queen's Close, even in spite of the impromptu nature of the party. The Stoddards were among the first to send back their acceptances. Victor gave orders to his staff to prepare the guest chambers, allotting the best three to Lady Anne, her mother, and her brother, the Earl of Stoddard. On a clear day in early October, the carriage bearing the Stoddard coat of arms drew up before the portico of Queen's Close, and Victor went out to greet his bride-to-be.

The first person to exit the carriage was the Dowager Lady Stoddard. Regal of bearing and commanding of figure, the Dowager stepped down from the carriage and stood looking about her with an air of critical approval. Next came Lord Stoddard, complaining loudly of being "shaken to bits across that damned rough cart path Caldwell calls a drive."

Victor, looking at his future brother-in-law, could not find him a prepossessing figure. Lord Stoddard was a small man with bad teeth and a habitually ill-tempered expression. There was obstinance in the set of his jaw and self-indulgence visible in every feature from his bloodshot eyes to his sensual mouth. Victor was glad to turn his scrutiny from the Earl to his sister, who had just stepped down from the carriage.

During the three Seasons that had elapsed since her coming-out, Lady Anne had been frequently called the most beautiful woman in London. The appellation was a just one. She was a small, exquisitely slender woman, and she moved with a grace that made all her actions appear part of some stately dance. Her dark hair was invariably coiffed in a Grecian style, the better to emphasize the classical regularity of her features. Her eyes were large and blue and her teeth as flawless as her brother's were faulty.

She smiled at Victor now, disclosing her teeth in all their pearly splendor. Victor smiled back, conscious of relief as well as admiration. Lady Anne was every bit as beautiful as he remembered. He was sure that with such a woman about, he would soon forget his irrational obsession with Catherine.

"Welcome to Queen's Close," he said, bowing first to the Dowager, then to Lady Anne and her brother.

"Thank you, my lord," said the Dowager, bowing in return with stately condescension. Lady Anne smiled again and dropped him a curtsy enchanting in its studied grace. Lord Stoddard, however, ignored Victor's greeting, being more intent on his own personal comfort.

"It's hot," he said, his tone as accusing as though Victor had been guilty of personally ordering the weather. "Damnable weather for October. I'm as dry as the Sahara. I hope you've got something in your cellars worth the drinking, Caldwell."

Victor regarded him with astonishment and a rising indignation. Although he had frequently visited the Stoddards' home in Grosvenor Square, it had never fallen to his lot to have many dealings with Lord Stoddard. The Earl had always been a background figure in his own household, referred to frequently and deferentially by his mother and sister but seldom figuring in their lives. This was hardly surprising, considering the Earl's tastes in entertainment. While the Dowager and Lady Anne were passing dutifully from ball to opera party to Almack's assembly in the Season's prescribed round of gaieties, Lord Stoddard might be seen whiling away his own leisure hours in gaming hells, cockpits, and other, even less reputable places.

Victor, who had some acquaintance with such places himself, had never previously held this taste against the Earl. Now, however, as he looked into Lord Stoddard's peevish, self-indulgent face, he realized it was representative of his whole character. The man was a boor, nothing more nor less. And this was the man who was to be his future brother-in-law! Victor made no answer to Lord Stoddard's inquiry about his cellars, but only went on looking at him steadily. The Dowager, perhaps divining

Victor's state of mind, gave him a smile that would have been apologetic in anyone less self-assured.

"You must forgive poor Stoddard, Caldwell. Carriage travel always makes him unwell. I am afraid our journey today has quite knocked him up." Addressing her son in reproving accents, she continued. "My dear, be sure Lord Caldwell's cellars are all they should be. If you will only take a blue pill and lie down until dinner, I am persuaded you will feel much more the thing."

Lord Stoddard damned blue pills and lie downs with a fine impartiality and demanded brandy instead. "Or gin if you haven't any brandy, Caldwell," he added generously. "I'm not partial to one above the other, truth to tell."

"I'll see that some brandy is sent to your room immediately," said Victor in a stiff voice. He could scarcely conceal his disgust as he turned away from Lord Stoddard. But he was a little mollified when Lady Anne laid her slim gloved hand on his arm.

"You have a charming home, my lord," she said, smiling up at him. "I am so pleased to be finally seeing it for myself. Mama was quite laughing at me, for I was all of a flutter during our drive here. I was, indeed."

Victor smiled indulgently, looking down into her lovely, flowerlike face. It was hard to imagine Lady Anne being all of a flutter about anything. Her beauty was of the serene and unflappable sort; even her voice was calm as she described her supposed emotional turmoil. It struck him that she was just the sort of rational, well-bred woman he wanted for his wife. He slipped her hand within his arm.

"I hope you will like it here, Lady Anne. If you do not, it will not be for want of trying, I assure you. Let me take you into the house now, and my housekeeper will show you to your rooms."

Eight

By dinnertime, Victor had recovered from his momentary qualms.

The other house party guests had arrived, and as he took his place at the table with the Dowager at his left hand and Lady Anne at his right, Victor was conscious of a feeling of satisfaction. On this occasion there would be no Lord Stoddard to provide a jarring note. The Earl was seated at the other end of the table beside Lady Caldwell. It did occur to Victor to wonder what his mother would make of the Earl as a dinner partner, but he pushed the thought away from him. Of course his mother could be depended on to behave civilly to anyone. And by now Lord Stoddard would probably be in a more pleasant frame of mind than had been the case earlier. Traveling disagreed with many people, and it stood to reason that the Earl would not have been at his best after an all-day journey in a closed carriage.

Lady Anne was looking very beautiful in her dinner dress of ivory crepe. Victor's eyes lingered on her with pleasure. He also took pleasure in the Dowager's appearance, which was as usual a trifle severe but undeniably elegant. He felt the Stoddard connection was altogether one to do him credit, and he served forth the soup with a swelling of pride in his heart.

Despite this promising beginning, however, the dinner proved less enjoyable than he had anticipated. One of the other lady guests was an authority on antiquities and insisted on question-

ing Victor throughout the meal about the history of Queen's
Close and its neighborhood. He was kept so busy answering her
questions that he had opportunity to exchange only a few remarks with Lady Anne. But she smiled at him whenever he
caught her eye, and on the whole Victor was satisfied.

He consoled himself with the thought that he would have
many days ahead in which to devote himself to his bride-to-be.
Besides, the evening was not over yet. There would probably
be time after dinner when he might take Lady Anne apart for
a little private conversation. If the opportunity presented itself,
Victor meant to propose to her that evening. He was eager to
get the matter settled now that he had made up his mind, and
Lady Anne looked so lovely that his eagerness was given an
additional spur.

Of course it would have been more correct to approach her
brother first, as her closest male relative. But many people were
dispensing with that convention nowadays, and Victor had determined to do the same. He had no desire for a private interview with Lord Stoddard. Nor could he see that such an
interview was really necessary. The Stoddards appeared to be
as eager for the connection as he was, to judge by the way they
had snapped at his house party invitation. He felt sure they
would not trouble themselves over a trifling deviation from
traditional etiquette.

The dinner dragged to a close at last, and the ladies filed off
to the drawing room. Decanters of port and Madeira were set
out, and Victor resigned himself to the inevitable half hour or
so of masculine conversation. He was resolved to keep the interval no longer than that, for he was anxious to have his interview with Lady Anne. But here Lord Stoddard served to thwart
him.

"Damned good Madeira," he said approvingly, draining his
glass and presenting it to be refilled. "Not a bad wine at all,
Caldwell. Give me another glass, and I'll tell you how I managed
to get the whole of old Babcock's cellar last year when his place

was under an execution. Cost me a pretty penny, but it was worth it."

Victor was made to listen to an interminable story of how Lord Stoddard had used a mixture of deceit and extortion to force a bankrupt acquaintance into selling him the contents of his cellars at a loss. It was followed by another interminable story about a wager he had made with a mutual acquaintance and still another concerning his current mistress.

None of these stories reflected much credit on their narrator. Victor found his disgust for the Earl growing. He was even more disgusted when he looked at the clock and found more than an hour and a half had gone by since the ladies had left the table. Already many of the gentlemen had left the dining room, encouraged no doubt by Lord Stoddard's monopoly on the conversation. Victor would have liked to follow their example, but his position as host, together with his hoped-for connection with the Stoddards, forced him to maintain at least a semblance of politeness.

"Well, shall we join the ladies?" he asked as Lord Stoddard paused in his conversation in order to finish off his fifth glass of Madeira. "Your mother and sister must be wondering what has become of us."

"Damn the ladies," said Lord Stoddard thickly, draining his glass and slamming it down on the table. "I don't have any use for ladies. Give me a girl that's pretty and willing is what *I* say, and leave the ladies to themselves. This is damned good Madeira, Caldwell. Give us another glass, and I'll tell you how I put one over on old Sedgewick at Newmarket last year."

Victor, looking at his flushed and leering face, experienced a revulsion of feeling. Host or no host, he felt he could endure no more of Lord Stoddard's stories. Pushing the decanter toward the Earl, he stood up. "Forgive me, I must join the ladies now. I'll see you in the drawing room later on." Not waiting to see Lord Stoddard's reaction to this speech, he left the room without a backward glance.

A moment later he was entering the drawing room, where the

ladies and most of the gentlemen were dispersed in groups about the room. His mother was the first person to hail him as he entered. "There you are, Victor," she said with relief in her voice. "I was beginning to wonder whether you meant to join us at all!"

Victor bent to kiss her. "I was detained, Mama, " he said lightly. "Our noble friend Lord Stoddard took such enjoyment in my Madeira decanter that I could not persuade him to relinquish its company."

He observed that his mother's expression changed at the mention of Lord Stoddard. He smiled at her ruefully. "I'm afraid the Earl is rather a rough diamond, Mama. I was sorry you were obliged to sit next to him at dinner, but I hope he did not bore you too much."

"Oh, no, he did not *bore* me," said Lady Caldwell with some emphasis.

Again Victor smiled ruefully. "I know Lord Stoddard is perhaps rather crude," he said. "Just between you and me, Mama, I confess I do not care for him myself. But his sister fortunately bears no resemblance to him. She is very lovely, isn't she?"

"Yes, she is lovely," agreed Lady Caldwell. In a reserved voice, she added, "Indeed, she seems a very sweet girl. Very sweet and—and innocent."

Victor was annoyed by this faint praise. Inwardly he cursed Lord Stoddard once again. Of course it must have been the Earl's fault that his mother was unenthusiastic at the prospect of an alliance with the Stoddards. Lady Anne herself was so obviously above reproach: beautiful, and well mannered—and, yes, very sweet and innocent. Victor consoled himself with the thought that his mother must inevitably come to recognize her good qualities, while her brother's bad ones must as inevitably recede into a distant memory. Victor could only wish that the Earl's visit to Queen's Close was ended, so he might be reduced to a memory as soon as possible.

Excusing himself to his mother, he made his way across the drawing room to where Lady Anne sat beside her mother. She greeted him with one of her dazzling smiles, and Victor's heart warmed to see how sincerely glad she seemed to see him. He found himself thinking how different was this reception from that generally accorded him by Catherine, who, if she did not look actually dismayed at his approach, at least always looked wary and reserved.

"Good evening," he said, taking Lady Anne's hand in his and bowing over it.

"Good evening, my lord," she said, giving him another of her dazzling smiles. Charmed, Victor inquired if she was enjoying herself. Lady Anne knit her brows together.

"Yes, to be sure, my lord. Although Mama and I have not been doing much besides sitting here this past hour or so. But this is a very pretty room, and I like it very much."

"Lady Anne would like any room that contained a pianoforte," put in the Dowager with a fond smile toward her daughter. "She is inordinately fond of music."

"Perhaps she will play for us then," said Victor. "I am fond of music myself." He was eager to exorcise the memory of the last lady who had played at the pianoforte.

Lady Anne rose obediently and went to the instrument. As Victor settled down to listen, he told himself triumphantly that Catherine was not the only young woman in the world who refrained from making a parade of her abilities by false modesty. Here was another, and one whose abilities were undoubtedly far superior to those of his tiresome cousin!

Yet his enthusiasm suffered a check when Lady Anne began to play. Her fingers moved over the keys in perfect time and with admirable accuracy, but it seemed to Victor that her performance had a mechanical quality he had never noticed before. It was better when she sang, for she had a very sweet voice and she invariably finished each song by smiling at him. Enchanted by these tributes, Victor told himself that she was undoubtedly a superior performer to Catherine.

"I am sorry you do not have a harp," said Lady Anne as she left the pianoforte to rejoin Victor and her mother on the sofa.

"I play the harp, too, as well as the pianoforte. And if I do not have a harp to practice on, I will soon grow dreadfully rusty. At home, Mama makes me practice my music three hours a day."

The Dowager, looking displeased, emitted a shrill laugh. "Nonsense, my dear! I am sure it is rather that I must *restrict* you to practicing three hours a day. This child is so foolishly fond of music, Caldwell, that I do not believe she would stop to take her meals if I did not make her. Would you, my dear?"

"No, Mama," said Lady Anne obediently.

The Dowager gave another shrill laugh. "Indeed, Caldwell, Lady Anne is a most dedicated musician. But she will have to manage without a harp for these next few weeks, seeing that you do not have one here at Queen's Close."

Victor was made slightly uncomfortable by this exchange. "Perhaps one of the neighbors has a harp we might borrow," he suggested diffidently. "I could make a few inquiries if you like."

The Dowager said approvingly that this would be a splendid solution, and Lady Anne thanked him with a smile. Still, Victor continued to feel uncomfortable. He told himself it did not matter if Lady Anne's love of music was real or assumed. There were undoubtedly many young ladies who chose to cultivate their musical abilities merely because it was the fashion. But somehow the picture of Lady Anne laboring at the harp and pianoforte three hours a day stayed with him for the rest of the evening, up till the time Lord Stoddard came staggering into the drawing room and provided an unwelcome diversion.

"There you are, Caldwell," he said, fixing a bleary eye on Victor and stumbling over a footstool that happened to lie in his path. "Wondered where you went off to. I've been wandering around your house for an hour trying to find you. Damned maze of a house—damned confusing, 'pon my word. If your butler hadn't given me a hand, I'd never have found my way here."

Victor found himself wishing his butler had not been quite so officiously helpful. It was evident that Lord Stoddard was more than three parts intoxicated. In that condition he was even less likely to be an addition to the party than in his natural state. The other guests were all looking at him—some with amusement, others with open disgust. Mrs. Watt, the antiquarian lady, said austerely that it was time she and her daughters sought their beds. Several of the other lady guests followed her lead, and this was the signal for a general exodus from the drawing room as one guest after another professed fatigue and begged to be excused.

Victor was irritated to see his party dispersed in this manner. Not that he had wanted so much to prolong it, for he had been hoping all evening that he might get a few minutes alone with Lady Anne. But now, with Lord Stoddard's advent, it seemed that he would not only be denied his tête-à-tête with Lady Anne, but would be forced to endure one with her obnoxious brother instead. He reckoned without the Dowager, however. As the last guest murmured an adieu and left the drawing room, she turned to her son.

"Stoddard, I fear you are still unwell after that long carriage drive," she said in a commanding voice. "You look extremely flushed. Come upstairs with me, and I will get you one of my headache powders."

In a thick voice Lord Stoddard damned his mother's headache powders, but he was no match for the Dowager. Remorselessly she drove him from the drawing room, pausing to address a few words to her daughter on the way out. "Anne dear, I will see you upstairs in a few minutes. Mind you do not sit up too late."

"I think I shall retire now, too, Victor," said Lady Caldwell, taking the hint. "Good night, my love." Forcing a smile to her lips, she added, "Good night, Lady Anne. No doubt I shall see you in the morning."

"Good night, ma'am," said Lady Anne, returning Lady Caldwell's smile with a dazzling one of her own. She waited till one of the footmen had wheeled Lady Caldwell's wheelchair out of the room; then she turned to Victor. "I suppose I ought to be retiring, too, my lord," she said. Having spoken these words, she paused and regarded Victor expectantly.

Victor recognized his cue and spoke in his turn. "No, don't go yet, Lady Anne. There was something I wished to say to you—something I would rather say while we are alone."

"Yes?" said Lady Anne, gazing up at him with wide blue eyes.

The moment was perfect, and Victor wondered why he felt so strange and awkward as he brought forth his prepared speech. "Dear Lady Anne, you must know I have always had the highest respect and admiration for your character," he recited rapidly. "As I have come to know you better during these last few months, I have learned to care for you most sincerely. It would be the greatest happiness to me if you would consent to become my wife."

Lady Anne beamed. "Oh, my lord, it would make me very happy, too," she said. "Indeed, I have always liked you very well. I cannot think of anyone I would rather marry."

"Well, that's settled then," said Victor. He felt a bit blank, but told himself he was merely overcome by happiness. Looking down at his bride-to-be, it occurred to him that he ought to kiss her. He tried to do so, but Lady Anne evaded his lips, not with any air of distress or embarrassment, but rather as though she were performing a necessary duty.

"Indeed, the matter is not *quite* settled yet, my lord," she said gently. "You must know that until Mama and Stoddard have given their consent, I cannot agree to marry you."

"Why not?" said Victor in surprise. "I had supposed they knew I meant to propose to you when I invited you here."

"Yes, they know *that,*" said Lady Anne, looking amused. "But they do not know yet what settlement you mean to make upon me. And until that is agreed upon, I cannot consent to marry you."

She spoke with the air of a pupil reciting a well-learned lesson. Victor looked at her, hardly believing what he was hearing. "Of course I am willing to make a fair settlement upon you,

Lady Anne," he said stiffly. "I would have thought that went without saying."

A smile bloomed forth once more on Lady Anne's face. "Then there will be no difficulty about our marrying, my lord," she said. "But you must understand that I cannot marry unless the settlements are in order. Poor Stoddard has so many debts!" She shook her head gravely. "It's dreadful how his creditors hound him. Once we had a bailiff staying at our house for weeks and weeks. It was very unpleasant, I give you my word. But if you are willing to make a fair settlement, then I am sure Mama and Stoddard will have no objection to our marrying."

Victor, looking into her smiling face, experienced a second revulsion of feeling. He wanted Lady Anne for his wife, of course—wanted her enough that he was willing to take her with only a token dowry or even with no dowry at all. But to obtain her at the cost of subsidizing Lord Stoddard's debts was an idea that struck him as highly distasteful.

Lady Anne seemed to sense something of his thoughts. Her expression became anxious. "You *will* speak to Mama and Stoddard about it, my lord?" she asked, laying her hand on his arm. "Once the settlements are agreed upon, you know, then our engagement can be announced."

Victor sought to equivocate with this unwelcome request. "I will speak to your mother, of course," he said carefully. "I had intended to do so anyway if you agreed to my proposal."

"And to Stoddard?" prompted Lady Anne, still looking at him anxiously. "You will speak to Stoddard, too?"

Victor knew he ought to allay her anxieties, but he simply could not bring himself to agree to a meeting with Lord Stoddard. He could imagine so clearly what the Earl's demeanor during such a meeting would be. Again Victor equivocated. "Perhaps, as it is merely a matter of business, it would be best if I called in my attorney," he told Lady Anne. "He could meet with your brother, and together they could come to an agreement on the subject of the settlements."

"Oh, yes, I daresay that *would* be best," agreed Lady Anne

happily. "I will tell Mama that it is all arranged." She then wished Victor good night and left the room, flashing one of her lovely smiles at him as she went out.

Nine

In the days that followed, Victor found himself very far from enjoying the undiluted happiness he had anticipated as the betrothed husband of Lady Anne Stoddard.

He had sustained an interview with the Dowager on the morning after his proposal to Lady Anne. Lady Stoddard had begged the privilege of a few words with him after breakfast; and Victor had acceded, acknowledging to himself that this request was quite in order. It was natural that a mother would wish to speak to the man who had solicited her daughter's hand in marriage. But he hoped fervently that Lord Stoddard would not be present at this interview. It did not seem likely, considering the Earl's excesses the night before, but if such excesses were a regular thing with Lord Stoddard (as appeared only too likely), then it was possible he might be so accustomed to their aftereffects that he considered them no bar from rising early.

As it developed, Victor's fears were needless. The Earl had not yet come downstairs when at last he and Lady Stoddard had their interview. Yet it proved not altogether a comfortable interview, even in spite of this undoubted advantage.

"My daughter tells me you have made her an offer of marriage," said the Dowager, commencing her campaign with admirable directness. "Let me say first how happy I am, Caldwell. Lady Anne is my only daughter, so of course I take a particular interest in her welfare. I do not think she could have won the regard of any man better disposed to provide for her future happiness and well-being."

Victor murmured that he was very much obliged to Lady Stoddard for her good opinion. Yet he was fairly sure this was only a prelude to the real object of her speech. Surely enough, after a little more polite persiflage, the Dowager got down to business.

"Of course you will wish to make a settlement on my daughter at the time of your marriage. Lady Anne comes of a very ancient family, as you must know, and her connections on both sides are most illustrious. This must naturally be taken into account in fixing the amount of the settlement. In speaking to Lady Anne last night, I learned you and she had spoken of this matter, and that you had indicated you were willing to make the necessary concessions?" The Dowager fixed Victor with a basilisk eye.

"Yes, we did speak of the matter, as you say," said Victor, striving for an easy air. "But of course the amount of the settlement must be an issue for the lawyers to settle. Lady Anne and I could hardly be expected to arrange it all between us last night!"

He gave the words a jocular tone, hoping to ease the discomfort of the situation. The Dowager accorded his witticism a brief, humorless smile. "To be sure, Caldwell. But you know I cannot permit Lady Anne to enter into any formal engagement until the matter of the marriage settlements has been resolved. This is one of those issues on which a mother must be wise enough for both herself and her child. Anne is so fond of you that she would willingly injure herself on your behalf, but you must see I would not be doing my duty as a mother if I were to allow her to do such a thing."

"As it happens, Lady Anne is quite as careful on her own behalf as you could wish, ma'am," said Victor dryly. "She told me the exact same thing."

"Then you are willing to meet with Stoddard this afternoon?" said the Dowager with ill-concealed eagerness. "Of course the details can be left to the lawyers, but you and Stoddard could come to a general agreement about what you were willing to do for Anne. And then, once an agreement had been reached, we could announce your engagement."

Victor was eager enough to announce his engagement, but he resented the Dowager's attempts to manipulate him using this lure. His resentment caused him to become obstinate. "I would be most uncomfortable entering into any financial agreement without my attorney present," he said with finality. "I would prefer to wait until he can attend me before speaking to Lord Stoddard."

"Then the announcement of your engagement shall have to wait, too," said the Dowager with an air of vengeful triumph.

"Very well," said Victor with a shrug. "Of course you must act in what you believe to be your daughter's best interests, ma'am. I will be happy to withdraw my proposal until such time as you are satisfied I am willing to provide for her."

The Dowager, looking alarmed, sought to retract her ultimatum. "Oh, there is no need to be hasty, Caldwell! You understand I am only trying to protect Lady Anne's interests."

"Yes, I understand that," said Victor dryly.

The Dowager gave him a long, frustrated look. She appeared to be weighing the advantages of a baron in the hand versus a generous settlement in the bush. That this was indeed the case was made clear by her next words. "Well, if you will give your word as a gentleman that you will act generously by Anne, I suppose I would have no objection to announcing your engagement immediately."

"I fail to see what would be the good of my giving my word on such a matter," said Victor in an icy voice. "The nature of my intentions toward Lady Anne must be implicit in my proposal. And if you consider that to be insufficient security—"

"Not at all, not at all," said the Dowager hastily. "We will announce the engagement immediately." She hesitated, but could not resist adding, "When do you think your attorney will be able to wait on Stoddard?"

"I shall write him immediately. But it may be that he canno leave London for a week or two. Perhaps it may be as much a several weeks. He is currently busy with some other matters have in hand."

The Dowager accepted this with a chastened nod and wen away, presumably to inform her son and daughter of what hac transpired. Victor, watching her go, reflected that his statemen to her was a true one as far as it went. He had written hi attorney two weeks ago asking him to investigate the affairs o the late Mr. Everhart. Only that morning had he received thi reply:

> Crabtree and Peppard,
> Bartle Square, Middle Temple

My Lord,

In accordance with your lordship's request, I have made a preliminary investigation into the affairs of the late Matthew Everhart, Esq.

Although it is impossible to be conclusive at the present time, I am of the opinion that your apprehensions of misconduct on the part of Mr. Everhart's partner are probably correct. I have had several interviews with Mr. Carr, and his explanations concerning the terms of his partnership with Mr. Everhart as well as the dispersion of their joint assets following his death are unsatisfactory, to say the least. But I do not think Mr. Carr can be persuaded to make good his defalcations without an action or at least the threat of one. If your lordship wishes me to undertake such an action on your behalf, please inform me and I will be happy to set the process in motion. I am,

> Yours sincerely,
> Joshua Crabtree, Esq.

Victor immediately wrote back, requesting Mr. Crabtree to undertake an action against Mr. Carr on behalf of Mr. Everhart's widow and daughter. He sealed and addressed the letter with a feeling of satisfaction.

Of course Mr. Carr might crumble at the first prospect of a lawsuit, but then again he might not. If the matter came to trial, it would inevitably absorb weeks, if not months, of Mr. Crabtree's time. And that would provide Victor with an excellent excuse to further delay his meeting with Lord Stoddard.

Victor supposed he was being childish in wishing to put off the inevitable in this way. But he had taken a strong dislike to the methods of the Stoddards, and he wished to frustrate them as far as possible. Of course he bore no grudge against Lady Anne in all this. She was an innocent victim, the pawn of her mother and brother, and she could not be held accountable for their actions. But it did hurt Victor a little that she seemed to care so much more for their interests than his own.

Well, never mind, he told himself. *I'm committed now and must make the best of it.* This struck him as a poor attitude for a newly engaged man, and he tried to soothe his fretted spirit with the thought of Lady Anne's incomparable beauty. But somehow, he found more comfort in picturing the delight of the residents of Crossroads Cottage should he be successful in recovering some part of their lost fortune. All afternoon he entertained himself with an elaborate daydream in which Catherine, with expressions of penitence for her past transgressions, threw herself at his feet and declared herself forever indebted to the generosity of her noble cousin.

That night at dinner, Victor's engagement to Lady Anne was announced to the company.

There were many expressions of congratulation from the other guests. All the ladies kissed Victor and told him he was getting a sweet bride, while the gentlemen thumped him on the back and called him a lucky dog.

Victor supposed he was a lucky dog. Lady Anne certainly looked dazzlingly lovely in her dress of cerulean blue sarcenet, and even Lord Stoddard behaved with unusual circumspection, contenting himself with only two or three glasses of the champagne Victor ordered served to celebrate the occasion.

Of course he made up for it afterward when the gentlemen were alone in the dining room with the port and Madeira decanters. But Victor no longer felt obliged to stand upon ceremony with his future brother-in-law. When Lord Stoddard began to grow offensive and hint that Victor might advance him some part of his sister's settlement to pay his most urgent debts, Victor got up abruptly and left the dining room.

He joined the ladies in the drawing room, where they were all gathered in a congratulatory group around Lady Anne. Lady Anne smilingly held out her hand to him, and Victor took it, finding some pleasure in this perquisite of his new status.

"We have been talking about the wedding, my lord," she said with childish pleasure.

"Aye, we have settled all the details among us, my lord," added one of the other ladies, laughing. "You need not do a thing except put on your best clothes and appear at the church at the proper time!"

"No, he also needs to give a ball to celebrate his engagement," contradicted another. "I have assured Lady Anne that her position entitles her to a ball, and she has agreed she will be content with nothing less!"

"I suppose I might give a ball," said Victor, smiling. "Indeed, I had intended to give a party anyway while you are all here so that you might meet some of my neighbors." He looked at his mother. "Mama, can we put together a ball in the next couple of weeks?"

"To be sure, my love," assented Lady Caldwell. With a slightly ironic smile, she added, "I am growing used to putting together parties on short notice."

Victor ignored this gibe and turned to his betrothed. "Then you shall have your ball," he told Lady Anne. She clapped her hands in delight, and the other ladies murmured their approval. The rest of the evening's conversation revolved around the newly affianced couple and their betrothal ball. Victor was able to take pleasure in his new status and to think that there was, after all, something in the business of being engaged.

The next morning at breakfast, Victor asked Lady Anne to drive with him into the village. "I have a small errand there, but it won't take more than a minute of my time. After that, we would be free to spend the afternoon as we liked. There are several decent shops, and the parish church is generally held to be worth a visit. As it is such a lovely day, I mean to drive myself in my curricle."

Lady Anne, whose face had brightened at the mention of shops, fell at these last words. "No, I cannot ride in a curricle, my lord," she said, with a shake of her head. "Thank you, but I believe I would rather stop here at Queen's Close."

"Why cannot you ride in a curricle?" said Victor, disappointed by her refusal. "I assure you it is perfectly safe. I've been driving one for years, and I've never had an accident."

"I'm sure you are a splendid driver, my lord," said Lady Anne warmly. "But you see my hair always gets dreadfully mussed in an open carriage. And I must think of my complexion, too. It would not do for me to get freckled or sunburned, you know. I don't believe I care to risk it, my lord. But if you were willing to take a closed carriage, I suppose I might go." She looked at Victor hopefully. "A closed carriage would really be better anyway, because then Mama might go with us—and Stoddard, too, perhaps."

Victor, who had been about to accede to her request, felt a shudder go through him at these words. "Perhaps another time, Lady Anne," he said hastily. "I have already ordered my curricle, and I don't care to put the servants to the work of changing the horses over. We will drive to the village another day."

Lady Anne pouted at this, and her pout grew even more pronounced when her mother told her it was better that she should stay home and practice her music rather than gadding about the village. "Now that Lord Caldwell has been good enough to procure you a harp, you have no reason for not practicing," she said autocratically. "I would have you in your best form so you may play for him tonight if he likes."

"To be sure," said Lady Anne, but it was plain that she was less than enthusiastic at the prospect. The memory of her sullen face stayed with Victor as he made his solitary way to the village.

That memory disturbed him more than he cared to admit. It was yet another flaw in the image he had formed of Lady Anne prior to their engagement. He could not quite get over his disappointment to find she was not all he had imagined her.

Of course it did not matter that Lady Anne practiced music only in order to appear accomplished. It likewise did not matter that she refrained from riding in open carriages for fear of ruffling her hair or spoiling her complexion. But these facts, immaterial in themselves, had begun to seem merely part of a larger picture, a picture that Victor did feel mattered and one that caused him a good deal of disquiet.

Of course women are pretty much all artificial—take it one way or another, he told himself. *I don't suppose Lady Anne is any worse than the rest of them.* But this statement, true though it might be, brought him small comfort.

As he drove toward the village, it occurred to him that it would be very little out of his way to drive by Crossroads Cottage. He had refrained from taking that route for the past week or two, but there could be no objection to his doing so now. He was safely engaged to Lady Anne, and so his obsession with Catherine must pass off as the harmless infatuation it was. If he should happen to see Catherine, say, reading on the porch or working in the garden, it would do no harm to stop and exchange a few words with her. Indeed, it would be only polite to inform her and her mother of his engagement, seeing that they were relations.

Having rationalized his desires in this manner, Victor turned his curricle into the lane that ran past Crossroads Cottage. When he reached the cottage, however, he was disappointed to see no sign of Catherine about the place. He considered stopping and making a formal call, but in the end decided against it. His business in the village was fairly pressing, and it would be better to call sometime when he would not feel hurried. So he whipped up his horses and continued on into the village.

His business there was easily settled, and within an hour, he was remounting his curricle and turning his horses' heads toward home. As he drove along the village high street with its rows of shops and businesses, he debated whether he ought to stop at Crossroads Cottage on his way home. There was a guilty pleasure in the idea that warned him that his infatuation with Catherine was not as dead as it ought to be, but he told himself he was a grown man and he could be trusted to restrain his feelings now that he had a sufficient reason to do so.

As Victor weighed the pros and cons of the idea, he became aware that a gentleman on the sidewalk opposite had halted suddenly and was regarding him with a look of startled recognition. Victor, returning his gaze curiously, was astonished to recognize him as Sir Simon Debrett—a gentleman whom he had often met in London but whom he had certainly never expected to see treading the humble sidewalks of his own home village.

"Simon?" he said in disbelief.

Sir Simon sketched a bow—the same graceful gesture that had distinguished him in the drawing rooms of London. Yet his face wore a distinctly guilty expression. Victor observed it and was puzzled anew. He brought his horses to a halt, and Sir Simon, seeing his intention, came over to speak to him. But he came almost reluctantly, and his greeting to Victor was not the cheerful, inconsequential affair it would have been in London.

"How d'you do, Caldwell? Fine day, isn't it?"

Victor ignored both these inquiries in order to voice the question that was uppermost in his own mind. "What the deuce are you doing here, Simon?" he asked. "I had thought you were to accompany your mother to Bath this autumn."

"Yes, I did accompany her there, but after a week or two I decided I'd had enough of it. Bath's a pretty slow place, you know."

"And this isn't?" said Victor with a disbelieving smile.

A flush appeared on Sir Simon's handsome face. "It isn't London, of course," he said. "But you know it's really not a half-bad village, Caldwell. I'm staying at your inn over there." He pointed toward the modest hostelry that stood across the street.

Victor looked at him, unable to picture the fastidious Sir Simon Debrett staying contentedly at the Pig and Poke. "But why are you here?" he asked again. "You must have had some reason for coming here, out of all the villages in England. And I already know it wasn't because you wanted to see me! You looked positively cag faced when you saw me just now."

The flush on Sir Simon's face deepened. "Perhaps I did, but you mustn't believe I was sorry to see you, Caldwell," he said earnestly. "Of course I knew you lived somewhere hereabouts. It just caught me off guard when I saw you coming down the street a minute ago. As to why I'm here—well, that's a personal matter, and a rather complicated one, too. I hope you won't take it amiss, Caldwell, but I don't really care to talk about it just now. Later on, perhaps, once I have everything settled—but not now."

Victor could readily believe there was some mystery about Sir Simon's presence in the village. He had already shown by his looks and manner that he was embarrassed at being discovered there by his friend. And his motive for coming to Leicestershire had obviously been a very pressing and powerful one, for his presence in such bucolic surroundings was inexplicable under any normal circumstances. A noted bon vivant, renowned for his discriminating taste in food, drink, and dress, Sir Simon lived in London year round save for those occasions when he was obliged to accompany his widowed mother to Bath or Brighton or some other resort.

Altogether, Victor's curiosity was roused by his friend's eccentric behavior. He did not mean to pry into Sir Simon's personal affairs, of course, but he reasoned that as long as his friend was in the neighborhood, it was only natural to invite him to Queen's Close. And once at Queen's Close, it might be possible to stimulate him into revealing more about his mysterious errand.

All these thoughts went through Victor's head as he regarded his friend. Sir Simon looked back at him anxiously. "I hope you're not offended, Caldwell," he said. "If I thought it wouldn't jeopardize my business here, I wouldn't mind taking you into my confidence. But as it is—"

"Be sure I am not offended by that," said Victor heartily. "What does offend me, Simon, is that you did not see fit to come to Queen's Close and ask for lodging when you found you were to be in the neighborhood. It cuts me to the heart to see you prefer the hospitality of Mrs. Harriwell at the Pig and Poke to my own."

A sheepish grin appeared on Sir Simon's face. "Well, I don't know that I prefer it, Caldwell," he said. "But you know I came here hoping to get my business settled as quickly and quietly as possible. And to that end, I thought I'd better stick with Mrs. Harriwell rather than bothering you over at Queen's Close. You've a party staying there just now, don't you?"

"Yes, but there's always room for one more, Simon. Indeed, I think you had better give Mrs. Harriwell notice and come stay with us. Mama will be glad to see you, and I've some Malmsey Madeira that's better than anything they have in the cellars of the Pig and Poke."

Sir Simon brightened perceptibly at these words. "Have you, by Jove! I must say that tempts me, Caldwell. If you're sure I won't be in the way—"

"Not at all. And if you want to taste my Madeira, I'd advise you to come as soon as possible. At the rate Stoddard's putting it away, I won't have any left in another week."

"Oh, Stoddard," said Sir Simon with a contemptuous face. "You might as well give him Mrs. Harriwell's homebrew as waste your Madeira on him, Caldwell. I don't believe he'd know the difference."

"Indeed, I am sure you are right, Simon. But it looks as though I must endure him for the next few weeks, so I suggest you make haste if you wish to sample my dwindling supply of Madeira. Shall we drive over to the Pig and Poke and tell Mrs. Harriwell she must relinquish your company?"

Sir Simon was amenable to this suggestion and returned to the inn to inform his landlady that he was quitting her premises. Leaving his servants to pack his bags and follow after in his own carriage, Sir Simon took his place in the curricle beside Victor. Together the two men set off for Queen's Close.

Ten

Sir Simon proved a useful addition to the house party. His manners were good, he knew all the latest gossip, and his fastidious appreciation of the Malmsey Madeira was gratifying to Victor after Lord Stoddard's indiscriminate guzzling. Sir Simon was willing to make conversation with the ladies by the hour, and he participated cheerfully in all the entertainments Victor's mother had planned for the company.

At the same time, however, he remained very reticent about his reasons for being in the neighborhood. Almost daily he would absent himself from Queen's Close for an hour or two, then return looking downcast and chagrined. Victor could see that his business, whatever it was, was not prospering. But what that business might be he could not guess. He questioned Sir Simon delicately once or twice on this subject, but Sir Simon, while reiterating his wish to confide in Victor, maintained that he would rather wait until his business was settled before making any confidence. And with this answer Victor had to be content.

Victor had enough to occupy his thoughts just then, even putting aside Sir Simon's mysterious behavior. He had his guests, his engagement, and his preparations for the ball to keep him busy. In the days following the announcement of his engagement, both the Dowager and Lord Stoddard had made efforts to speak to him about the marriage settlements, but he had resolutely refused to discuss the subject until his attorney could be present. Happily, Lady Anne did not seem to partake of her relatives' anxieties. Save for an occasional attack of pettishness when her mother insisted she give up some more enjoyable activity to practice her music, curl her hair, or endure a session with the backboard, she remained as beautiful and serene as ever. By dint of dwelling largely on her beauty and serenity, Victor was able to regard his engagement in a not-too-unhappy spirit.

But still he could not help thinking about Catherine now and then. Indeed, after the first excitement of his engagement with Lady Anne had worn off, it seemed as though he thought about her more than ever. There was a vague undertone of guilt in his thoughts. Victor found this puzzling, for it seemed to him he ought to feel guilty on Lady Anne's behalf rather than Catherine's. It was surely wrong for an engaged man to be thinking so much about a woman other than his fiancée. But of course Catherine was a relative of sorts, and he assured himself that it was solely as a relative that he thought of her. It had been almost a month since he had called at Crossroads Cottage. He felt it would be perfectly proper for him to call there again now, both to announce the news of his engagement and to deliver the invitation to the upcoming ball.

"Mama, I think I shall call on the Everharts today," he announced at breakfast. "Have you any message you want to send them?"

Lady Caldwell looked up with pleasure. "Are you going to Crossroads Cottage? I am so glad, Victor. I am afraid we have been neglecting Martha and Catherine lately, though of course I had told them we were to have guests staying with us. But my conscience has been troubling me that we have not had them both to Queen's Close since the night of our dinner party."

"I thought you had asked them on several occasions since then," said Victor, looking surprised.

"So I have, dearest, but only Martha has been able to come. Of course I was very glad to see her, but I should like to see Catherine, too. Such a lovely girl and so very charming in her manners. I took a great fancy to her."

Lady Anne, who had been languidly consuming a piece of toast, looked up at these words. "Who is Catherine?" she asked.

"A cousin of mine," said Victor rather shortly. "She and her mother live in a cottage here on the estate."

"Oh, a poor relation," said Lady Anne, dismissing the subject without interest.

"Perhaps it would be as well if you accompanied Caldwell on his call, Anne dear," said the Dowager in a honeyed voice. "Of course you must meet your new husband's relations sometime. And if they are indigent relations, all the better that you should make their acquaintance now. After you are married, you know, it will be your duty to call upon them and render them any little services that might be necessary. And you will be less apt to be taken in if you know beforehand what to expect."

Lady Caldwell looked as though she wanted to make an indignant rejoinder to this speech. Victor forestalled her by making one of his own. "Lady Anne need not fear to be taken in by the Everharts, ma'am," he said hotly. "I assure you that they are very good, genteel people—quite as genteel as yourself. As for being indigent, they are not rich, certainly, but they insist on paying rent on their cottage and so moderate their expenditures as to have no debts. In that, they must be considered superior to a great many people who live in a much larger way."

The Dowager's eyes snapped angrily at this speech. However, she judged it better not to risk further provocation by replying to it. Lady Anne merely yawned and said, "It must be very tiresome to live in a cottage and moderate one's expenditures. I am sure I should die if I were obliged to do so."

Lady Caldwell gave her a pained look, but refrained from making any comment. Instead she turned to Victor. "No, dearest, I have no particular message to relay to the Everharts," she told him. "Merely give Martha and Catherine my love, and be sure to tell them they must come to our ball. I shall be quite disappointed if they do not both attend."

Victor promised to convey these messages and left the table precipitately. He was afraid that, if he lingered, the Dowager might make another effort to send her daughter along with him. In the normal way, of course, he would not have minded Lady Anne's company, but today, on this particular errand, he preferred to be alone. Not that he planned on saying or doing anything that his fiancée might not perfectly well have witnessed, as Victor assured himself. But somehow, he felt he would like to have one last private interview with Catherine. It would be in the nature of a final indulgence, and then he would be ready to put behind him the obsession that had held him in its grip for the past month or two.

He chose to walk to the cottage, using the path through the woods he had taken on his first visit. His reasons for this were several. The walk would give him time to compose himself, for he felt almost nervous at the prospect of seeing Catherine again. It would also give him a chance to plan how best to break the news of his engagement to her. Of course there was no reason why Catherine should care if he was engaged, but he still felt it important that the thing should be done in a proper manner. His third reason was to prolong his time away from Queen's Close. The constant presence of guests there, and in particular the Stoddards, was beginning to wear upon him. He still maintained his loyalty and affection for Lady Anne, naturally, but there was no doubt he would be glad to escape for a while from the Dowager and Lord Stoddard.

As he approached the cottage, Victor slowed his steps, looking about him at the changes that had taken place since his last visit. Autumn had advanced by leaps and bounds, dimming the gay colors of the garden, but brightening those of the trees above him. He observed with approval that the Everharts had trimmed some of the trees and cleared away much of the brush and shrub growth that had flourished unchecked during the cottage's vacancy. There was even fresh paint on the shutters and eaves and a fresh coat of whitewash on the fence that enclosed the cottage garden. Victor thought to himself that the place had never looked better, and once more he fulminated on Lady Stoddard's remarks about poor relations. This was clearly the residence of gentlewomen, and he vowed that, whatever the Dowager might say, her daughter should never be allowed to patronize Catherine and her mother.

As he came around the corner of the house, the first thing that caught Victor's eye was Catherine. She was standing on the porch with her back to him, but there was no mistaking that statuesque figure and head of ginger hair. Victor's heart gave a curious little leap within his breast. "Hallo, Cousin," he called.

Catherine swung round at the greeting. There was a harried look on her face, which changed to a look of consternation when she saw Victor. "Oh, dear," she said, then added violently, "No, I cannot. This is simply too much on top of everything else. You must excuse me, both of you, if you please." And with these words, she ran into the house.

Victor was surprised by this behavior, but his surprise was amplified a hundredfold when he saw that Catherine had not been alone on the porch. A gentleman stood there, his hat in his hand and an embarrassed expression on his face. Only the most cursory of glances was necessary to identify him to Victor as Sir Simon Debrett.

"Simon?" ejaculated Victor. "What the deuce!"

Sir Simon flushed up to the roots of his fair hair. "It's you, is it, Caldwell?" he said. "I suppose this was bound to happen. But it might have happened at a better time for my purposes, let me tell you."

Victor stared at him in bewilderment. "Your purposes!" he said. "What purpose could you have in calling on my cousin?"

Sir Simon glanced at the cottage in a nervous manner. "I'd as lief not tell you here," he said in a low voice. "It's a complicated story, and I'm afraid I don't cut any too favorable a figure in it. If you want to walk back with me to Queen's Close, Caldwell, I'll tell you on the way. It seems there's no point in my staying here any longer today."

"I will gladly walk home with you, but first I must deliver a message to my cousins," said Victor. "If you wouldn't mind waiting here while I speak to them—"

"No . . . No, I believe I'd rather start back now," said Sir Simon with another nervous look at the cottage. "Indeed, you had better just leave a note for your cousins, Caldwell, and come with me. Mrs. Everhart isn't in, for one thing, and Catherine—well, as you've seen, she's in no mood for visitors right now. You'd better just write down your message and come along."

Victor was very loath to accept this advice. But when he sought to summon Catherine to the door, his summons produced no one but a flustered maidservant, who informed him self-consciously that Miss Everhart was indisposed. Victor therefore demanded paper, pen, and ink, and he wrote down his message while Sir Simon hovered nervously outside on the porch.

As yet no inkling of the truth had dawned upon Victor. As he and Sir Simon left the cottage and set off through the woods together, he impatiently demanded to know what had been his friend's business at the cottage. "And let me tell you, Simon, that I want to hear no more talk of your wishing to keep the matter confidential. If your business involves my cousin, then I think I have a right to know it."

"That's a matter of opinion," returned Sir Simon with dignity. "But in fact I've no objection to telling you, Caldwell. Indeed, I had nearly decided to make a confidant of you anyway, in hopes you could make Catherine see reason."

"It seems to me you make pretty free with my cousin's name, Simon," said Victor, eyeing him askance. "What gives you the right to call her Catherine?"

"She gave it to me herself. The fact is, we were once engaged to be married, Caldwell. Has she never spoken of it?"

Enlightenment broke over Victor like the dawning of a belated sunrise. He recalled Mrs. Everhart's remarks concerning Catherine's engagement and the gentleman for whom she still allegedly cherished a regard. This then was his cousin's former fiancé, the man who had basely abandoned her when Mr. Everhart had been revealed to be a pauper.

"You!" he exclaimed, regarding his friend with revulsion. "You are the suitor who cried off after her father died?"

Sir Simon flushed. "It's not so bad as that, Caldwell. I didn't actually cry off from the engagement, you know. Catherine released me from it."

"It comes to the same thing," said Victor hotly. "I have no doubt you made it plain you weren't eager to marry a girl with no portion. What could she do but release you from the engagement?"

Sir Simon's flush deepened. "You needn't read me a lecture, Caldwell," he said sullenly. "I know I behaved like a cad—"

"Yes, you did behave like a cad," said Victor in an uncompromising voice. "And knowing that to be the case, I should think you'd be ashamed to show your face around my cousin now. Haven't you caused her trouble enough?"

"But it's not like that, Caldwell. I don't mean to cause her any more trouble. In fact, my whole purpose in coming here was to persuade her to take me back as her fiancé."

Victor gazed at Sir Simon in stupefaction. Sir Simon, having made this announcement, appeared to feel the worst was over. He went on speaking, his voice growing more confident with each word. "So you see, Caldwell, it's not as though I were here to cause Catherine trouble. On the contrary, my intentions toward her are nothing but good. I'm willing to make her my wife as soon as she says the word. But until we have matters settled between us, I thought it best not to say anything to anybody else."

Victor looked at him for a long moment. "And you seriously expect to resume your engagement with my cousin, just like that?" he asked. "After the way you behaved before?"

Sir Simon looked annoyed. "Dash it, Caldwell. You don't have to keep rubbing it in," he said. "I know I behaved badly before, but that wasn't intentional. The fact is, I was caught off guard by the whole business. When I proposed to Catherine, it was with the understanding that she would have something pretty considerable when we married—and then all of a sudden I was told she wouldn't have a groat. Do you wonder that I shied a bit?"

"I don't wonder that *you* did, Simon," said Victor with gentle sarcasm. "But I hope you do not mean to imply that all gentlemen would behave so. Personally, I would consider it poor conduct to jilt a lady while her father was barely cold in his grave."

"That's easy for you to say, Caldwell," said Sir Simon, looking nettled. "Everybody knows you're rich enough to buy an abbey. But I've got to scrape along on only a few thousands a year. That's not poverty, of course, but you must see that Catherine's portion would have been very welcome."

"Yet apparently you have made up your mind to do without it now," pointed out Victor.

"Well, yes." Sir Simon looked slightly abashed. He cast a sideways look at Victor as they went along the path together. "I can't tell you how it is, Caldwell," he said after a minute. "I suppose you don't see it, being her cousin and all, but the fact is that Catherine's a very attractive girl. I thought so the first time I saw her there at the Bath assemblies. That's where we met, you know. I was escorting the Mater there for her annual dose of the waters."

Victor nodded. "Yes, of course," he said. "I should have guessed you met Catherine in Bath. The Everharts did not go to London for the Season, so you could hardly have met her anywhere else."

"That's right. And I tell you plainly, Caldwell, I fell for her hard right from the start. I asked her to marry me just a few weeks after we first met. And though I was anxious enough to be free of the match when it turned out her old man had been playing Merry Andrew with the family fortune, the fact is I haven't been able to get her out of my mind since. As I said, she's a very taking girl. You might have heard I was making up to Marianne Ridgeway this last Season. I did my best to convince myself it might answer, but when it came to the point I couldn't go through with it. Marianne can't hold a candle to Catherine, and that's the truth."

"I see," said Victor. Sir Simon gave him another sideways glance.

"So after I got the Mater comfortably installed in Bath, I asked around until I found someone who knew where Catherine and her mother had gone to. I didn't know till then that she was a relative of yours, Caldwell. That took me back a bit, but I couldn't see that it made any difference in the long run. So I made up my mind to come here and tell Catherine I didn't care if she had a marriage portion or not."

"Generous of you," said Victor in an ironic voice.

Sir Simon, however, took the words at face value. He nodded solemnly. "Yes, I think it was, Caldwell. Not many fellows would care to marry a girl who hadn't any fortune at all. But Catherine's something special, and I'd rather have her with no portion than Marianne Ridgeway with twenty thousand pounds." He looked speculatively at Victor. "Of course, if Catherine *did* have a portion—even if it were only a thousand or two—that would be so much to the good. I don't suppose you'd care to dower her yourself, Caldwell? You are her nearest male relative, after all."

"Disabuse yourself of that idea instantly," said Victor harshly. "I may be Catherine's nearest male relative, but I don't intend to dower her by so much as a penny."

Sir Simon accepted this refusal philosophically. "Well, it's no great matter," he said. "As I told you before, I'm willing to take her without a portion. Of course it's what you might call selling myself at a loss, but I've made up my mind that I shan't let that deter me. Catherine is something pretty special, and that being the case, I can afford to be generous on the subject of a dowry."

Victor, looking at Sir Simon's self-satisfied face, felt his fists clench involuntarily at his sides. He was surprised by the wave of hot anger that swept over him. It was evident that Sir Simon fancied himself the most generous and disinterested of suitors. He obviously saw himself as Catherine's savior, sweeping down to rescue her from a life of poverty and obscurity.

Victor supposed there was some justice in this viewpoint. Yet it made his gorge rise to hear Sir Simon talk so complacently about marrying Catherine—just as though she were a horse or a snuffbox or some other possession he was planning to acquire. And how incredible that Catherine should tamely submit to such treatment! Without thinking, Victor voiced his reflections aloud. "Am I to understand my cousin has consented to this arrangement, Simon?"

Sir Simon looked slightly embarrassed. "Well, not in so many words, Caldwell. Mind you, I don't doubt she intends to in time—but just at present she's still a bit annoyed with me."

Victor recalled Catherine's face when he had seen her on the porch. "Yes, she did look annoyed," he said dryly.

Sir Simon brushed this comment aside without rancor. "She has a right to be, of course. You know I don't begrudge her that, Caldwell. I behaved like a fool before, and if she chooses to punish me a bit now, I daresay it's no more than I deserve. But all the same, I don't doubt she means to take me back in the end. It doesn't become me to say so perhaps, but the fact is she used to be dashed fond of me. And I've no reason to believe her feelings have changed."

Sir Simon looked more complacent than ever as he made this statement. Once again Victor found his fists clenching. He was spared making any comment, however, for Sir Simon suddenly turned to address him in a wheedling voice.

"As a matter of fact, I was hoping you might say a word to her about that, Caldwell. It's all very well for her to keep me up in the air this way, but now I've made up my mind to have her, I'd as soon get the business settled. If you wouldn't mind speaking to her, perhaps you could convince her to give over her pique and set a date for the wedding. It's bound to come to that in the end, of course, and by delaying, she's merely cutting off her nose to spite her face."

"You are quite convinced she means to accept you then?" said Victor, looking Sir Simon full in the face.

Sir Simon nodded, looking surprised by the question. "Yes, to be sure. Only consider what her alternative is, Caldwell! She's a handsome girl, but without a portion who's going to want to marry her?"

"You want to marry her," said Victor with an edge to his voice.

"Yes, well, I explained all that. But in the ordinary way she's not likely to receive many offers. And you can't tell me she wants to spend the rest of her life living with her mother in a squalid little cottage! Well, I don't mean to say squalid exactly," he temporized, seeing Victor's quick frown. "But if you'd seen the Everharts' house in Bath, you'd realize what a comedown this must be for her."

Victor said nothing. Sir Simon regarded him with a mixture of anxiety and impatience. "So will you speak to her about it, Caldwell? As I said, I'm eager to get the matter settled."

Slowly Victor shook his head. "It would do no good, Simon," he said. "I have no authority over Catherine—a fact of which she is quick to remind me at every turn. If I were to recommend her to marry you, it would only inspire her to do the exact opposite. Besides—"

"Besides what?" prompted Sir Simon, looking disappointed.

"Besides, I would rather not meddle in the affair. If Catherine chooses to marry you after the cavalier way you have treated her, then I have nothing to say to it. But I would not care to put pressure upon her to do anything she felt contrary to her principles."

"I see," said Sir Simon coldly. He said nothing more after that, and Victor said nothing more either. The rest of their walk home was accomplished in perfect silence.

Eleven

In the days following his conversation with Sir Simon, Victor found himself in a most dark and desolate state of mind.

Sir Simon's revelations had come as a shock to him. There was no denying it, and Victor did not attempt to deny it. But what he did deny was that the idea of Catherine resuming her engagement to Sir Simon had disappointed him in any personal sense. He told himself that he had supposed his cousin had too much pride to behave in such a spiritless way. He would have predicted that a girl of her temperament would have sent Sir Simon away with his ears stinging had he ever dared show his face near her again.

But Sir Simon continued to go every day to Crossroads Cottage and to return apparently none the worse for the experience. Victor could only suppose that his visits there must be welcome. Hence it followed that Catherine must indeed mean to fulfill Sir Simon's predictions and take him back as her fiancé.

This idea bothered Victor more than he cared to admit. He could see only two reasons for Catherine's behavior, and neither of them was a reason that reflected well on her, as far as he was concerned. In the first place, Catherine's leniency toward Sir Simon might be motivated by simple financial distress. She found life in a cottage uncongenial and was willing to grasp at anything that offered an escape. Victor supposed he could understand such behavior, but still he was disappointed by it.

Of course everyone knew that women, with a few exceptions,

were all more or less mercenary. Even Lady Anne, sweet and elegant creature that she was, had shown flashes of the mercenary spirit. But Victor had supposed Catherine to be one of the rare exceptions. She had certainly not been mercenary when she rejected his offers of financial help before, and he found it bewildering that she would behave in such an inconsistent manner now.

Yet distasteful as the idea of a mercenary Catherine might be, it was still better than the second explanation that presented itself to Victor. This explanation, which haunted his darkest hours, was simply that Catherine still loved Sir Simon so much that she was willing to forgive him anything. Victor could not say why this idea bothered him so much, but whenever he envisioned Sir Simon's smug face repeating, "She used to be dashed fond of me," he felt a renewed urge to knock him down.

So tormented was Victor by these thoughts that in the days that followed he sought to escape them by any means that offered. He immersed himself in work and sport, returning barely in time to eat dinner with his guests. He attempted once or twice to seek solace in Lady Anne's company, but though her artless conversation ought have served to divert him, he found increasingly that it only irritated him. And the fact that the Dowager usually managed to work in a little jab about the still unresolved issue of marriage settlements did nothing to soothe his temper.

By the time the night of the ball arrived, Victor was in a thoroughly unsociable mood. He cursed the necessity that lay before him that evening as he donned his black evening clothes, silk stockings, and dance pumps.

"I'd as lief I'd never agreed to give a ball," he muttered through his teeth, as he arranged his neckcloth before the glass. Yet little as he was anticipating the evening ahead of him, he did have a curiosity to see Catherine. It would be the first time he had seen her since the day of his abortive call at the cottage. He knew she would be present, for she and her mother had sent in their acceptance some days before. Victor, as he put the finishing touches on his toilette, wondered if she would appear as

striking to him as she had the evening of the dinner party. He
wondered even more how she would conduct herself in regard
to Sir Simon.

Later, as he stood in the ballroom waiting for the guests to
appear, he found himself asking this question once again. Sir
Simon was standing to one side of the ballroom, conversing
negligently with Mrs. Watt. Victor surveyed him morosely, trying to see him as he must appear to Catherine. Sir Simon's fair
head gleamed as bright as gold in the light of the chandeliers.
His blue coat sat faultlessly across his elegant shoulders, and
his satin breeches and delicately flowered waistcoat were both
masterpieces of their kind. There was no denying that he was a
handsome man. Nor was he a mere tailor's dummy, for at the
moment he was holding his own in a most scholarly discussion
about medieval architecture. And though he might not be so
wealthy a man as Victor, by his own admission, his income
amounted to some thousands a year. It would be no wonder if
Catherine chose to claim so tempting a matrimonial prize.

Restlessly Victor turned his eyes away from Sir Simon. In
doing so, he caught the eye of Lady Anne, who happened to be
standing nearby. She immediately gave him a dazzling smile.
Victor—who had received countless such smiles during the past
few weeks and had come to suspect they were a mere mechanical
gesture rather than any particular sign of favor—forced himself
to smile back, but inwardly he felt almost annoyed. Yet Lady
Anne looked very lovely tonight, her slim figure robed in a gown
of *eau-de-nil* taffeta shot with gold and open over an ivory satin
petticoat. A diadem of pearls sat atop her dark head, giving her
an almost regal air. Any man might be proud to own her as his
bride-to-be.

But then there was her family. Morosely Victor turned his
eyes from Lady Anne to Lord Stoddard. The Earl looked more
respectable than usual tonight, no doubt owing to the fact that
his usual after-dinner session with the Madeira decanter had
been curtailed on account of the ball. But still he was not a
figure to make one proud to own him as a relation. His coat was

an exaggerated affair with broad lapels and padded shoulders, and his tight-fitting knee breeches emphasized the paunch that was the natural result of his self-indulgent lifestyle.

The Dowager, standing beside him, was by far the more noble figure. Yet Victor, surveying her with the knowledge born of closer acquaintance, thought now that there was something gross and displeasing about her appearance, too. Perhaps it was the haughty angle at which she bore her plumed head or the lines of avarice about her mouth that gave her a disturbing resemblance to a bird of prey. Whatever it was, Victor was glad to turn his eyes away from her to greet the party of guests whom his butler had just admitted into the ballroom.

For the next half hour, Victor was kept busy exchanging greetings with friends, neighbors, and acquaintances. The Langleys came in, all three generations of them, from old Mrs. Langley in her stiff brocade robes to Cordelia, resplendent in pink gauze and rosebuds. The Miss Scotts fluttered in, smiling and gay, and proceeded to make a dead set for Lord Stoddard.

"Not bad-looking gels, but a bit countrified, don't you know," confided Lord Stoddard, who had strolled over to give Victor his unsolicited opinion of these proceedings. "The little blonde in pink's more to my taste." He looked with lecherous approval at Cordelia Langley, who was flirting nearby with a handsome militia officer. Then suddenly his face changed, and he let out a low whistle. "Or better yet, the gal that's just walked through the door! Now there's a girl I wouldn't mind knowing better—a good deal better, heh, heh! Introduce me to her, won't you, Caldwell?"

With a strong sense of inevitability, Victor looked toward the door.

There on the threshold stood Catherine, with her mother beside her. Mrs. Everhart was dressed in unrelieved black, with a frilled headdress of jet beads crowning her gray head. Of course this somber dress was merely a badge of her still recent widowhood, but it might have been divinely inspired as the perfect foil for Catherine's. That lady was all in white: purest glittering white with touches of snowy lace that lay here and there on her arms and bosom like frostwork.

It took Victor a moment or two to adjust his eyes to this dazzling vision. Once his eye had adapted, however, he perceived that there was plenty more to render Catherine's costume striking besides its color. The bead-and-lace-encrusted bodice of her dress was cut low in front and back, and that part of her figure not revealed openly in this manner was sufficiently hinted at by the clinging silken draperies that served her as skirts. Her red-gold hair was a mass of waves and curls, crowned by a wreath of lace intermingled with pearls. In this costume she managed to look both spiritual and sensuous—lovely as an angel, but with an appeal that was frankly earthy. Victor could not wonder at Lord Stoddard's besotted expression. He himself felt besotted as he watched her look curiously about the room.

Eventually her gaze came to rest on him. Victor could tell the exact moment this happened by the change in her expression. She did not frown, precisely, but her eyes flickered and her brows drew slightly together. Victor thought there was an almost defiant look on her face as she came forward to where he stood.

"Good evening, my lord," she said, with a formal curtsy. "I hope I find you well?"

"Yes, very well," said Victor. Mrs. Everhart had come forward at the same time as her daughter and was greeting Lady Caldwell, who sat in her wheelchair nearby. Seeing that the two of them were fully occupied, Victor ventured another remark. "You look very handsome tonight, Cousin," he said. "That is a very lovely costume. I must say I prefer it to the one you were wearing when we first met."

He smiled as he spoke, hoping to encourage her into smiling also. But it was evident Catherine had taken his remark as other than a joke. Her brows drew together. "I generally do try to dress in a manner fitting to the occasion," she said in a cold voice. "For a ball I wear a ball dress—and for beating rugs I wear a cap and apron. I hope you have no objection to that, my lord? It would take a sad toll on my good clothes if I were forced to wear them every day."

"No, no, of course I have no objection," said Victor hastily. "I was merely joking." He felt that he had bungled the situation abominably.

To make matters worse, Lord Stoddard chimed in before he had a chance to recover himself. "So this is your cousin, eh, Caldwell? I must say, you've been keeping her devilish dark all this time." He gave Catherine a friendly leer. "I'm Stoddard, ma'am. You must know I've been staying with Caldwell these last few weeks. And in all that time he's never once mentioned he had a beauty like you tucked away on his estate. I'm very glad to make your acquaintance, ma'am, upon my word."

"This is Lord Stoddard, Cousin," said Victor stiffly. "He is brother to Lady Anne, my fiancée. Stoddard, this is Miss Everhart."

"I am very pleased to meet you, my lord," said Catherine, curtsying politely.

"So am I glad to meet you, Miss Everhart," returned Lord Stoddard, his eyes fixed greedily on her décolletage. "You're a sight for sore eyes and no mistake. Do you care to stand up with me for the first two sets? I'd be honored to have you as my partner."

Catherine hesitated, then assented with a reserved smile. "Certainly, my lord. Let me first pay my respects to Lady Caldwell. Then I will be happy to dance with you." Bestowing a cool nod on Victor by way of farewell, she moved over to where her mother stood talking to Lady Caldwell.

Lord Stoddard trailed after her, a foolish grin on his face and his chest thrust out in a self-important strut. Victor watched gloomily as he took Catherine's arm to lead her onto the floor. Just then Mr. Banks, Catherine's admirer from the dinner party, came rushing over with his face wreathed in smiles.

"By Jove, don't you look ravishing, Miss Everhart!" he exclaimed. "You take the shine out of every other girl in the room—stap me if you don't. Care to stand up with me for the first set?"

"Miss Everhart is engaged to me for the first set," Lord Stoddard informed him, thrusting out his chest yet further.

Mr. Banks looked disappointed, but compromised by requesting Catherine's company for the second set of dances. Catherine had just smilingly assented to this request when Sir Simon came hurrying over to where she stood.

"Here, Catherine. They're just about to start the dancing," he told her, taking her arm in a proprietary grasp. "We must take our places in the set."

"She ain't standing up with you for the first set, Simon," said Lord Stoddard, seizing Catherine's other arm and regarding Sir Simon with a scowl. "She already told me she'd dance the first two dances with me."

"And the second two with me," chimed in Mr. Banks.

Sir Simon turned a look of surprise and indignation on Catherine. "But how can this be?" he demanded. "You knew that I meant to dance the first set with you, Catherine. Why, I was speaking of it only yesterday when I called on you and your mother."

Victor, watching Catherine, saw a slow and rather malicious smile spread across her face. "Perhaps you did speak of it, Sir Simon," she said gently. "But you know that, in dancing as in other things, an engagement cannot be considered binding unless it is entered into with the full consent of both parties. Even then, it is by no means immutable—but we need not discuss that now. On this occasion my consent was neither sought nor given, and so I felt free to engage myself elsewhere."

This speech made Sir Simon flush and look for a moment both angry and confused. But he managed to get the better of these emotions and summoned up a dry laugh. "Very well," he said. "Perhaps I was rather presumptuous. But I hope you will forgive my presumption and consent to dance with me sometime this evening, even if you cannot favor me for the first two dances."

"Oh, sometime, to be sure," said Catherine with an offhand nod. "You may have the two dances after Mr. Banks if you want them." And with these words, she took Lord Stoddard's arm and went out onto the floor.

Victor, who had been watching this byplay, was startled to feel a touch on his arm. Turning, he found Lady Anne standing at his side.

"I thought, as the dancing was to begin, we ought to be taking our places," she explained. She looked with curiosity after Catherine's retreating figure. "Who is that girl? I saw you watching her just now, and I see that Stoddard means to stand up with her."

"That is my cousin, Miss Everhart," said Victor.

Lady Anne's delicate brows rose on her forehead. "Indeed?" she said. "The one who lives in a cottage? Well, she is not such a patterncard of economy after all. Those beaded silks are very dear, and that is real lace on her corsage if I mistake not. But I daresay she bought it all secondhand. Low dresses of that sort are quite outmoded nowadays. I am sure no one has worn them in London for at least two Seasons."

Victor felt a strong urge to defend Catherine. To his eyes there was nothing wrong with her dress, even if it were not in the latest mode, and he thought Lady Anne's criticisms rather catty. It occurred to him that he had never heard her abuse another woman before. She had always seemed to be above such pettiness, or so he had assured himself. But the past few weeks had shown Lady Anne deficient in several of the virtues he had previously credited to her account. There was a melancholy feeling in his heart as he took his fiancée's arm and led her onto the floor.

The first set consisted of country dances—both of which Victor danced with Lady Anne and both of which Catherine danced with Lord Stoddard. From Lord Stoddard, Catherine passed on to Mr. Banks and then to Sir Simon. Victor watched her closely during her dances with this last gentleman, trying to see what footing she might be on with her former fiancé. It was evident from the speech he had overheard that she had not forgiven him entirely, but at the same time, it did not seem that she was trying very hard to discourage him.

So intent was he on observing his cousin that he had little time or thought for anyone else. His preoccupation was remarked on smilingly by several people and unsmilingly by the Dowager, who addressed some words to him on the subject when he encountered her in the refreshment room later that evening.

"You seem a trifle *distrait* tonight, Caldwell," she said. "I hope you are not feeling unwell?"

"Not at all," said Victor, smiling and hoping to leave the matter at that.

But the Dowager, scenting his discomfort, bore down on him relentlessly. "There is a young lady here tonight—a red-haired young lady in a white dress. Someone told me she was a relation of yours."

"Yes, that would be my cousin, Miss Everhart," said Victor. He did his best to make his voice sound matter-of-fact, but that was difficult with the Dowager's eyes boring into him.

She regarded him without speaking for a moment or two. "Your cousin, you say. Would that be a cousin on your mother's or father's side?"

"On my mother's," replied Victor. "Technically, I suppose, she is a cousin once or twice removed. Her mother is first cousin to mine."

"I see," said the Dowager. She paused a moment, as though considering how best to prosecute her inquiry. "Is this the same cousin you spoke of the other day at breakfast? The one whom you said was in impoverished circumstances?"

"I did not say she was impoverished," said Victor sharply "Neither she nor her mother is wealthy, to be sure, but they are not paupers."

"They certainly do not dress like paupers," said the Dowager dryly. "I say nothing about Mrs. Everhart, for her dress is at least suitable, if a good deal more elaborate than her circumstances would warrant. But I confess I was surprised to see Miss

Everhart dressed as finely as she is tonight. I suppose you must have been surprised, too, Caldwell. 1 noticed you looking at her a great deal." She fixed Victor with a penetrating stare.

"Was I?" said Victor, giving her stare for stare. "I suppose I was merely thinking how handsome she looked."

The Dowager's lips thinned. "Yes, I suppose one might call her a handsome girl. But what a pity her hair is that unfortunate ginger color! Most unattractive—and of course quite without remedy, poor thing."

"I think her hair very attractive," said Victor boldly.

The Dowager disregarded this remark, however, and went on with her critique as though she had not heard him. "And then there is that figure of hers. I do not wish to be indelicate, Caldwell, but I own that I would be very much surprised to find it was natural. Being a man, you would not know the artifices practiced by young women seeking to entrap men into marriage."

Victor was tempted to reply that he had become quite familiar with such artifices since his engagement to Lady Anne. But such a comment would be disloyal to his bride-to-be, and so he held his tongue. This became increasingly difficult to do, however, as the Dowager went on speaking.

"Of course there is nothing artificial about my dearest Anne," she said, bringing forth this astounding falsehood without batting an eye. "You may not realize how lucky you are to have obtained such a prize, Caldwell. Beautiful, wellborn, and with manners such as must grace the highest station—"

"Lady Anne is without peer, of course," said Victor impatiently. "I do realize that, ma'am, I assure you."

"Do you?" The Dowager smiled a thin-lipped smile. "Then I have concerned myself for nothing. But you know, Caldwell, when I saw your evident admiration for Miss Everhart just now, I could not help feeling a trifle disturbed. My daughter has led a very sheltered existence. I would not like her exposed to the ruder aspects of male behavior—either now or after you are married. And since Miss Everhart actually lives on your estate—well, you must admit it has a peculiar appearance."

Victor would have laughed at this speech if it had not made him so furiously angry. Certainly it was laughable to suppose that any girl growing up as sister to Lord Stoddard could be sheltered from the ruder aspects of male behavior. But less laughable was the Dowager's insinuation that Catherine's residence on his estate must necessarily expose her to the suspicion of being his mistress.

"As Miss Everhart resides with her mother, I should think that would render her immune to such contemptible suspicions," he said coldly. "But of course there are always plenty of mean-minded people about who are ready to think the worst." Giving the Dowager no chance to reply, he turned and walked out of the refreshment room.

Twelve

The first person Victor encountered on returning to the ball-room was Catherine. She was just coming off the floor with Sir Simon. There was a smile on her face, and she was listening with the appearance of interest to something Sir Simon was saying. Victor was still feeling raw and irate after his interview with the Dowager. The sight of Catherine smiling at Sir Simon seemed to spur him to a kind of madness.

"Dance this next dance with me," he said, addressing her impulsively. Catherine turned to regard him with astonishment.

Sir Simon regarded him with astonishment, too, and a touch of indignation. "Devil a bit she will, Caldwell!" he exclaimed. "Catherine's engaged to dance this next dance with me. In fact, I shouldn't wonder if you hadn't waited too late to dance with her at all. She's bound to be completely booked up by now, the way the beaux have been besieging her all evening."

Victor said nothing to this speech. He merely looked at Catherine. She looked back at him, a hint of irresolution in her eyes. At last she spoke.

"It is true I am engaged for most of the other dances," she said. "But I can give you a country dance, I think, if I put off Lord Stoddard. And that ought not to be difficult. He has been partaking of your champagne so liberally that I doubt he remembers our engagement anyway."

"Very well," said Victor. "I shall claim you for the next country dance." Bowing, he walked away and took a vacant seat near the edge of the dance floor.

He ought, he supposed, to stand up with one of his other lady guests. There were plenty of ladies around who were looking hopefully in his direction. The Miss Scotts even made an excuse to come over and talk to him, under the guise of telling him how much they were enjoying his delightful party. But in the end they were forced to abandon their efforts and take the floor with inferior partners.

It seemed a very long dance to Victor, as he sat watching from his bench. He saw Catherine whirl past him seemingly countless times, a blur of glittering white draperies and flying red-gold curls. He saw Lady Anne, too, waltzing less exuberantly but nonetheless gracefully in the arms of a young guardsman. He saw Lord Stoddard stagger past, loudly damning those members of the crowd who had the effrontery to get in his way. Victor did not reflect on any of these things, but merely observed them. And when the dance was over, he was waiting at the edge of the floor to take Catherine's arm.

"You will eat supper with me?" said Sir Simon jealously as he relinquished Catherine to Victor.

She smiled and shook her head. "No, I have already a partner for supper, Simon. Thank you very much all the same."

"Who is it?" demanded Sir Simon.

Catherine did not hear the question, or at least she pretended not to. Instead she gave her arm to Victor, and together they went onto the floor.

Victor looked at her as they took their places opposite each other at the top of the line. There was a hint of color in Catherine's cheeks, perhaps caused by Sir Simon's words, perhaps merely by the exertion of dancing. "You seem to be much in demand tonight, Cousin," he said.

"I suppose I am," she agreed calmly. Victor went on studying her as they began to go through the movements of the dance. She returned his gaze levelly. "I met your fiancée earlier," she emarked as they went down the line together. "And I must give you my congratulations, my lord. She is a very lovely girl."

"Yes," said Victor. He waited a moment until the movements of the dance brought them together once more. "But though Lady Anne may have been the inspiration for tonight's party, she cannot be said to be its belle. That honor must rest with you, Cousin."

"Must it?" said Catherine, looking amused.

Victor thought her question disingenuous and was irritated by it. "Of course it must," he said sharply. "You cannot fail to see what a furor you have caused among my male guests. Simon and Jack Banks have been trailing after you like children after a lollipop woman, and I have no doubt Stoddard would have done the same, had not your attractions been eclipsed in his eyes by those of my champagne."

Catherine said nothing. Victor regarded her with growing frustration as he went through the figures of the dance. She looked so lovely and yet so distant, as if she were thinking of something else. With her other partners she had been smiling and gay, even flirtatious, but now that she was dancing with him, she seemed hardly aware that she had a partner. Victor knew a reckless impulse to goad her out of her reserve.

"You say nothing, Cousin," he said with a dry laugh. "But surely you are not unaware of your attractions?"

Catherine gave him a surprised look. "I don't know that I am aware of them particularly," she said.

"Ah, but this must be false modesty, Cousin. You can hardly have failed to realize the sensation you would make, appearing here tonight in such a costume."

Victor was pleased to see that these words brought a flash of anger to Catherine's eyes. "That is the second time this evening you have presumed to criticize my dress," she said tightly. "May I ask what you find wrong with it, my lord? It seemed to me a suitable dress for the occasion."

"No doubt it is. But I cannot help suspecting that most young ladies in your position would have contented themselves with a less striking costume."

"Do you think so, my lord?" said Catherine. Surprisingly, her anger seemed to have left her. Her voice was once more calm, even a little uninterested.

Somehow this angered Victor even more and spurred him to further recklessness. He gave a disagreeable laugh. "Why, yes, I do think so, Cousin. It seems to me surprising that you would choose to spend your mother's modest income on what appears to be a very expensive costume."

"Appearances can be deceiving, however," retorted Catherine. Her voice trembled slightly as she added, "I spent not a penny of my mother's income on this dress, my lord."

"Indeed?" said Victor with a disbelieving smile.

"Indeed, yes, my lord. This dress was made for me well over a year ago. And though it is now a trifle outmoded, I did not wish to part with it."

"Because it suited you so well, no doubt," said Victor jeeringly. "I am sure you won countless admirers whenever you had occasion to wear it *before.*"

"As a matter of fact, I have never worn it before tonight; my lord. This was to have been my wedding dress." And having made this statement, Catherine burst into tears.

Victor stared at her aghast. Never in a thousand years had he anticipated such a response as this. And it was clear that the storm he had provoked would not soon subside. Catherine wept silently but steadily, the tears flowing down her face with childlike abandon.

"Oh, Catherine, I'm sorry. Please don't cry," begged Victor.

Catherine merely shook her head as the tears continued to flow. Victor looked about in an agony of guilt and embarrassment. No one else seemed to have noticed her tears as yet, but it was inevitable that they soon must. Grasping her arm, he hurried her from the floor, shielding her as much as he could from the gaze of the other guests. One or two people looked after them curiously, but it was obvious that most had merely sup posed them desirous of sitting out the rest of the set. Victor was able to hustle Catherine into a nearby parlor without any interference or remark.

Catherine's tears did not subside once she and Victor were alone in the parlor. On the contrary, they seemed to flow even faster. She wept as though her heart were breaking, her breath coming in little gasps.

"Oh, Catherine, I'm sorry," said Victor, his heart wrung with remorse. "I'm so sorry, Catherine. My dear, I didn't mean to hurt you. I ought to be kicked for saying such things to you." He got out his handkerchief as he spoke and clumsily tried to wipe the tears from her face. "Don't cry, my dear. Please don't cry. I didn't mean to criticize your dress. It's a beautiful dress, Catherine—a beautiful, wonderful dress. I'm an ass for saying what I did."

"It was the only appropriate dress I had," said Catherine, still weeping copious tears. "I sold all my proper ball dresses before we came here because I didn't suppose I'd need them, living in the country. So when the invitation to your ball came and Mother said we must accept, it was either wear this dress or have a new one made. And I couldn't see buying a new dress when we must watch every penny as it is—"

"Of course, of course," said Victor soothingly. "I see it all perfectly now. I was an idiot not to have seen it before." But these words did not seem to comfort Catherine. She continued to weep as though her heart was breaking.

Victor, watching her, was overcome by guilt and remorse. He came a step nearer, putting his arms around her. "Don't cry," he begged. "Oh, my dear, don't cry. Don't cry, Catherine. Please, please don't cry anymore."

Catherine made no objection to this treatment. On the contrary, it seemed to Victor that her sobs subsided slightly. Heartened, he pressed her more closely against him, stroking her hair and murmuring a mixture of endearments, apologies, and self-denunciations. At what point exactly his comforting turned into lovemaking he could not have said, but eventually it dawned upon him that he was holding Catherine in his arms—the same Catherine who had haunted his thoughts by day and his dreams by night for the past several weeks. It struck him that it felt very pleasant to hold her in his arms and that he would not mind holding her in his arms for the duration of the evening or even longer. And when Catherine presently raised a tearstained face to his, it seemed the most natural thing in the world to lower his lips to hers and kiss her.

Catherine thought it natural, too. There had been a kind of unreality about the last hour or two that had tended to disarm her usual defenses.

Victor's remarks about her dress had been the starting point. Those remarks were not significant in themselves, yet somehow they had seemed to touch her on the raw. She had known, of course, that in wearing such a conspicuous costume she was courting disapproval. She had come fully prepared to endure a certain amount of criticism that evening, and when she had overheard the Dowager remarking acidly on her décolletage, or observed Cordelia Langley eyeing her with jealous dislike, she had been able to shrug it off with a wry, inward smile.

Even Victor's remarks had in the beginning caused her more anger than distress. Her tears had merely been an expression of her anger—inconvenient, to be sure, but fairly typical of those occasions when her temper was strongly roused. Yet somehow, once she had begun to cry, she had found it impossible to stop. It was as though all the trials and tribulations of the past year, endured stoically at the time, had suddenly combined to crush her under the impetus of Victor's unthinking criticism.

But though Victor had precipitated the storm, it did not immediately occur to Catherine to blame him for it. Her distress was at first so general and overwhelming that it was beyond her power to do more than simply give way to it. In this mood, she was hardly aware of Victor, except to be grateful to him for getting her so quickly out of the ballroom. And when he had taken her in his arms in the seclusion of the parlor she had clung to him instinctively, feeling an insensible comfort in his physical presence.

In her present unthinking misery, it was easy to succumb to such comfort. Catherine did succumb to it, shutting her eyes and allowing Victor to draw her closer. All the while she was vaguely aware of his voice in her ear, speaking in a tone both penitent and impassioned, but his words reached her as a mere soothing murmur. Still, there could be no doubt that it *was* soothing. It was pleasant to be held and caressed in such a way. She had not felt so comfortable in years. The comfort was not so much a mental as a physical thing, which her body received as gratefully as it would have received food after a prolonged fast or water after a long, hot walk.

By some insidious process, this state of passive acceptance gained ground as her emotional turmoil subsided. When at last her tears ceased and she lifted her face to look at Victor, she was not actually expecting to be kissed, nor was she surprised or shocked when he did kiss her. It seemed quite the natural and proper thing to do. She shut her eyes once more, feeling a fierce surge of pleasure in the demand of his mouth seeking hers, enjoying the strength of his arms and the warmth of his body as he crushed her against him.

Had Catherine remained a few minutes more in this passive state of mind and body, the sequel might have been quite different. As it was, however, her ordinary awareness began to assert itself almost immediately. Perhaps it was the sound of voices in the hall outside the parlor that first awoke her to the impropriety of her situation. In any event, her sleeping conscience awoke, became aware of what she was doing and was appalled accordingly.

"My lord!" she gasped, and the words were such an unmistakable rebuke that Victor instantly released her. For the next moment they merely looked at each other. On Victor's face was a look of growing consternation, on Catherine's an expression of growing anger.

"Just what do you think you're doing'?" she demanded in a breathless voice.

Victor searched his mind for an answer. What was he doing? As nearly as he could remember, he had taken Catherine in his arms with the idea of comforting her. But what he had been doing a moment ago had clearly gone beyond comforting. It had also, as he realized with dismay, gone well beyond the bounds of gentlemanly behavior. To kiss a young lady in such circumstances would have been a questionable act at any time, but for him to do so now, on the night he and his guests were celebrating his engagement to another young lady, was the act of a blackguard—behavior for which there could be no possible excuse.

"I beg your pardon," said Victor. He felt at once how inadequate these words were to the occasion, and it was obvious from Catherine's curled lip that she felt them inadequate, too. Victor tried again. "Please accept my apologies, Cousin," he said in a stiff voice. "My conduct was quite inexcusable, but I beg you will excuse it this once. Rest assured it shall not happen again."

He wondered as he spoke how it had happened in the first place. It had seemed almost as though he had been drawn to kiss Catherine by some unseen and incalculable force. One moment she had been sobbing in his arms; the next he had been kissing her with a passion as unexpected as it was impossible to resist.

He looked down at Catherine with perplexity. She avoided his eye, however, and turned away. "I trust it will *not* happen again," she said. "Shall we go back to the ballroom now, my lord? It is time and more that we were returning."

Victor was relieved to escape with no more than this mild rebuke for his sins. Yet as he led Catherine back toward the ballroom, he continued to puzzle over what had prompted him to sin in the first place. He could not say that Catherine had encouraged him to kiss her, could he? No, not in any way he could put his finger on—unless one counted her ravishing appearance in the white dress as an excuse. And that was plainly nonsense, for one could not go about ravishing young ladies merely because they looked ravishing. He had certainly never done such a thing before, even on occasions when palpable lures had been cast his way.

This made it all the more incredible to Victor that he could have acted as he had with no encouragement at all. And as he tried to sort through his jumbled impressions of that moment when he had first pressed his lips to Catherine's, there was one that occupied him more than the others. Had it been his imagination, or was it possible that Catherine, for a moment, had actually kissed him back?

Stealing a look at Catherine's stony face, Victor decided it must have been his imagination. He was probably trying to justify his actions by suggesting that Catherine had encouraged him to kiss her. *And it wouldn't matter even if she had encouraged me,* Victor told himself gloomily. *It would still be I who was in the wrong, for I am the one who's engaged to someone else. I ought to have thought of Lady Anne and abstained on her account.*

Yet it was the injury done to Catherine rather than Lady Anne that preoccupied him as he reentered the ballroom. He sought to apologize once more, but Catherine cut him short.

"Never mind, my lord," she said. "Let us forget it if we can. I am engaged for this next set and must be taking my place."

She gave Victor a nod, then took the arm of Jack Banks, who had come hurrying over as soon as he saw her. Together they went onto the floor.

Thirteen

For Victor, the rest of that evening was trying in the extreme. After his experience in the parlor with Catherine, he would have preferred to abandon the party altogether and retire to his bedchamber. He did attempt a withdrawal shortly after reentering the ballroom, but this attempt was foiled by Lady Anne, who saw him leaving and promptly hauled him back in again.

"Oh, Caldwell, this is too bad of you," she said, seizing his arm with a pretty air of childlike reproach. "You must not think of quitting the party again so soon. It's bad enough that you should run off with your cousin and stay away for two whole dances, but now I find you running off again! If I did not see Miss Everhart out on the floor this minute, I should think you and she must have an assignation of some sort." Lady Anne flashed her pearly teeth in one of her trademark smiles as she made this statement, but her voice sounded a little nettled. "You must dance with me now, or everyone will say you are neglecting me most shamefully."

Because Victor knew this to be true—and because he was feeling guilty about his behavior in regard to Catherine—he acquiesced to Lady Anne's request. But with such motives to inspire him, he could not hope to obtain much enjoyment on the dance floor. The sight of Catherine dancing nearby with Jack Banks was both a goad and a reproach to him. He tried not to look at her, but he was conscious nonetheless of her every word, every look, and every movement. He observed with inward gloom that she seemed to have recovered her spirits almost the instant she was away from him, for she laughed, smiled, and chatted a great deal with Mr. Banks.

Nor did she become noticeably more reserved while dancing with subsequent partners. Of these there were a great many, for her early popularity continued unabated until the close of the evening. Even Lord Stoddard came lurching forward to bid her farewell as she and her mother were taking their leave.

"Dashed pity you're leaving so early, Miss Everhart," he said, regarding her décolletage with a bleary and regretful eye. "Thought we was engaged to dance another set together this evening. Ah, well, another time. No doubt I'll be back to visit again once Anne and Caldwell are buckled."

"No doubt," agreed Catherine and turned away rather quickly.

Victor was reluctant to emulate the Earl's example, but he could not resist the urge to put himself in Catherine's way and speak a few words to her before she left. "Good evening, Cousin," he said, bowing and attempting a smile. "I am glad you were able to attend our party this evening."

Catherine gave him a brief look, nodded, and dropped a curtsy. "Good evening, my lord. I thank you for your hospitality," she said, her eyes fixed on the floor.

As she was speaking, a maidservant came hurrying up with a bundle of green cloth. "Here's your cloak, miss," she said, offering the garment to Catherine. Catherine took it from her with a word of thanks.

"Let me help you with that," said Victor, stepping forward to take the cloak from her hands. Catherine did not resist, nor did she acclaim Victor's offer of help. She stood like a statue, her eyes still fixed on the floor, as he arranged the cloak carefully over her shoulders.

"Thank you," she said when he was done. "Good evening, my lord." She did not look at Victor again or address another word to him, though her mother spent a considerable time expressing her gratitude for his hospitality before finally taking her leave.

Had Victor but known it, Catherine's mood was little different from his own. Since leaving the parlor, she had been in a state of perturbation that allowed little enjoyment in the subsequent events of the evening.

What could have possessed me to behave like such a fool? she asked herself over and over even as she danced, smiled, and made conversation with Mr. Banks and her other partners. *To cry and carry on like a wet goose merely because Lord Caldwell made a rude remark about my dress! He's made a deal of rude remarks to me before now, and yet I never felt like crying about any of them. Why should I have done so tonight?*

But even more disturbing to Catherine than the disgrace of weeping in public was the memory of that kiss in private. She could not imagine how she had come to permit such a thing—for that she *had* permitted it, she knew very well. Unlike Victor, she was under no delusion that he had acted without encouragement. She had been wrong to let him take her in his arms in the first place, although that might have been excusable had matters gone no further. But to allow him to kiss her, when he clearly neither loved nor respected her—nay, when he was actually engaged to someone else! That was an act that must sink her in the eyes of all right-minded people.

"Of course I did it without thinking," Catherine told herself. "I was upset and unhappy, and I let him take advantage of me in a moment of weakness. That's all there was to it." But she very much feared that was *not* all there was to it. She did not cherish anything like a *tendre* for her cousin, of course; such an idea was ridiculous when she found him insufferable in so many ways. But there did seem to be a hint of ambivalence in her feelings toward him—an ambivalence that had resulted in the fatal interlude just past. And if his behavior on that occasion were any indication, it seemed he must cherish similar feelings toward her.

"Very well then," Catherine told herself. "It's just an infatuation of sorts—a mere physical attraction with nothing real behind it. That is perfectly understandable, for of course he is very attractive. But still he had no business to take advantage of me in such a way—and on the night of his own engagement party, too!"

It was this last circumstance that disturbed Catherine more than anything. She stole frequent looks at Lady Anne throughout the rest of the evening, observing her beauty, grace, and elegance. This was the girl Victor had chosen to marry, while he had chosen to treat Catherine like a common flirt—or something worse. Shocking though it was, Catherine rather encouraged herself to dwell on this aspect of the affair, as it was more effective than anything else in rousing her anger toward Victor. Anger was a much safer emotion than envy or hurt or desire.

On the carriage ride home, her mother gently discoursed on the evening just past. "I hope you had as good a time as I did, dearest. It was delightful to see Queen's Close looking so festive." She scrutinized Catherine's face. "You looked as though you were enjoying yourself, but I was not quite sure. Indeed, I thought at one point you had been crying. But I made sure you were only flushed from the heat of the room. It was certainly a warm night for October."

"Yes, it was," said Catherine, who had no wish to discuss what she privately declared a fit of uncommon foolishness.

Mrs. Everhart continued to probe, however, with motherly concern. *"Were* you crying, dearest? Did someone say something to hurt you? I know I overheard Lady Stoddard making a very spiteful remark once—something about your being overdressed, I believe. As though you had not a perfect right to dress as finely as her daughter—who, though a very pretty girl, seems not to have two words to say for herself, by the by. I tried to talk with her for a few minutes this evening, but found it very uphill work. However, that's neither here nor there. As I said, I heard Lady Stoddard making a very derogatory remark about you, so I just gave her a look, and she shut up immediately. But I was afraid you might have overheard what she was saying, too, and been hurt by it."

"No, I was not hurt by Lady Stoddard's criticism," said Catherine, smiling in spite of herself. "But if I was, I know I might depend on you to defend me, Mother. A tigress could not be more ferociously protective of her young than you are of me!"

"Well, I don't know about that, dearest, but I hope I should always do my best. And indeed, I thought it remarkable that Lady Stoddard should criticize the conduct of someone else's child when the conduct of her own left so much to be desired. Not Lady Anne, of course, for she seems a nice enough girl. But everyone could see Lord Stoddard was positively inebriated."

"He was, of course," agreed Catherine. "I stood up with him for a couple of dances, and it was all he could do to remain on his feet."

Her mother eyed her carefully. "Yes, I saw him dancing with you. He seemed to admire you very much. Of course you were obliged to be polite to him on this occasion, but in the future I think it would be better to refuse him if he asks you to dance. A man who drinks heavily cannot be depended on to keep the line."

Catherine acceded to this statement, though she could not help thinking that on this occasion it was not Lord Stoddard who had stepped outside of the line. "I doubt I shall see Lord Stoddard again anyway, Mother," she said. "I gathered from one or two remarks he let fall that he is not a frequent visitor to rural society."

"Perhaps not. But you know that his sister is engaged to marry Lord Caldwell. It's likely that Lord Stoddard may come to visit them from time to time after they are married, and if he does, you will probably see him at parties now and then."

Catherine said nothing. Her mother went on, a note of musing in her voice. "Poor Lord Caldwell! Of course Lady Anne is very beautiful, but if I were him, I would think twice about marrying into such a family. To have a man like Lord Stoddard as one's brother-in-law cannot be at all pleasant. And Lady Stoddard, too—she seemed a most ill-natured woman. I was not at all impressed by what I saw and heard of her."

Catherine smiled crookedly. "You only say that because she

presumed to criticize me, Mother! I daresay Lady Stoddard is a most delightful and amiable woman once one comes to know her. At any rate, she ought to make Lord Caldwell a very suitable mama-in-law." Mrs. Everhart opened her mouth to protest this, but Catherine went on, a note of finality in her voice. "And it would not matter even if she were not suitable. Lord Caldwell has made his bed with regard to the Stoddards, and now he will be obliged to lie on it, willy-nilly. He could hardly cry off at this point without causing a scandal."

"That is true," agreed Mrs. Everhart and fell into a pensive silence for the rest of the drive.

Back at Queen's Close, Victor was simultaneously bidding farewell to the last few lingering ball guests while trying to prevent Lord Stoddard from making any further depredations on his wine cellar.

"Jus' one more bottle," urged Lord Stoddard, swaying on his legs and blinking owlishly up at Victor. "What say we ring your butler and have him bring up a bottle of the Malmsey Madeira, Caldwell old man? Here, I'll do it for you." Seizing the bellpull, he gave it such a violent tug that it came down in his hand. He looked at it stupidly. "Damned thing broke! This damned house of yours is falling apart, Caldwell. Ought to pull the whole damned place down and build it over again."

"Yes, I daresay," said Victor shortly. "Just sit down on the sofa over there, would you, Stoddard? I'll see to ordering the wine."

Dropping the severed bellpull, Lord Stoddard obediently collapsed onto the sofa. But the wine he had already drunk proved after all to be sufficient to his needs. By the time the butler arrived in answer to Victor's summons, Stoddard was snoring loudly on the sofa, his mouth wide open and a thin trickle of saliva issuing onto his own shirtfront.

"What shall we do with him, my lord?" said the butler, eyeing him dubiously.

"Just leave him there," said Victor, looking with distaste a the Earl's sprawled figure. "If he wakes up, he can get himsel upstairs as best he can."

The butler coughed discreetly. "Perhaps it would be as wel if he were conveyed to his own room, my lord," he said. "Ther is a very fine rug in this room, and a good deal of valuabl Chinese porcelain. I am informed that there has already bee an—ahem—accident to the rug in his own room. If I were t summon a couple of the footmen, they could carry him upstair with very little trouble."

Victor acquiesced gloomily to these measures and the quickly betook himself to his own rooms, so that he was no obliged to witness the sight of his footmen struggling upstair with his future brother-in-law. He undressed, made a brief pre tense at washing, and then fell into bed with the disheartene feeling that his house really was falling apart around him.

It was not to be expected that he would sleep well after th events of the evening, nor did he. He tossed and turned for wha seemed like endless hours before finally falling asleep. In spit of this, he awoke a good hour before his usual time and foun sleep had irretrievably fled his couch. Ringing the bell for hi valet, he wearily got out of bed and began to dress. It seeme to him that he might at least try to accomplish a little work sinc there was no other solace left him. As soon as he was dressed he went to his study and began to turn over the pile of corre spondence that had been delivered the day before, but which he had neglected in the excitement of the ball.

As he shuffled through a stack of solicitations, he found hi mind returning tenaciously to the subject of Catherine. Over an over he reviewed what had passed between them the previou night, trying to decide what, if anything, he ought to do now Of course, the problem was really that he had done too muc already, but it did not seem to him that he could leave matter as they presently stood. He had made Catherine no proper ex planation for his actions the night before and only the sketchies of apologies. That there could be no proper explanation for ac-

tions of that sort did not occur to Victor. He seized with relief
on the excuse afforded him for seeing Catherine again. Of course
he ought to call on her as soon as possible and render her a
formal apology.

Victor accordingly made short work of his correspondence.
As soon as the hour was far enough advanced for a formal call,
he set out for Crossroads Cottage.

It did occur to him, before setting out, that Catherine might
be reluctant to see and speak to him after what had passed between them the night before. She had not seemed unduly angry
at the time—indeed, he had seen her far angrier on other occasions—but there could be no doubt that she had been displeased
with him. It seemed prudent to provide himself with a pretext
for calling on her. Fortunately, he had one in the form of a letter
from his attorney that had been among the day's correspondence.
The letter detailed the actions Mr. Crabtree had taken against
Mr. Carr on behalf of the Everharts. With this excuse in hand,
Victor felt tolerably assured of at least a civil greeting, if not a
warm one.

As he walked through the woods, he was planning what he
would say to Catherine and what she would likely say in return.
By the time he arrived at the cottage, he had it all settled to his
satisfaction and felt he was prepared for any contingency, from
immediate forgiveness to furious reproach.

But as he came around the corner of the cottage, he realized
that there was one contingency for which he was not prepared.
In all his imaginings, he had pictured Catherine as being alone
or at least attended by no more intrusive companion than Mrs.
Everhart. But on this occasion Catherine was not alone. She was
sitting on the front steps of the porch with Ginger in her lap,
and seated beside her was Sir Simon Debrett.

The sight of Sir Simon made Victor stop dead in his tracks.
Sir Simon and Catherine were so deep in conversation that they
did not at first notice his presence, but Ginger did. He lifted his
head, his ears very slightly laid back and his eyes fixed suspiciously on Victor.

Catherine observed the cat's gaze, glanced around, and saw Victor, too. "Oh!" she said. Her voice was not angry, or embarrassed, or even contemptuous. It was merely blank. Her expression was blank, too, and Victor could not guess what her thoughts might be.

Sir Simon's thoughts were easier to guess: He looked irritated by the interruption and also a trifle sheepish. But he rose and greeted Victor with a semblance of his usual urbane manner. "You're out early today, Caldwell," he said. "I would think after all the excitement last night you'd have been glad to keep to your bed a little longer."

"You're out early, too," said Victor pointedly. He observed that Catherine's cheeks had gone pink, perhaps in reference to Sir Simon's remark about the excitements of the night before. He looked at her, but she leaned over to stroke Ginger, avoiding his eye. "And Catherine is out early as well. We seem to be a trio of early risers altogether."

"Aye, I just thought I'd drive over and see how Catherine was," said Sir Simon, striving for an airy tone and not altogether succeeding. "After dancing so much last night, I feared I would find her completely knocked up."

"Gammon," said Catherine loudly. Both Victor and Sir Simon looked at her with surprise. She colored again but lifted her chin defiantly. "As though I were to be knocked up by a little thing like that! I am sure I could dance a dozen dances every night without ill effects. And you at least ought to know that, Simon, for I am sure you have seen me dance in Bath often enough." She glanced briefly at Victor, then looked away again. She rose to her feet as she spoke and began to move toward the cottage door. "As for Lord Caldwell, I can forgive him for his concern, for he does not know me and my constitution so well as you do. But I assure you both that, if it is concern for my health that has brought you here, then your errand was needless. I am perfectly well and happy to be able to set your fears at rest."

Sir Simon rose, too, looking more sheepish than ever. "Very well then," he said. "I am glad you suffered no ill effects from

last night, Catherine. Caldwell, I can give you a seat in my rig
if you care to drive home instead of walk."

Victor paid no attention to this speech. He hurried up the
porch steps and laid his hand on Catherine's arm. "Just a minute,
Cousin," he said. In his hurry to reach her, he inadvertently trod
on Ginger's tail. The cat let out an explosive hiss and vanished
beneath the nearest wicker chair.

Catherine spun around, looking furious. Victor instinctively
withdrew his hand, but the next moment he had recovered himself. "I beg your pardon," he said with dignity. "And—er—I
beg your cat's pardon, too, Cousin. But you see you are laboring
under a misapprehension. I did not call today out of concern for
your health, although I am very glad to hear you are feeling
well, of course. But it happens there is another matter I wished
to discuss with you."

Catherine surveyed him with an irresolute face. "What matter
is that?" she asked.

"It concerns your late father's affairs, specifically his partnership with Mr. Carr. Perhaps your mother has mentioned that
she spoke with me some weeks ago about having my attorney
in London look into the matter for her." Victor produced his
letter as he spoke and showed it to Catherine, keeping his eyes
fixed on hers. "I just received this report from my attorney today.
If you can give me ten minutes, Cousin, I can sit down and
explain it all to you. There is no reason why Simon need stay,
however," he added maliciously.

"Yes, you may as well go, Simon," agreed Catherine, her eyes
on the letter in Victor's hand.

Sir Simon went, but reluctantly. "May I call on you tomorrow?" he asked Catherine as he took the reins from his groom
and remounted his phaeton.

"If you like," she said. She watched as he drove off, then
turned to Victor. "Shall we step inside, my lord? I must fetch
Mother so she can hear your report, too. After all, this business
concerns her as much as it does me."

"Why do you encourage him like that?" said Victor.

Catherine, who had been about to enter the cottage, turned to look at him with raised brows. "I beg your pardon?" she said.

"Why do you encourage Simon like that?" repeated Victor with a hint of anger in his voice. "Don't tell me you don't encourage him, Cousin. You danced with him three times last night, and I never come here anymore but I find him running tame underfoot. After the way he treated you before, I should think you would rather send him about his business than dance with him."

Catherine regarded Victor a moment with an inscrutable expression. "You think that, do you, my lord?" she said. "And just what business is it of yours how I behave to Sir Simon?"

Victor tried to think of an answer and failed. "It is none of my business, of course," he said stiffly. "But I could not help wondering. I had thought—well, it seemed so out of character for you to behave in such a way. I would not have expected it of you."

"Possibly you are unacquainted with my true character," suggested Catherine.

Victor thought it better not to respond to this statement, which he suspected to be a pointed comment on his behavior the night before. He merely shrugged and said, "I do not pretend to know your inmost thoughts and feelings, Cousin, if that is what you mean. I can only say that if it were me, I would prefer not to put my trust a second time in a person who had once disappointed me."

Catherine went on looking at him steadily. "You know sometimes one is compelled by circumstance to put one's trust in vessels that are known to be faulty," she said.

"Yes, perhaps that is true," said Victor. "But is this one of those circumstances? To throw yourself away on a man who has shown himself so unworthy of you! I cannot like to see it, Cousin. You deserve better than such a man as Sir Simon Debrett."

A faint flush rose to Catherine's cheeks. "You are very eloquent on my behalf, my lord," she said. "But I think you concern yourself needlessly. It is true that Sir Simon is not the strong and stainless character I once thought him, but as a suitor he possesses advantages that dispose me to overlook his failings."

Victor was angered by her coolness and found himself wishing to anger her in turn. "What advantages are those?" he asked. "His title and fortune?"

Catherine's eyes flashed, but her voice remained provokingly cool. "No, although those are desirable things, to be sure. But of course you already know that, being a gentleman of title and fortune yourself."

"Certainly!" said Victor, made reckless now by anger and frustration. "Indeed, my title and fortune must be counted far superior to Simon's. I cannot think why you do not choose to encourage me rather than him."

Catherine looked at him for a long moment. "You cannot be serious," she said.

"I *am* serious," said Victor doggedly. "Why should you prefer him to me? If you were mine, I'd never be fool enough to let you go as Simon did. He isn't half good enough for you."

"That may be," said Catherine, speaking with great deliberation. "But I must question your intentions in telling me this, my lord. Seeing that your engagement to Lady Anne was announced only last night, I fear they can hardly do either of us much credit. And that is where Sir Simon must have the advantage of you. His intentions toward me are honorable, you see."

There was a long silence. "I beg your pardon," said Victor unhappily.

He felt the futility of all speech at that moment. It seemed to him that no man had never been in such a terrible predicament. Here he was, longing to justify himself to Catherine, wishing to refute the reproach of her words by assuring her that his intentions were as honorable as Sir Simon's. But that course was impossible to him. He was engaged to Lady Anne and could not speak of his feelings for Catherine without dishonoring both women. Indeed, he had already said enough to brand himself a knave, and to say more would only confirm his knavishness. He was in fact helpless—hamstrung by convention and by the engagement he himself had foolishly entered into and now regretted with all his heart.

"I beg your pardon," he said again, speaking with an effort. "You are right to reproach me, Cousin. Of course I should not have spoken as I did." With would-be jocularity, he added, "It seems I am always apologizing to you when we meet."

"It seems so," agreed Catherine. She spoke dryly, yet her voice was a little unsteady.

Victor, looking into her eyes, was seized by a sudden, startling conviction. "Catherine?" he said. "Catherine!"

A smile ineffably sad touched her lips. "No, certainly not, my lord," she said, answering his unspoken question as though he had voiced it aloud. "It is all conceit and imagination on your part, and you had better put it out of your mind."

"Catherine!" said Victor again and took a step toward her. "By God, I don't believe it is my imagination!"

"If it isn't, it ought to be," said Catherine, retreating from his outstretched arms. Her voice was grave as she added, "Indeed, I think you must agree that we have discussed this matter quite enough, my lord. Any further discussion would be unprofitable as well as improper. So let us go into the house. I will call Mama, and you can tell us what your attorney in London has discovered."

Fourteen

As if in a dream, Victor followed Catherine into the cottage.

Ginger followed, too, and while Catherine went off to fetch
Mrs. Everhart, the big cat perched himself atop the parlor sofa.
From this perch he sat regarding Victor with deep suspicion.
Victor was hardly conscious of his feline nemesis's baleful stare,
however. His thoughts were absorbed by the amazing truth Catherine had just revealed to him. When she returned presently with
her mother, he tried to rouse himself from his abstraction and
make himself agreeable to Mrs. Everhart, but he felt all the while
as though he were acting and speaking in a dream.

Fortunately he had his attorney's letter, which was so clear
and detailed that it largely relieved him of the necessity of speaking. Handing it to Mrs. Everhart, he sat back and watched as
she read it through. Catherine, leaning over her mother's shoulder, read it through, too. She then picked up Ginger and retired
to the window, where she stood looking out at the frost-ravaged
cottage garden.

"A legal action!" said Mrs. Everhart, looking up from the
letter. "But will that not be very expensive, my lord?"

"It's nothing," said Victor absently, watching Catherine at the
window. "I am obliged to retain several attorneys full time anyway to handle my affairs. I might as well keep them busy as
not." To himself, he added silently that he had a powerful incen-
tive for wishing to keep his legal advisors busy with other mat-

ters just then. The idea of marriage with Lady Anne had never seemed as distasteful to him as it did at the present moment.

"But surely there must be costs associated with bringing the matter to court," persisted Mrs. Everhart. "It doesn't seem right that you should have to spend money out of your own pocket to help us."

"But I want to, ma'am," said Victor. "I want to very much. In fact—" He stopped suddenly, a bemused smile spreading across his face.

"In fact what?" said Mrs. Everhart, looking at him inquiringly.

"In fact, I must insist that you let me handle this in my own way, ma'am," said Victor, still smiling in a bemused manner. "Now I come to think of it, it is in my interests as well as yours that I should bear the costs of the suit at this time."

"Indeed?" said Mrs. Everhart. She glanced nervously at her daughter. Catherine said nothing, however, and continued to stand looking out the window, her back to Victor and her mother. "Well, I don't know, my lord. Of course it is very generous of you to wish to bear the costs of the lawsuit, but I do not know that I can allow you to do such a thing for us. Not without making you some kind of compensation, at any rate."

"But I will accept compensation very willingly, ma'am. Only I beg you will wait until everything is settled before we discuss what its details should be. Can you trust me so far as that, just for these next few weeks? I promise your trust shall not be abused."

Victor raised his voice as he spoke these last words, so as to be sure to reach Catherine at the window. If she understood them, however, she gave no sign. Mrs. Everhart merely smiled and said, "I am sure we can trust you, my lord. Although I must say that I cannot see how it should be in your interests to pay our legal expenses!"

"It is," said Victor fervently. "I assure you it is, ma'am." Rising, he took Mrs. Everhart's hand. "I shall let you know as soon as all is settled. Of course, if the matter comes to trial, it may be necessary for you and Catherine to go to London in order to testify. Should that be the case, I will accompany you there and give you lodgings in my town house during your stay. But I think it will probably be as my attorney says, and Carr will prefer to settle out of court. We should know within the next week or two."

"You have been very good to us, my lord," said Mrs. Everhart, smiling at him tremulously.

"Not at all, not at all," said Victor with some embarrassment. "I assure you, I shall profit quite as much as you in this matter. Indeed, it may be that my profit shall be even greater than yours. As my attorney says, there is no guarantee Carr will be able to restore your funds even if it is proven that he misappropriated them. But we will hope there is something left that will enable you to go on more comfortably than you do now."

As he spoke, Victor glanced wistfully at Catherine, wishing she would acknowledge his words or at least come over to say good-bye to him. But she continued to stand at the window without speaking. "Well, good afternoon, ma'am," he told Mrs. Everhart. "And good afternoon to you, too, Cousin," he added, addressing Catherine's unresponsive back.

"Good-bye, my lord," said Catherine from the window. Victor was forced to take his departure without further parley and without touching or saluting her hand, as he had hoped.

As he made his way home, he pondered what Catherine's coolness might mean. She had as good as admitted she cared for him when they had been standing together on the porch. Yet thereafter she had seemed to distance herself from him, as though regretting or even recanting her admission.

"Well, it stands to reason that she should," Victor told himself. "As long as I am engaged to someone else, it is hardly likely she would encourage me to make love to her. But surely she understands that I mean to get free of my engagement to Lady Anne as soon as I can so that I will be able to marry her. Yes, she must have understood that. And if she does not, I shall see it is made clear to her within the week."

But a week proved insufficient for this purpose, much to Victor's annoyance. He waited impatiently for the Stoddards to approach him once again about the marriage settlements, but though they had been harassing him regularly on the subject for the past few weeks, they now seemed to have entered into a conspiracy of silence. The Dowager complacently spoke of his and Lady Anne's upcoming nuptials without one mention of jointures or pin money. Lady Anne smiled her sweetest and was sulky only when her mother ordered her to practice her music or when one of the other guests failed to pay her the deference she expected as the future mistress of Queen's Close. Even Lord Stoddard limited his demands for money to a request for a loan of fifty pounds and seemed hardly disappointed when it was refused.

Never mind, Victor told himself. *They will say something about the settlements soon, no doubt.*

But day succeeded day without the Stoddards making any further mention of the subject. It appeared that they had either resigned themselves to the situation and were willing to trust him to make a fair settlement when the time came; or, more sinisterly, they had divined his desire to free himself from his engagement and were taking this course to thwart him.

Victor, who had counted on disagreements about money as an excuse for ending his engagement, began to be seriously alarmed as the days went by and no disagreement took place. If the Stoddards did not choose to make an issue of the settlements, then he would have no excuse for breaking his engagement to Lady Anne. Of course if worse came to worst, he could break with her without an excuse, but such an action would inevitably reflect badly on him, as well as on any woman he might subsequently take up with. And since he had every intention of taking up with Catherine as soon as the matter could conveniently be arranged, this was naturally a consideration.

Then, too, there was Lady Anne to be considered. Victor was under no illusion that Lady Anne would be heartbroken if he did not marry her. It had been made abundantly clear to him during the last few weeks that she had accepted him only for his money and position. Morosely contemplating her beautiful, vacuous face, he doubted sometimes whether she was capable of caring for any man except the bestial elder brother for whom she seemed perfectly willing to sacrifice herself.

But since he had made his proposal to Lady Anne in good faith and been accepted in the same spirit, Victor did not feel he could expose her now to the humiliation of being jilted. It would be much better if matters could be arranged so it appeared they had mutually agreed to dissolve the relationship. And if his bride-to-be were not agreeable to such civilized measures, Victor was even willing to let it be said that she had jilted him, for it seemed to him the least he could do to pay for the error of taste and judgment that had led him to propose to Lady Anne in the first place.

Whether or not he would be allowed to get off so lightly was a question, however.

The house party was finally drawing to an end. There remained less than a week now until the time arranged for the guests' departure. And still the Stoddards had not broached the subject of the marriage settlements. Victor was nearly frantic, for he felt he must not let Lady Anne depart while there was still the pretense of an engagement between them. The Dowager made it clear that as soon as she and her family returned to London, she intended to set immediately about interviewing clergymen, ordering wedding invitations, and purchasing Lady Anne's bride clothes—all measures Victor wished desperately to avoid. But he hesitated to announce baldly that he intended to make no settlement. There was a fear in the back of his mind that the Stoddards might call his bluff and say that Lady Anne might marry him even without settlements. In that case, he would be in twice as awkward a situation as before.

He felt altogether that it would be better if the first move came from the Stoddards. Still, he could hardly restrain his impatience to have the matter settled. He could not forget the reserved way Catherine had taken leave of him the last time he had visited the cottage. Nor could he avoid seeing that Sir Simon still paid regular visits there and appeared as confident as ever that Catherine would eventually marry him. Might it be that Sir Simon was right? Might it be that Catherine would succumb to his persistence, even in spite of the feelings she had confessed for him?

The mere idea was enough to send Victor into a panic. In this mood he had small patience for playing the role of genial host. So when Mrs. Watt began speaking about visiting some monastic ruins that lay a short distance from Queen's Close, he responded without any noticeable enthusiasm.

"To be sure, the old abbey lies only an hour or two from here, ma'am. But I assure you its ruins are wholly unspectacular. Indeed, they are very *ruined* ruins, hardly recognizable as an abbey at all."

Mrs. Watt smiled indulgently. "Ah, my lord, it is easy to see you are not an antiquarian!" she said. "To those of us who claim that title, no ruin can be too scant to afford us interest. And I am sure the young people would find much to interest them in it, too, if they cared to go."

One or two young ladies immediately declared that they adored ruins, and this statement was echoed by others in the party.

"You must go, too, my dear, so you may add a sketch of the ruins to your portfolio," the Dowager instructed Lady Anne. "As nicely as you draw, it would be a shame to miss such a picturesque subject."

Lady Anne was heard to mutter under her breath that she cared nothing about fusty old ruins. But a stern look from the Dowager wrung a reluctant, "Yes, Mama," from her lips.

"And once you have made the sketch, perhaps you can work up a copy in watercolors for Lord Caldwell," continued the Dowager, smiling at Victor in an ingratiating way. "I am sure he would value such a work, even if its subject does not stir him to enthusiasm."

Victor felt obliged to say, "To be sure, ma'am," but his desire for such a work was as scant as Lady Anne's desire to create it. It seemed clear, however, that the party had set its collective heart on seeing the site of the old abbey. Lady Caldwell, trying to be helpful, began to suggest ways and means for the trip.

"The gentlemen can ride, if they like, but you will need carriages for the ladies. It's a long ride from here to the abbey. I will have Marie-Claude put up a picnic luncheon for your party. It's a bit late in the year for alfresco dining, of course, but we will hope this nice weather holds so you will be able to dine out-of-doors without too much discomfort."

The older members of the party, save for the antiquarian Mrs. Watt, looked unenthusiastic at the prospect of picnic dining in late October. Most of them chose to bow out from the planned expedition, and so did several of the younger gentlemen, including Lord Stoddard. But Victor, as host, was obliged to pledge his support, and Sir Simon, too, said he would come.

"Are you sure, Simon? It's a stiff ride to the old abbey. Hardly worth it to see a lot of weed-grown ruins," said Victor.

"Oh, as for that, I thought I would drive my phaeton. That way I could take Catherine, too, you know." There was a hint of defiance in Sir Simon's voice as he brought forth this statement. "I hope you've no objection, Caldwell? I'm sure she would like to see the ruins, too."

Victor took a long time answering this question. "No, I've no objection to your inviting Catherine, Simon," he said at last. "But I doubt she will come." He could not decide in his heart if he wanted Catherine to come or not. For her to accept Sir Simon's invitation, after what had passed between them, would be tantamount to declaring she put no faith in his declarations and intended to return to her former suitor. But he had a great longing to see her again, and he could not help wishing that he, rather than Sir Simon, was in a position to invite her as his special guest.

His mother, predictably, reacted with pleasure to Sir Simon's proposal. "That is so kind of you, Sir Simon," she said, beaming at him. "I do hope Catherine can go. She deserves a little recreation now and then."

Lady Anne put down her wineglass with a bang. "Well, I hope
she *cannot* go," she said.

Everyone looked at her in astonishment, Victor not excepted.
"I hope she cannot go," repeated Lady Anne defiantly. "If we
must drive for hours just to see some boring old ruins and eat a
nasty picnic luncheon out-of-doors, then we want no one but
our own party."

"Yes, but Miss Everhart is in a rather special position, my
love," said the Dowager, addressing her daughter in honeyed
tones but betraying a hint of steel beneath the honey. "She is a
relation of Lord Caldwell's, you know."

"Yes, a poor relation," said Lady Anne disdainfully. "I don't
see why she need tag along on an expedition like this one. It's
bad enough we should have had to invite her to our betrothal
ball."

One of the other young ladies at the table leaned over and
whispered something to her neighbor. The other girl nodded,
giggled, and shot a look at Lady Anne. Lady Anne glared at
them both.

"Indeed, my dear, I don't think you're being very civil," said
the Dowager, still trying to pour oil on troubled waters. "It's not
as though Miss Everhart's presence will discommode you in the
least. She will be riding with Sir Simon, after all." The Dowager
looked appealingly at Sir Simon, who smiled and nodded.

"*If* she goes," said Victor jealously.

He would have found it hard to say at that moment who annoyed him more, Sir Simon or Lady Anne. Lady Anne's spite
toward Catherine was certainly very annoying, so much so that
he found himself wishing Catherine would put his bride-to-be's
nose out of joint by accepting the invitation. But of course, if
she did accept it, it would mean that she was still favoring Sir
Simon as a suitor. And that would mean he would be forced to
sit by and watch Sir Simon pay court to her, while he was obliged
to dance attendance on Lady Anne. Gloomily Victor played with

a forkful of roast pheasant and wondered what the outcome would be.

He had not long to wait, for Sir Simon drove to Crossroads Cottage early on the following day to issue his invitation.

Both Catherine and her mother were home and seated in their parlor sewing when Sir Simon was announced. Mrs. Everhart at once laid aside her needlework and rose to greet Sir Simon politely. "So you are still here, are you, Sir Simon? I had thought you must be leaving Queen's Close pretty soon. I am sure Sophronia told me the party was to break up around the end of October."

Sir Simon fidgeted and looked rather sheepishly at Catherine. "So it is, ma'am. I believe most of the guests are leaving next week. However, I haven't decided yet whether I will go or stay in the neighborhood a little longer." He paused, looking once again at Catherine, but she continued to ply her stitchery, her face quite impassive.

"So you have come to take leave of us?" suggested Mrs. Everhart helpfully.

"No, oh, no," Sir Simon made haste to say. "No, as a matter of fact I'm here on quite a different errand. We've decided that before our party breaks up we'd like to pay a visit to the old abbey over near Nettisford. Are you familiar with it, ma'am? Most of the young people are going, and I thought I'd see if Catherine would like to go, too."

"Indeed," said Mrs. Everhart, looking surprised. "No, I am familiar with no abbey in this neighborhood. But it sounds a very enjoyable expedition."

"Yes, it does, doesn't it?" said Sir Simon enthusiastically. "I thought Catherine would not like to miss it. We're going to explore the ruins, then have a picnic luncheon." Again he paused and looked at Catherine.

Catherine placed another stitch with great deliberation, then looked up from her sewing. "And you say I am invited to make up one of this party, Simon?" she asked.

Sir Simon smiled a self-satisfied smile. "Oh, yes, I saw to that," he said. "You're invited right enough."

Catherine continued to survey him thoughtfully. "Are you sure the other members of your party do not mind my accompanying them on this expedition?" she said.

Sir Simon looked a trifle self-conscious. "Oh, well, Lady Anne jibbed a bit," he said. "But that's only to be expected. She considers she should always be the center of attention, you know, because she is engaged. And I think you annoyed her the other night at the ball by attracting more attention than she did! Indeed, you looked very beautiful, Catherine."

Catherine brushed this praise aside impatiently. "So Lady Anne did not want me to come," she said. "I suppose Lord Caldwell opposed the idea, too?"

"Not at all," Sir Simon assured her. "And even Lady Anne came round in the end. Somebody—I think it was Caldwell— told her you would be riding with me, and that seemed to satisfy her."

"I see," said Catherine. Her mind was working rapidly. In the days that had passed since Victor's call, she had spent much time pondering the words he had spoken to her, trying to guess their meaning. At one point it had seemed almost as though he was signaling his intention of breaking off his engagement to Lady Anne in order that he might pursue her instead.

But though Catherine would have been happy to interpret Victor's words in this manner, when she examined the matter rationally, she could hardly believe she had understood him aright. He was engaged to marry Lady Anne, after all—not merely courting her or flirting with her, but formally engaged. And that was a solemn and binding agreement that a gentleman could not simply break as though it was a dinner engagement. If he did, it proved he was no gentleman. And any sane woman ought to think twice before putting her trust in a man who was not a gentleman.

So Catherine had told herself, and she had spent some unhappy hours wondering how she would respond if Victor did jilt

Lady Anne. But it began to look now as though her worrying had been unnecessary. It was plain from Sir Simon's words that Victor had known and approved of his plan to drive her to the abbey. What could that mean but that he was content with the status quo? If he had intentions toward her that went beyond friendship or flirtation, he would hardly invite her to a party that included Sir Simon and Lady Anne!

All this flashed through Catherine's head in the space of a moment. She hardly paused before responding to Sir Simon's speech. "I suppose I might go if Mother does not need me," she said. "What day is your expedition planned for?"

"We hope to go tomorrow if it is fair. I know that is short notice, but we wanted to go while the weather holds. Would that be convenient for you, Catherine? If it is not, I daresay we could put the expedition back a day or two."

Sir Simon made this last statement rather doubtfully, and Mrs. Everhart was quick to reassure him. "You need not put it back on my account, at least," she said. "I have nothing planned for tomorrow that requires Catherine's attendance."

"Yes, tomorrow should do very well," agreed Catherine.

"Tomorrow it is then," said Sir Simon, smiling his broadest. He went on to make a great many protestations of gratitude and pleasure at having secured Catherine's company for the following day. He did this at such length that Ginger, atop the sofa, yawned, curled himself in a ball, and went to sleep. Catherine found herself envying the cat's easy escape. But at last Sir Simon took leave of her and her mother, promising to call at ten o'clock the following morning to take her to the abbey.

Fifteen

After Sir Simon had gone, Mrs. Everhart turned to her daughter. "My dear, I do not understand you," she said.

"What do you mean?" asked Catherine. Her voice was innocent, though she had a pretty good idea what her mother meant.

"What I mean is that your behavior is dreadfully inconsistent," said Mrs. Everhart sternly. "You have hardly given Sir Simon the time of day for the past month. And now, when he asks you to go on what will almost certainly be an all-day expedition, you agree as though it were nothing out of the ordinary!"

Catherine said nothing. She picked up her needlework, which had been laid aside during Sir Simon's leave-taking, and began to sew once more.

Her mother surveyed her with frustration. "Indeed, Catherine, I would give a good deal to know what you mean by your behavior," she said. "Do you intend to marry Sir Simon or not? I am neither blind nor stupid, and I can see he has come here to mend matters with you if he can."

Again she paused, but still Catherine said nothing. After a minute Mrs. Everhart went on, a touch of asperity in her voice. "My dear, I asked you a question. I beg you will do me the honor of answering it. Do you mean to marry Sir Simon or not?"

Catherine hesitated, then parried the question with another question. "Do I act as though I mean to?" she asked.

"Since you ask me, no. You act rather as though you have lost your mind," said her mother roundly. "You dance with Sir Simon three times at Lord Caldwell's ball, but hardly speak a word when he comes to call on you. You will not even exert yourself to give him a civil greeting when you meet, but treat him as though he were of less account than the butcher's boy. And yet you agree to spend the day with him tomorrow when you have turned down a dozen similar invitations in the last fortnight! It's inconsistent—that's what it is."

Catherine looked up, a hint of fire in her eye. "You are quite right, Mother," she said. "But then Simon has been a trifle inconsistent in his behavior, too, hasn't he? I can remember him swearing the most extravagant vows of eternal devotion to me back in Bath, and yet he was glad enough to dispense with eternal devotion when he discovered I had no dowry!"

"Then you have not forgiven him," said Mrs. Everhart with relief. "I did not think you had, but I could not be sure."

Catherine regarded her mother with a mixture of amazement and amusement. "Why, Mother, you sound quite pleased about it!" she said. "I would have supposed you thought it my Christian duty to forgive and forget."

"Up to a point, yes," said Mrs. Everhart seriously. "I should not like to think of your carrying a grudge, dearest, or brooding continually about Sir Simon's inconstancy. But at the same time I should not like to see you put your trust a second time in a person who has shown himself so utterly untrustworthy the first time around."

"I am quite of your opinion, Mother," said Catherine, smiling. "One would be a fool, or worse than a fool, to do that."

"Then you do mean to refuse Sir Simon?" said her mother.

Catherine shook her head, still smiling. "I didn't say that, Mother. I only said one would be a fool to trust a man who had once proven untrustworthy. Perhaps I *am* a fool."

"No, you are not a fool," said her mother firmly. "I know you are not, though to be sure you have behaved quite unaccountably about this business! I declare I have felt almost sorry for Sir Simon sometimes, the way you have blown first hot and then cold upon him. And he has borne it all like a lamb. Any man of ordinary patience would have given up and gone away long ago."

"His endurance has surprised me," agreed Catherine. "Clearly Simon thrives upon discouragement! I begin to think he never would have jilted me in the first place if I had abused him like a pickpocket all along."

Mrs. Everhart shook her head, but could not help smiling a little at her daughter's words. "Perhaps, but that is nothing to the point now, Catherine," she said. "If you mean to refuse Sir Simon, then you should do it at once and put him out of his misery. As it is, you remind me of Ginger playing with a mouse!"

Catherine laughed and reached out to tickle the cat beneath the chin. "Ginger and I are a good deal alike, I suppose," she said. She sat musing a moment, absently stroking the cat's fur as the smile gradually faded from her face. "I suppose I must have it out with Simon sometime," she said at last. "But you know I cannot refuse to marry him until he asks me, Mother. And up till now he has simply assumed that I am bound to take him back without ever considering I might refuse him."

"Of all the conceit!" said Mrs. Everhart indignantly. Catherine smiled at her indignation, but her face soon grew pensive again.

"I assure you, Mother, that if Sir Simon had ever come out and said, 'Catherine, will you marry me?' I would have turned him down long ago. As it is, I admit it's been rather amusing to see how long he is willing to persevere without encouragement. But the game has begun to pall lately, and I agree with you that it's time to put a stop to it. I expect tomorrow Simon will say something again about renewing our engagement, and then I will tell him that what he wishes is impossible. Will that satisfy you?"

"Yes, to be sure, my dear," said Mrs. Everhart. She looked at her daughter wistfully. "I only hope it satisfies *you.*"

"As much as anything could, I suppose," said Catherine. She

continued to stroke Ginger, her expression pensive. "Tell me, Mother, are you happy here?" she asked suddenly.

"Happy?" said Mrs. Everhart with surprise. "I suppose I am tolerably happy. It is pleasant to be where I can see Sophronia from time to time, and I feel as though we are gradually building a circle of friends and acquaintances in the neighborhood. If I have any complaint, it is that this cottage is a trifle cramped and lacking in modern conveniences. But of course that would probably be the case with any house we could afford."

"Not necessarily,," said Catherine. She hesitated, then went on with spurious gaiety. "You forget the lawsuit that Lord Caldwell is undertaking on our behalf. If it should prove successful, then we might have money enough to move to a larger house in some other neighborhood."

Mrs. Everhart shook her head dubiously. "Perhaps so," she said. "But I can hardly believe the lawsuit *will* prove successful. And even if it does, I daresay most of the money we get will have to go to pay legal costs."

"But if it should not, would you mind moving again, Mother?"

"You seem very eager to move," said Mrs. Everhart, regarding her daughter with surprise. "Don't you like living here, Catherine? I had thought we were settling in quite happily in the neighborhood of Queen's Close."

"So we are, I suppose," said Catherine, turning away. "Never mind, Mother. It was only an idea, and I can see you do not like it."

Observing that her daughter's spirits were dejected, Mrs. Everhart exerted herself to be both cheerful and entertaining for the rest of the day. Catherine saw and appreciated the effort, but still her spirits remained low. When her mother offered to press the dress she was to wear to the abbey the following day, she chose a gown at random out of her wardrobe and was indifferent to her mother's concern that it might not be warm enough. "You know it is almost November now, even if the weather has been more like August," Mrs. Everhart cautioned. "If you intend to wear nothing warmer than a light muslin, you must be sure at least to wear a thick shawl or pelisse over it."

"Yes, Mother," said Catherine listlessly.

Yet it was a fact that when Sir Simon arrived the next morning to take her to the abbey, she forgot all about these maternal solicitations. The sky was so blue and the sun so bright that they seemed irrelevant anyway. Having tied a broad-brimmed hat over her curls, draped a light scarf over her shoulders, and snatched up a fringed and tasseled sunshade, Catherine hurried out to the phaeton, already regretting that she had committed herself to the expedition.

She was not the only one in a joyless mood. Victor, from atop his favorite bay mare, watched with a sad and envious heart as Sir Simon helped Catherine into the phaeton. He thought she looked very lovely in her flowered muslin dress and ribbon-trimmed hat. It seemed to him he would have given anything in the world to have been riding in the phaeton beside her rather than escorting the carriage that contained Lady Anne and the other lady guests. His betrothal and betrothed were wholly distasteful to him at that moment: distasteful because he feared they would tie his hands until it was too late to win Catherine, but also distasteful on their own account.

For Lady Anne, too, was in a bad mood that morning. She had come down to breakfast in an elaborate toilette of fur and velvet, in which she looked most disarmingly lovely. But the moment she had opened her mouth, the effect was spoilt. She complained that the toast was too brown, the tea too weak, and the service too slow and stupid to be borne. When her mother ventured to reprove her for her ill humor, she snapped, "I suppose I have a right to complain if I want to, Mama. This is to be my house, after all, and the servants will be my servants someday. And if they want to please me, they will have to be a little quicker about obeying my orders."

Victor could see that this speech had not sat well with the

servants. It appeared to sit equally ill with his mother, who was regarding Lady Anne with open repugnance. "My dear, you must learn that servants are human, too," she told the pettish beauty. "They may make mistakes, but unless the mistakes are a regular thing it is better to pass them by without comment. And you should learn, too, that when criticism is necessary it is better given in private rather than trumpeted at the breakfast table. Nobody does his best when subjected to public humiliation."

The footman who had been slow about refilling Lady Anne's water glass gave Lady Caldwell a grateful glance. Lady Anne, on the other hand, thrust out her lower lip and flashed her future mother-in-law a look of venomous dislike. Nor did she respond well when Mrs. Watt, in a spirit of helpfulness, criticized the costume she had chosen to wear.

"Those thin shoes will never do, my dear. You will need stout boots if you are to explore the ruins properly. And your dress, too—it is very lovely and becoming, of course, but hardly suitable for the kind of rough sight-seeing we are to do. If I were you, I would change it for something simpler."

"But you are not me, are you, ma'am?" said Lady Anne with an ugly thrust of her chin. "I thank you for your advice, but I don't choose to make a dowd of myself even if I am going on a picnic."

Shocked silence succeeded this speech. Mrs. Watt was a favorite with the whole party, and there were many besides her daughters who resented Lady Anne's snub. Both Lady Caldwell and Sir Simon, with the same charitable intention, began to talk loudly about the weather. The Dowager, after a glance at her daughter, joined in this discussion with enthusiasm.

By talking interminably through the rest of the meal, the three of them managed to gloss over Lady Anne's childish fit of temper. But the memory of it stayed with Victor, and it was strong in his mind now as he watched Catherine settle herself in Sir Simon's phaeton.

"Of course, Catherine has a temper, too," he reminded himself. "She has raked me over the coals half a dozen times during the course of our acquaintance." But Victor found little satisfaction in this kind of sour-grapes philosophizing. For he recognized now what pride and egoism had kept him from seeing before: On every occasion when Catherine had lost her temper with him, there had been ample justification for her doing so.

It had been his own fault that their acquaintance had gotten off on the wrong foot. The fracas with the dog did not count, of course, for that had been merely an unfortunate accident. But his subsequent actions did not bear such an innocent interpretation. He had been offended by the Everharts' desire to remain independent and had sought to impose his generosity on them, even against their will. He had been heavy-handed, obstinate, and insufferably overbearing.

And even this had not been his worst fault. When he found that he had been wrong in his initial opinion of Catherine and that she was not only witty, charming, and lovely, but the woman divinely fashioned to suit him, had he recanted his errors and humbly enrolled himself among her admirers? No, his pride had been such that he could not allow himself to admit he had made a mistake. He had chosen instead to deny his attraction and precipitate himself into an engagement with Lady Anne.

And now here he was, in the bitterest of all bitter predicaments. He was engaged to a woman he did not love and forced to stand by while the woman he did love was courted and perhaps won by another man.

What made it worst of all was that he felt sure in his heart that he could have won Catherine himself if he had tried. Victor tried to dismiss this as merely another instance of pride and egoism. But he was haunted by the remembrance of Catherine's face the other day and the way she had implied it was too late for them both.

As he rode along beside the carriage with Lady Anne and the other ladies, the remembrance continued to haunt him. Up ahead rode Sir Simon in his phaeton, with Catherine beside him. Victor stole frequent glances at the two of them, trying to determine what their relationship might be. In his heart he feared to witness some exchange of tenderness or intimacy between Catherine and her ex-suitor. But there was nothing of that kind to be seen, nor did their attitudes provide any clue as to what footing their relationship might be on. Victor took what comfort he could from this negative evidence, but he wished it had been possible for him to hear as well as see what passed between them during the drive.

If he had been able to hear, undoubtedly he would have been comforted. Catherine, still regretting her consent to Sir Simon's invitation, made short replies to his conversational overtures. But Sir Simon was not at all daunted by her reserve. He merely took it as encouragement to talk about his favorite subject— himself—which he did cheerfully and without interruption all the way to the ruined abbey.

"I've been having some repairs done to my home," he confided to Catherine as they drove. "Not my town house or the house in Bath, but my seat down in Berkshire. As long as I've got to live there, I felt I might as well do something with the wine cellar. The kitchens, too, were pretty hopeless."

"Indeed," was Catherine's polite response.

Sir Simon regarded her out of the corner of his eye. "I thought you'd like to know that I'm having the place brought up to date. It would make things much easier for you if the offices and reception rooms were in order before you move in."

Catherine threw him an incredulous glance. "Before *I* move in?" she said. "Upon my word, I think you go too fast, Simon. I have no plans to move into your house."

Sir Simon laughed, but at the same time looked rather irritated. "Now, Catherine, don't be missish. You know I'm talking about marriage. I wouldn't be bothering about fixing up the house if I wasn't."

"You relieve me," said Catherine ironically.

Sir Simon paid her no heed, but went on talking in an animated voice. "Of course the old place is a bit of a barracks, but I don't despair of making it livable. I never bothered with it before now,

for I didn't see the sense in wasting time and money on a plac
I didn't visit more than once in a twelvemonth. But after we'r
married, I expect we'll be living there most of the year, so w
might as well be comfortable."

Catherine gave him another incredulous look, which cause
Sir Simon to laugh once more. "Now, Catherine, don't say I'r
going too fast for you again! I've already said what are my in
tentions. If you want a proposal in form, you shall have it, bu
since we went through all that business last time around
thought we might dispense with it now."

"Indeed, I think we might," agreed Catherine, her brows draw
ing together.

This was too subtle for Sir Simon, however. There had bee
times during the last few weeks when he had come close t
despairing in his courtship, fearing that Catherine did not mea
to take him back, but on the present occasion his assurance wa
perfect. Had not Catherine accepted his invitation to drive to th
abbey? That must mean that she was softening and that her re
serve was only coyness, as he had first supposed. But he wa
leaving Queen's Close soon, and it was time to put an end t
such coyness. So he talked with complete assurance of his an
Catherine's future life together and detailed all the changes i
house and grounds that he had made on her behalf.

In truth, his loquacity could not have been said to advanc
his cause. Listening to him rattle on and on about patent stoves
curtain linings, and wine cellars, Catherine wondered how sh
could ever have imagined herself in love with such a man. I
was not so much that he took her consent for granted, thoug
that was certainly offensive. But his conversation never ros
above the purely material. His whole life seemed to cente
around an Epicurean desire to have the best of everything
whether it be food, drink, or the appointments of his home.

Of course this was not, strictly speaking, a fatal flaw. Cath
erine was not herself above the enjoyment of fine food and drin
and handsome furnishings. But she perceived for the first tim
that there was something missing from Sir Simon's personality

a touch of whimsy, as it were, or a capability of enjoying the ridiculous. When, for instance, he spoke of sending all the way to China for a special silk he wanted for his drawing room draperies, it was obvious he saw nothing humorous about such an act. It was merely the logical way to go about achieving his desires.

I don't believe he has a sense of humor at all, Catherine thought. *I wonder how I escaped noticing it before? But of course, I was so flattered to have such a sought after man courting me that I never realized he was essentially humorless. No wonder he has put up with my abuse all these weeks! I am merely another of his whims, to be achieved at great cost and then put on display like his drawing room curtains. I expect he would go all the way to China for me, too, if it were necessary.*

This thought made Catherine smile, but she determined not to put her suitor to such a test. She had already told her mother that she would bring an end to Sir Simon's courtship that day, and her determination to do so had been strengthened by his presumptuous behavior during the drive. But she felt it would be better to wait until later in the day to tell him the truth. Sir Simon would probably be angered by her refusal, and it would be awkward to go through the day with an angry man as her escort.

The day was likely to be awkward enough anyway, Catherine reflected gloomily, glancing back to where Victor rode beside Lady Anne's carriage. It would be far better to endure Sir Simon's presumptuous chatter for a few more hours if she could do it without actually committing herself. And since Sir Simon seemed to take her commitment for granted, she had only to keep quiet and endure whatever the rest of the day might bring.

Sixteen

The ruined abbey lay in a little valley nestled among some low hills to the east of Queen's Close. Centuries ago it had been surrounded by thriving fields and meadows, but nature had gradually encroached upon the site, so that only the top of the abbey belltower could now be glimpsed above the trees. The stream that had once provided the monks with water and power to run their mill now ran amid dense growth of beech, oak, and fir.

The thickness of the surrounding woods made reaching the abbey no easy task. There was only one road, and that road was little better than a cart track. It was so narrow and overgrown that Victor and the other gentlemen were forced to give up their place beside the carriage and ride behind it instead. In doing so, Victor lost sight of Sir Simon's phaeton, but when at last he and the others emerged from the woods, he saw it drawn up in a little clearing near the abbey's ruined cathedral.

"By Jove, this is quite a place," observed one of the gentlemen, looking about him. Victor nodded, but he was not looking at the abbey. He was looking toward Sir Simon's phaeton, trying to see where Catherine might be. Sir Simon he had already spied, standing near his horses' heads, but as far as he could tell Catherine was nowhere to be seen.

The other carriage had drawn to a stop by this time, and the young ladies came spilling out of it with exclamations of delight. The Dowager got out, too, moving stiffly as though walking pained her. Last of all came Lady Anne, carrying her sketchbook and pencil and wearing a mutinous expression on her lovely face.

"What a shabby place," she said, her voice rising clearly above the raptures of the other young ladies. "You can barely even see the ruins, Mama. I don't see how I'm to draw anything when there're so many trees around."

"The church is not so overgrown as the rest," said the Dowager in a determinedly cheerful voice. "That would make a charming subject, with the belltower in the background. Let us get your easel and stool from the carriage, and then you can get started. Where did those fools of servants put them, I wonder? Don't say they forgot to pack them after all my instructions!"

"I hope they did forget them," said Lady Anne, throwing down her sketchbook and seating herself petulantly on a heap of stones.

Victor cast a last, longing look toward the ruins where he knew Catherine must be. Then he turned and walked over to where his betrothed and her mother were standing. "May I help you?" he asked, forcing a smile to his lips.

"Yes, Caldwell, if you would be so good," said the Dowager, turning toward him eagerly. "I cannot find where the servants have put Lady Anne's easel and stool."

"They're right here, my lord," said one of the footmen, producing a folding stool and easel from the carriage boot. "Do you want the picnic things out, too?"

"Better wait a bit for those," decided Victor. "Everyone will want to explore the ruins first, I daresay. It may be an hour or two before we're ready to eat, and the food will keep better in the hampers than it will out in the open."

"Very good, my lord," said the footman with a bow. He helped Lady Anne set up her stool and easel, then retired to the carriage with his fellow servants.

"I think I shall return to the carriage, too, and sit down for a while," said the Dowager, addressing herself to her daughter. "Truth to tell, I'm not feeling quite the thing today, Anne dear.

I'll leave you to your sketching. You shall not want for my company, I know, with Lord Caldwell here to keep you entertained." With a nod and a smile at Victor, she began to hobble back toward the carriage.

There was a long silence after the Dowager had departed. Lady Anne slammed her sketchbook onto the easel and began to leaf through it impatiently, looking for a blank page.

"I hope your mother is not actually unwell?" said Victor, forcing himself to speak.

"No, it's only her rheumatism," said Lady Anne shortly. "She always has trouble with her joints when it's raining."

"But it's not raining today," said Victor with surprise. "The sky is quite blue, and I don't see a hint of a rain cloud."

Lady Anne threw him a look of hostility. "Perhaps not, but I daresay it will be raining before long," she said. "Mama's rheumatism is better than any barometer. Wait and see, my lord, and don't say I didn't warn you when it starts to rain."

"I won't," said Victor mildly. For several minutes he said nothing more, and Lady Anne said nothing either. She took up her pencil, traced a single vertical line on the paper, then furiously rubbed it out. This performance she repeated two or three times, until she had rubbed a hole in her sketch paper and had to turn over to a fresh page.

"I suppose these ruins are rather challenging to draw," said Victor by way of consolation. Lady Anne merely gave him a look of dislike and took up her pencil once more. "You know that if you do not care to draw, you need not do so," he suggested. "Perhaps we could join the others in exploring the ruins."

"Perhaps we could if I had not this horrid sketch to make," said Lady Anne, angrily rubbing out another vertical line. "I have you to thank for that, my lord. If you had not told Mama you wanted a sketch of this nasty, tumbledown heap of ruins, I would not have to sit here working while the others are enjoying themselves."

This was so unjust that Victor could only stare at her. Lady Anne drew two or three lines in quick succession, scowled at them, then rubbed them all out. "I never said I wanted a sketch of the abbey!" said Victor. "It was your mother who suggested I might like one. I did nothing but agree."

"It comes to the same thing," said Lady Anne, scrubbing angrily at her paper. "Everyone heard you and Mama talking about it, so now I've got to make a drawing whether I like it or not. And let me tell you, my lord, that the work would go a great deal quicker if you would go sit down somewhere and quit gawking over my shoulder. You're blocking my light completely."

Victor stared at her a long moment. "Perhaps you would rather I went away altogether and let you work in peace?" he suggested.

"Do whatever you like," said Lady Anne, still scrubbing away at her paper. Victor waited for no other permission. He walked briskly toward the ruined doorway, which led into the abbey cathedral.

There were several of the guests wandering about inside the cathedral, gazing up at its still lofty walls pierced by lancet windows. It took Victor only an instant to verify that Catherine was not there. Mrs. Watt was, however, and as soon as she saw him she came hurrying over with a beaming face.

"Indeed, my lord, this is a real treasure trove. A most interesting nave and an apse of really unusual design. A pity the piscina is so much damaged, but that is frequently the case with these old cathedrals. In general, Cromwell's men were only too thorough."

"Yes, a great pity," agreed Victor, trying to ease out of the nearest doorway. But Mrs. Watt took him firmly by the arm and gave him a personally conducted tour of the various unique points of the cathedral. This proved not entirely a waste of time, for while viewing the narthex at the west end he caught a glimpse of Sir Simon walking back and forth beside his phaeton.

Sir Simon's face was fretful, and every now and then he drew out his watch, looked at it, shook his head, and resumed his pacing. Victor could see he was waiting for something. It was not hard to guess what that something must be, seeing that Catherine was still absent from the scene. Victor was mystified to know where she had gone and why Sir Simon should not have accompanied her. But he was not disposed to look a gift horse in the mouth. As soon as he decently could, he excused himself to Mrs. Watt and hurried out of the cathedral.

The abbey was built in the form of a hollow square, with the cathedral forming the north side of it. Victor turned along the east side of the square—a range of rooms now mostly roofless and often reduced to little more than the crumbling outline of four walls.

There was so much underbrush and so many trees intermingled with the fallen stones that it took Victor a considerable time to negotiate this area. He began to feel rather like a child playing hide-and-seek. He also began to feel a certain anxiety as to Catherine's whereabouts. He could see a couple of young ladies out in the abbey courtyard examining the remains of a ruined fountain, but of Catherine there was no sign. Was it possible she had returned to the phaeton and Sir Simon? Just then he came around the corner, into the south side of the square, and there she was. She was standing motionless, watching a pair of rooks circling round in the sky above.

"Hallo, Cousin," said Victor, feeling suddenly rather shy.

Catherine turned to look at him. "Hallo," she said, and there was surprise in her voice. Victor imagined there was also a hint of constraint. She looked about as though searching for someone behind him. "Where is Lady Anne?" she asked.

"She's sketching," said Victor briefly.

"Indeed?" said Catherine and turned back to regard the rooks. "I am surprised you did not choose to stay and keep her company," she added casually over her shoulder.

Victor smiled grimly. "I did stay until I was accused of blocking the light and otherwise impeding the artist's progress. At that point I thought it better to relieve her of my unwanted presence."

"I see," said Catherine. She continued to watch the rooks with apparent absorption.

Victor stood a moment, watching her. "It seems you are without an escort, too, Cousin," he said at last. "Why did Simon not come with you? I saw him waiting by the carriage."

"When he saw the ruins, he decided he did not care to explore them," said Catherine. "I think he was afraid of damaging his boots."

Victor fancied there was a note of derision in her voice, and he was immeasurably cheered by it. "Well, I am not afraid of damaging *my* boots," he said. "Will you accept my escort in his stead, Catherine? You should not be exploring alone, you know, for you might stumble into a hole or twist your ankle on a loose stone or otherwise injure yourself in some way."

Catherine gave him a quizzical look. Victor felt sure she saw through his pretense of concern and understood his real motive, which was a simple desire to be with her. But all she said was, "I should be glad of your company, my lord. The ground is very rough hereabouts, no question."

"Yes, and there's no telling what wild animals may be lurking about," said Victor solemnly. "There might be badgers or snakes or even a bear."

"Or lions and tigers, no doubt," agreed Catherine with only a faint quiver of her lip. "It is reassuring to know you are willing to lay down your life to defend me from such dreadful perils."

"With the greatest pleasure," said Victor, executing a sweeping bow. "I must beg you to watch your step there, Cousin. I don't see any lions or tigers, but you are in imminent danger of snagging your gown on some brambles."

"My noble defender!" said Catherine, carefully lifting her gown free of the brambles.

Encouraged by this exchange, Victor offered her his arm. "It *is* very rough hereabouts, as you say," he said. "And we have a good deal of abbey yet to explore. I would not wish you to become weary betimes."

Catherine slanted him another quizzical look, but accepted the proffered arm. "There does seem to be a good deal of abbey," she said. "I must confess, however, that I can make little of it.

With no furniture and only the walls left standing, the rooms al
look much alike."

"We need Mrs. Watt to tell us which rooms were used fo
what," said Victor. "But, no. On second thought I believe w
may dispense with Mrs. Watt. It happens I have already bee
subjected to a tour of the cathedral under her guidance. An ad
mirable lady, Mrs. Watt, and extraordinarily well informed abou
medieval architecture, but she is an enthusiast, and these enthu
siasts tend to be deucedly long-winded when they get on th
subject of their enthusiasms. We will do better to bungle throug
on our own."

Catherine acquiesced, and together they went along, peepin
through ruined doorways, gazing up at crumbling pillars an
walls, and speculating on the purpose of different rooms.

"I believe this must have been a wine cellar," said Victo
peering with interest into a dark hole dimly visible beneath
fallen tree trunk. "Or, no, more likely it would have been an al
cellar. Growing grapes this far north is an enterprise fraugh
with peril, as my nurserymen could tell you."

"But they do it very successfully nevertheless," said Cather
ine, also inspecting the cellar with interest. "I never tasted suc
grapes as come from your hothouses, my lord. Yes, this doe
look like a cellar of some kind. See, here are some steps goin
down to it. If we had a lantern, we might explore a little belov
ground as well as above."

"Yes, and perhaps uncover a three hundred year old cask o
monastic beer for our efforts!" said Victor. "In truth, I could d
with a pint about now. Exploring ruined abbeys is thirsty work.

Catherine smiled at him. "Yes, it is. But we have no lanter
to locate your beer, and even if we did, I doubt whether thre
hundred year old beer would be worth drinking. You will hav
to make do with whatever beverage you yourself have provide
for our picnic, my lord."

"Alas, merely champagne," said Victor with pretended sor
row. In a more serious voice, he added, "You know, Catherine
I take it hard that you still insist on calling me 'my lord.' I hav

never hesitated to use your Christian name, and I think you might do the same with me. As we are cousins, there can be no impropriety."

Catherine looked at him, no longer smiling. "Perhaps not," she said. "But considering everything that has passed between us, I thought it wisest to preserve those formalities still remaining to us."

Victor did not pretend to misunderstand her. "You are talking about what happened the other night at the ball," he said. "Of course that was an unfortunate episode, but I am glad the subject has come up. I was wanting to discuss it with you anyway, Catherine. In fact that is one of the reasons why I sought you out today. I wanted to apologize—"

"You don't have to apologize," said Catherine, turning away. "I quite understood what happened and why. We discussed all that the other day."

"Did we?" said Victor gently. "I don't think we discussed quite *all* of it, Catherine."

Catherine was still a moment; then she turned around to face him. Her eyes were very clear and green as she looked at him, and Victor could have counted each individual freckle on her nose. He wondered irrelevantly how he could ever have thought them a disfigurement. It seemed to him that nothing could be lovelier than freckles and no woman more lovely or desirable than Catherine herself. He drew a deep breath. "Catherine, I—"

"Don't," said Catherine violently. "Please don't, my lord.

"Why not?" said Victor, looking at her in surprise.

"For the same reasons I gave before. It would be unproductive and—and improper."

"You're wrong," said Victor. "I don't deny that it was improper of me to have kissed you the other day. But all I want to do now is talk to you. May not I say what I feel?"

"It depends on what you feel," said Catherine, steadily returning his gaze. "Any feeling you would not mind owning to in front of Lady Anne would, of course, be perfectly proper to discuss with me."

Victor made an impatient gesture. "It's not so simple as that," he said. He was silent a long time after making this statement, and Catherine was silent, too. At last he gave her a twisted smile. "It's very unfair, isn't it? I believe the whole trouble with you and me was that our acquaintance got started on the wrong foot. We began wrong, and we've been out of step ever since."

Catherine nodded. She was having a difficult time keeping tears out of her eyes, but she was determined to speak lightly. "Yes, it is unfortunate," she said. "But I don't know that our first meeting had so much to do with it. People with such contrary personalities as you and I are bound to clash, just like cats and dogs."

"I don't see that," objected Victor. "I would say that, if anything, the problem is that our personalities are too much alike. We're both proud people who can't bear patronage and pity. And more than anything else, we can't bear having other people tell us what to do."

Catherine was silent. Victor looked down at her. "Isn't it true, Catherine?" he said gently. "Don't you see it, too? I have come to know you rather well this past month or two, I think. And the more I see of you, the more I feel that you are a woman after my own heart."

"That may be," said Catherine, blinking furiously. "But is not all this rather beside the point now, my lord? You are engaged to be married to Lady Anne—and Sir Simon thinks I am engaged to marry him."

"But you are not engaged to him, are you?" asked Victor.

"As to that, my lord, I can only reply by asking you, as I did before, what business is it of yours if I am?"

"None, I know," said Victor unhappily. "At least, I suppose most people would say it was none of my business."

"Then should we not end this discussion, as it can be in no wise productive?"

"Ah, but it can be productive! It can be if you will only listen."

"I'm listening," said Catherine.

Her expression was not encouraging, however, and Victor

paused before going on in a humble voice. "Catherine, I made a mistake. It was a great mistake, but not, as you suppose, an irretrievable one. If I can rectify it so as to place myself once more in my original position, would you—could you consider hearing me more fully on a subject that concerns us both?"

"What you are saying is that, if you can find a way to jilt Lady Anne, you would like to pay your addresses to me," translated Catherine.

A rueful smile appeared on Victor's face. "If you like to put it that way," he said. "But it's not as bad as it sounds, Catherine. Although it's not generally known, my engagement to Lady Anne was provisional in nature, dependent on our coming to agreement on the subject of the marriage settlements. And it has become increasingly clear to me in the past few weeks that no agreement will be possible."

"How foresighted of you to leave such a loophole to wriggle out of," said Catherine admiringly.

Victor ground his teeth. "Catherine, it was no such thing! You must know I entered into the engagement in good faith—though with only half a heart. Oh, I believe you are teasing me." He looked closely into Catherine's face. "Yes, you are teasing me! You see I know you well enough now to know when you are intentionally trying to provoke me."

"Perhaps I am," said Catherine, smiling a little. "At the moment, however, I think it better that you should be provoked."

"And why is that?" demanded Victor. Catherine shook her head, still smiling.

"You may feel you know me quite well by this time, my lord, but you see I have come to know you, too. During our acquaintance you have generally manifested one of two moods toward me: either angry or amorous. And as I wish to avoid any expression of the latter, I think it better to encourage the former."

A reluctant answering smile spread over Victor's face. "You do know me," he said. "But I don't think your plan is working, Catherine." He took a step toward her. Catherine, retreating a step, stumbled over a tree root. Victor hurried forward in time to catch her in his arms.

Catherine laughed weakly. "Now you are in truth my defender," she said. Victor said nothing, but the expression on his face made Catherine catch her breath. "You can let go of me now, my lord," she said in a small voice. "It is not necessary that you hold me any longer."

"Yes, it is. I'm afraid you'll slip away if I don't." Victor looked down at her searchingly. "You won't slip away from me, will you, Catherine?"

Catherine did not answer the question directly. Instead she rolled her eyes heavenward and sighed. "What a fool I am," she said.

"And I am another," said Victor. "But I mean to mend my foolish ways from now on, Catherine. And though it might not appear that way on the surface, I am convinced this is the best way to go about it."

Catherine arched an incredulous brow, but any reply she might have made was effectively stopped by Victor's mouth. "Oh, Catherine," he said, as his arms tightened around her. "I've dreamed about doing this, Catherine—ever since I did it the first time."

"Mmm," said Catherine, her eyes closed. She knew she ought to resist, but it felt so comfortable in Victor's arms—so comfortable and yet at the same time so tremendously exciting. The touch of his lips on hers seemed to leach all power of resistance out of her, leaving her weak and breathless. As Victor commenced another assault on her lips, she managed a feeble protest. "This is wrong, you know," she said.

He laughed. "It doesn't feel wrong to me," he said and kissed her again most thoroughly.

When at last Catherine managed to get her breath, she tried again. "But Lady Anne?" she said.

Victor paused, looking down at her. "I would rather die than marry Lady Anne," he said, speaking the words clearly and deliberately. "I came to that conclusion some weeks ago, but I never felt it so strongly as I do at this moment. Still, you need not feel guilty, Catherine. It's really two separate issues. I shall not marry Lady Anne—and I hope to marry you—but I shall not marry Lady Anne even if you do *not* marry me. I hope that you will marry me, however." He looked down at her earnestly.

"Is this a proposal?" said Catherine, torn between laughter and tears.

"No, merely due notice of my intentions. I shall come and propose to you properly as soon as it is appropriate for me to do so—that is, as soon as I am free of my other engagement. But in the meantime I shall kiss you again, just to give me the inspiration to carry on in the face of difficulties. There undoubtedly will be difficulties, Catherine." He stroked her face gently with one finger. "Still, I have no doubts I will overcome them. When I am kissing you, I feel I could conquer all the world, let alone a few Stoddards." And with this sweeping declaration, he proceeded to kiss Catherine again.

The kiss was a long one and might have been longer had not a loud rumble suddenly shaken the air. "What was that?" exclaimed Victor, lifting his head and looking around.

"It sounded like thunder," said Catherine. "Yes, there it is again, you see." She looked up at the sky. "Good heavens, how dark it has become! And I just felt a drop of rain."

"Rain," said Victor in a bemused voice. "Well, that is one up for Lady Anne, I suppose. Perhaps we had better be getting back to the carriages." He planted a hasty kiss on Catherine's lips. "Whatever happens, don't forget what we were talking about today. You won't forget, Catherine?"

Catherine laughed weakly. "I won't forget," she said.

As they spoke, a strong wind shook the branches of the nearby trees. Then as suddenly as it had started, the wind ceased, and the rain began to fall in earnest. With an exclamation of dismay, Victor caught Catherine's arm. "We must hurry," he said. "You'll be soaked! I wonder what is the quickest way to the carriages?"

"I hear voices over there," said Catherine, pointing through the trees. "I think they're calling for us."

She and Victor began to hurry in the direction of the voices. As they came nearer, they could clearly hear their names being called. "Lord Caldwell! Miss Everhart! Hallo, there! It's started to rain!"

"There's news for us," said Victor, squinting against the sheets of rain that were pouring down around them. Catherine giggled. She was trying to adjust her hat, which Victor had pushed back on its strings during their embrace. But the rain had taken so much of the stiffness out of its brim that she finally pulled it off and cast it aside.

"It's ruined anyway," she said in reply to Victor's questioning look. "The ribbons were bleeding onto the brim. If I wear it any longer, they will bleed onto my dress and ruin it, too."

"I'm sorry," said Victor. As they continued their stumbling progress toward the carriages, he pulled off his own hat and held it out to Catherine. "Would you care to wear mine? It doesn't seem to be bleeding, and it might give you a little protection from the rain."

Catherine laughed and shook her head. "I know how you like to confer benefits, my lord, but I beg you will not be offended if I refuse this one. Indeed, I prefer to brave the rain bareheaded."

They had almost reached the carriages by now. Victor helped Catherine over a low stone wall that intervened, then sprang hastily over himself. "I am not offended at your refusing my hat," he said, as they ran toward the carriages. "But I am offended that after my repeated requests, you still refuse to use my Christian name."

Catherine said nothing until they reached the carriages. Sir Simon was waiting there, and he came forward as soon as he saw her with an air of mingled relief and irritation. "There you are, Catherine! Upon my word, I was about to send my groom out looking for you. Where have you been?"

Catherine looked at him, then at Victor. Her hair hung in bedraggled ringlets about her face, and even her brows and lashes were wet, but there was a sparkle in her eyes. "Oh, I was with Cousin Victor," she said.

Seventeen

So exalted had been Victor's mood as he ran with Catherine
through the rain that he had considered nothing beyond the immediate objective of getting to the carriages. But once he and
Catherine were there, a difficulty arose. Sir Simon's phaeton
was an open one with not even a folding roof to protect him and
his passenger from the rain. As the rain was coming down in
buckets now, this was clearly not a desirable arrangement for
Catherine, yet the only alternative was for her to ride in the
closed carriage with Lady Anne, the Dowager, and the other
ladies. And this Lady Anne was determined she should not do.

"She must ride in the carriage—that's all," said Victor to Sir
Simon.

Sir Simon shot a harried look at the carriage. "Yes, that's what
I thought, too. In fact, I already said as much to the other ladies.
Mrs. Watt and most of the others were willing to double up a
bit so Catherine might have a seat, but Lady Anne wouldn't hear
of it."

"What?" said Victor incredulously.

Sir Simon nodded with gloomy relish. "Yes, that's right,
Caldwell. She said they were full enough in the carriage as it
was and she wasn't going to be crowded by a poor relation. Last
I heard, Lady Stoddard was trying to talk her round, but it didn't
look to me as though she was having much success."

Victor looked toward the carriage. Through the rain-spotted
window he could see the Dowager speaking to her daughter.

Although he could not hear what words were being said, it was easy to see from Lady Anne's mulish expression and from her frequent, violent head shakings that the Dowager's strictures were having no effect. "All right, Simon," said Victor. "I'll have a word with Lady Anne myself and try to make her see reason."

Striding over to the carriage, he swung open the door. "Forgive me for troubling you, but I must ask that you make room for one more," he said with an apologetic smile. "Miss Everhart cannot ride outside in this rain."

"No, to be sure she cannot," said Mrs. Watt warmly. The other ladies murmured agreement—all except Lady Anne, who turned to Victor with flashing eyes.

"I don't care if it is raining! She cannot ride here. We are crowded enough already."

As Victor was trying to decide how best to respond to this speech, Catherine came up beside him. Lady Anne looked at her with distaste. "Upon my word, you cannot really expect us to give her a seat, my lord! Only look at her. Why, she's soaking wet."

"Yes, and indeed I do not want a seat," returned Catherine before Victor could reply. "I am already so wet that a little more rain can do me no harm. Rather than put these ladies to inconvenience, I will ride back the same way I came, with Sir Simon."

Victor hesitated. "I cannot like to see you endure so much discomfort, Catherine," he said.

Catherine smiled. "I doubt I shall be much more uncomfortable outside than in, Victor. Until I can get out of these wet things, there is no helping a certain amount of discomfort. I see no reason why others should be made uncomfortable, too."

"Now I call that a very nice, unselfish attitude," said Mrs. Watt, looking pointedly at Lady Anne. Lady Anne turned her face to the window and pretended not to hear.

"Very well," said Victor after thinking a moment or two. "But indeed, Catherine, I cannot let you ride all the way to Queen's Close in the rain. I will give orders to have the coachman stop at the first inn we come to. There we can get your things dried off and perhaps have something to eat and drink while we are waiting. And with luck the storm will have blown over by the time we are ready to go on again."

This plan being agreed upon, the whole party set off down the narrow lane once more. As soon as they reached the broader high road, Victor spurred his horse so he might ride beside the phaeton instead of the carriage. "Only a little farther, Cousin," he called to Catherine. "I'm sure I remember an inn somewhere hereabouts."

"Yes, I seem to remember one, too," Catherine called back. There were raindrops hanging from her lashes, and her hair was plastered to her head in tight curls, but her manner was relaxed and cheerful.

Sir Simon, on the other hand, looked as out of temper as the proverbial wet hen. "A fine day you picked for your outing, Caldwell," he commented sourly.

"It has been a very fine day for *me*," said Victor with a sideways look at Catherine.

She colored slightly but her eyes sparkled with laughter. "Indeed, I do not mind the rain, Victor," she told him.

He shook his head with pretended wonderment. "Now I would not have expected that statement from *you*, Cousin." Catherine looked at him inquiringly, and he grinned at her. "You compared yourself to a cat once if you remember. And it is a well-known fact that cats dislike the rain and wet. How do you explain that anomaly, O Cousin Cat?"

"I don't explain it," said Catherine, laughing. "I only know it is so."

"Well, I know I'll be deuced glad to get out of this weather," said Sir Simon shortly, hunching his shoulders against the rain's onslaught. "How long till we reach this inn you were talking about?"

"Not much longer, I think. Indeed, I believe I can see the roof of it from here. Pray the landlord has room for us all!"

The inn, when at last it came in sight, proved to be a dilapidated building perched haphazardly beside the high road. It looked deserted as well as dilapidated, so Victor feared it might no longer be operating as a public hostelry. But when he pushed open the door with trepidation, he saw a tidy-looking middle-aged woman wiping down the shabby chairs and tables that lined one side of the room.

"Can I help you, sir?" she inquired civilly when she saw Victor.

"Yes, I have a party outside in need of food and a place to sit out of the rain. I have also a young lady in need of dry clothing. Can you supply me with these things?"

The woman looked dubious. "How many in your party, sir?" she asked.

"Fourteen, ma'am," said Victor.

The woman shook her head, looking around the room with its shabby furnishings. "You can sit here if you like, and welcome," she said. "But I misdoubt I can cook for so many, sir. Indeed, we haven't victuals enough for such a large party."

"Oh, but we have our own victuals," said Victor with sudden recollection. "There are several hampers of food out in the carriage. If you will only let us sit and eat our luncheon here, I will reimburse you for the time and trouble it will cause you."

Having amicably settled the terms for this arrangement, the woman turned her attention to the next item on Victor's list. "A young lady in need of dry clothing, you say. Is this the young lady?" she asked, looking over Victor's shoulder.

Victor turned. There stood Catherine, along with Sir Simon and several of the other guests. Catherine was laughing and shaking her head in reply to a question from Mrs. Watt. She was drenched to the skin, with little rivulets running off her hair and clothing, but instead of looking sodden or bedraggled, she looked quite unexpectedly magnificent. Victor looked and looked again. The other gentlemen were looking, too, and it was not hard to see why. Her wet dress clung to her figure, exposing every curve and refuting in the most inarguable way the Dowager's contention that it was artificial.

"Yes, that is she," said Victor in a reverent voice.

The landlady regarded Catherine appraisingly, then shook her head. "My things wouldn't fit her. She's a deal taller than me and not so stout. But I tell you what, sir. That's naught but a muslin dress she's wearing, and it wouldn't take a minute to iron dry. Let me go put the irons on this minute, and then I'll take her upstairs and let her wear my old wrapper while I see about drying her own things. I'll fetch her a towel, too, so she can dry off her hair a bit."

Victor agreed to these measures, and while the landlady bustled away to see to her irons, he walked over to where Catherine stood.

"You look a very wet Cat, Cousin," he said with a smile. "But our hostess has promised to dry your things for you, and there will be a fire for you to warm yourself by when you come back down."

"And a saucer of milk, I suppose," said Catherine, laughing and running a hand through her wet curls.

As she was speaking, the Dowager and Lady Anne came into the inn. Lady Anne looked about the room with aristocratic disdain and drew her fur-trimmed pelisse closer about her. Then her eyes alighted on Catherine. She drew in her breath, causing the Dowager to look round also.

The Dowager's thin brows drew sharply together. "Disgusting!" she said in an audible voice.

The landlady had returned by this time and was leading Catherine away with many cluckings and expressions of concern. Victor strolled over to the Dowager. "I beg your pardon, ma'am," he said politely. "Did you say something?"

"Disgusting!" repeated the Dowager, her eyes on Catherine's retreating figure. "A most improper display."

"But a *natural* one under the circumstances," said Victor wickedly.

The Dowager made no reply. Nearby, two of the gentlemen guests were discussing in a guarded way Catherine's appearance. "Like Aphrodite, rising from the waves!" declared one with poetic fervor.

Lady Anne heard his remark, too, and a faint flush rose to her cheeks. "I'm hungry," she said, turning abruptly to Victor. "When can we have our luncheon?"

Victor hesitated. "I thought I would order it served as soon as Miss Everhart returns," he said.

Lady Anne's face promptly wrinkled into an ugly scowl. "Why need we wait for *her?*" she said. "She's only a poor relation, for heaven's sake. I can't see why all of you make such a fuss about her. Aphrodite, indeed! Why, she hasn't even a Grecian nose."

Victor wanted to laugh, but it was clearly his duty to pacify his irate betrothed. He reflected guiltily that Lady Anne did indeed have cause to be jealous of Catherine, even if not for the reason she supposed.

"Indeed, you should not have to wait long, Lady Anne," he said soothingly. "The landlady said it would take only a few minutes to dry Miss Everhart's things."

"Well, I want my luncheon now," said Lady Anne in an uncompromising voice. "See that it is served immediately, my lord."

"I'm afraid that is impossible," said Victor in a voice as uncompromising as her own. "I understand that you are hungry, but I think my cousin should be present before I order the meal served."

The Dowager glanced at Victor in a troubled way, then at her daughter. "Anne, dear—" she began.

Lady Anne stamped her foot. "Stay out of this, Mama! It is time Lord Caldwell and I came to an understanding." She looked angrily at Victor. "My lord, I will not be slighted this way for a poor relation. I am your fiancée, and you ought to consider my wishes before anyone else's. If you do not order the luncheon served immediately, then you may consider the engagement between us at an end."

The Dowager drew in her breath in a sharp hiss. "Anne!" she said urgently. "My dear! You do not know what you are saying!"

"I know exactly what I am saying," said Lady Anne, lifting

her chin. "What is it to be, my lord? Will you have luncheon served immediately?"

Victor was stunned by this turn of events, but not so stunned as to neglect a heaven-sent opportunity. "Regretfully, I must still decline to oblige you, ma'am," he said, trying not to sound as jubilant as he felt. "If you choose to dissolve our engagement on such slight grounds, then I can only accede to your wishes."

"No, no," said the Dowager wildly, but Lady Anne merely nodded a cold assent.

"Very well, my lord," she said. "I will see the proper notices are sent to the papers immediately." Turning her back on him and the rest of the company, she retired to the far corner of the room.

All this conversation had of course been perfectly audible to the other guests. There were many whisperings, murmurings, and indignant looks cast at Lady Anne, and not a few sympathetic ones at Victor. Mrs. Watt was heard to audibly remark, "What a little termagant! I believe he is well rid of her." The Dowager gave Mrs. Watt a furious look, then stalked over to join her daughter in the corner.

At this interesting juncture, the door opened and Catherine reentered the room. Thanks to the landlady's skillful iron, her dress had been rendered almost as neat and crisp as when she had first set out that morning. She had combed and towel dried her hair so that, though still damp, it now hung in ordered ringlets. She glanced about the room as though sensing something strained in the atmosphere.

Victor came forward to take her arm, and he did not bother to disguise the triumph in his voice as he said, "Ah, here is Catherine! Now we may have our luncheon."

Eighteen

It might have been expected that a luncheon party containing two people who had broken their engagement only a short time before would have been a tense occasion at best. But for Victor, at least, it was a most festive and memorable meal, and he enjoyed every minute of it.

His chef had provided everything a picnic party could possibly need or desire, and Marie-Claude's efforts lost nothing by being laid out in a shabby inn parlor instead of a grassy meadow. Tablecloths of rich damask hid the stained and scarred wooden tables, and once they had been further embellished with Victor's own silver, crystal, and china, it was, as the landlady declared with admiration, "a spread fit for the King himself."

As for the food, that too was fit for a king. There was fricasseed chicken, cold roast turkey, two kinds of ham, and several pâtés and galantines. There was salad, with oil and vinegar in their individual cruets, ready to mix and toss; there was a great basket of apples, pears, grapes, figs, and damsons. There was bread and butter, cheese and nuts, and a vast selection of pastries, sweet biscuits, creams, cakes, comfits, and other sweetmeats.

Lady Anne and her mother partook but little of this sumptuous feast. They ate by themselves, at the end of a table apart from the other guests. Everyone else did full justice to the food, however, and to the champagne Victor had brought to wash it down.

"More champagne, Cousin Cat?" said Victor, offering the bottle to Catherine with a broad smile. "I'm sorry I can't offer you cream to drink, but the only cream I happen to have is in the form of chantilly."

One or two of the other guests had already whispered to Catherine the news of Victor's broken engagement. She had no trouble understanding his mood, but she felt obliged to murmur a reproof to him as he refilled her glass. "Victor, I must beg you to conduct yourself with a little more sobriety. For a man who has just broken his engagement, you look quite indecently happy!"

"I *feel* indecently happy," returned Victor and daringly pressed his knee against hers under the table. However, he moderated his spirits during the rest of the meal, so that Catherine was only once or twice obliged to give him reproving looks.

When at last the party reached the stage where they could do no more than nibble at nuts and cheese, Victor excused himself to go check on the weather. He found that the worst of the storm had passed, but rain was still falling steadily. "If I was you, m'lord, I'd wait another hour or so before setting out," said his coachman, who was also squinting up at the sky. "Looks to me as though it's clearing a bit to the south. If we wait a while longer, we may be able to drive home as dry and pleasant as you please."

"Very well, we will wait," assented Victor. Now more than ever he wished to spare Catherine the necessity of a ride through the rain—or the even worse necessity of sharing a carriage with Lady Anne. He went back into the inn and announced the news to the party. Warm, dry, and replete with good food, they were quite amenable to the idea of lingering a little longer.

"We can play games to pass the time," cried one of the young ladies. "I know a lovely game, only you need paper and pencil to play it. Has anyone paper and pencil?"

Several of the party did, but most expressed little enthusiasm for the young lady's "lovely game."

"I'd as soon have a game of cards," declared one of the gentlemen. "I'd play a hand or two of whist, if we could make up a table—and if we had some cards."

The landlady was appealed to and obligingly produced several decks of grimy cards. The paper-and-pencil party retired to a corner to pursue their simple pleasures while a couple of tables were hastily cleared for cards. Lady Anne and her mother took part in neither of these two activities, but sat sullenly apart, not talking even to each other.

"Do you care to play cards with us, ma'am?" Victor asked the Dowager, feeling that politeness obliged him to make this inquiry.

"No, thank you, Caldwell," said the Dowager in frosty accents. "I am in no mood for diversion right now."

Victor bowed politely, then retired with alacrity to the whist table. He had contrived to be at the same table as Catherine, though this circumstance was not unalloyed with irritation. Sir Simon, having dried out a bit, had regained his usual good humor, and along with it his old possessive attitude toward Catherine.

"Of course you and I must be partners, Catherine," he remarked as he took his seat at the table.

"No, I am to be her partner," said Victor at once. Sir Simon gave him a surprised and indignant look.

"Upon my word, Caldwell, I don't see where you get that idea," he said. "Catherine must be my partner, of course. That goes without saying."

"No, it doesn't go without saying," contradicted Victor stubbornly. "I have already asked her to be *my* partner."

Mrs. Watt, the fourth member of their party, surveyed them with the indulgent smile of one witnessing a children's squabble. "Let us draw to see who will be partners," she suggested.

The two gentlemen assented unwillingly to this proposition. The cards were drawn, and Victor emerged the winner, a fact that so much delighted him that he could not resist throwing a look of triumph at his rival.

Sir Simon shot him a dark look in return, but his manners were too nice to dispute the matter further. He smiled at Mrs. Watt. "Well, it's you and I against Caldwell and Miss Everhart, ma'am. I don't know about you, but I intend to reduce them to penury in short order."

Catherine said nothing during all this. Victor tried to catch her eye once or twice, but she kept her gaze fixed demurely on the floor. Her manner changed slightly, however, when the cards were dealt. She took up her hand, gave it a quick, comprehensive glance, then looked across at Victor: Deliberately she laid three fingers against her cheek. It looked like a casual gesture, but Victor, an experienced whist player, recognized it with astonishment as a signal.

"Have you played whist much before, Cousin?" he asked.

"A little," she replied with a trace of a smile hovering about her lips. "My father used to be very fond of the game. But it has been more than a year since I have played it."

Notwithstanding this circumstance, she proceeded to lay down her cards with such skill that she and Victor were the winners by a comfortable margin during the first rubber. "Luck, merely luck," decreed Sir Simon as he gathered up the cards. "You shall see that the tide will turn during the second rubber."

But this prophecy proved a false one. He and Mrs. Watt went down even more heavily during the second rubber despite their most earnest efforts.

"What was that you said about the tide turning, Simon?" inquired Victor maliciously as he gathered up the cards.

A reluctant smile appeared on Sir Simon's face. "And so it would have, if it weren't for your partner. As far as I can see, she has saved your groats half a dozen times." He looked admiringly at Catherine. "By Jove, Catherine, you're quite the cardsharp, aren't you? I begin to think the rest of us are mere flats by comparison."

"And I have the same suspicion," said Mrs. Watt, also smiling at Catherine. "Indeed, you are a very clever player, my dear. That was a nice trick you played on us by holding back the queen."

Catherine laughed and shook her head. "Yes, but I took an

awful risk in doing so, ma'am. It might just as easily have resulted in disaster."

She took up the hand that had just been dealt her, absently running her fingers through her hair as she studied the cards. Her hair was drying by this time, and Victor was fascinated to see the returning sheen of copper in her curls as her hand moved through them, fluffing and separating the individual strands of hair.

She looked up and encountered his eye. "You are not attending to your cards, Victor," she said severely.

"No more I am," agreed Victor meekly. He picked up his own cards, but as he attempted to study them he could not resist the urge to watch Catherine out of the corner of her eye. He thought she was aware of his surveillance, and a moment later he was sure of it, for as she laid down her first card she gave him a look at once challenging and laughing.

"See if you can follow that, Cousin! I doubt you know even what suit we play."

Victor opened his eyes. "Hearts, isn't it?" he asked innocently, but Catherine laughed, colored, and shook her head.

"The suit is clubs, my lord, and diamonds are trumps," Mrs. Watt informed him kindly as she laid down the knave of clubs. Victor said nothing, but as he played his own card he smiled at Catherine. She smiled back at him, and there was a light in her eyes that filled him with exultation.

So absorbed was he in the joint pleasures of cards and Catherine that he was oblivious to the passage of time. It was not until a young lady at the next table inquired plaintively if they might soon be able to start back to Queen's Close that he thought to look at his watch. "Good God! However did it get so late? We shall have to start back immediately if we are to reach home before dark. Has the rain stopped?"

"It stopped near an hour ago," volunteered the landlady, who had come into the room to watch the cardplay. "I thought about saying something, but I didn't like to bother you when you was having so much fun with your game."

"Some of us were having fun," said Sir Simon, sourly inspecting the scorecard. "And others of us were merely lambs for the fleecing. Mrs. Watt, we must be glad we were only playing for penny points. As it is, those two have physicked us out of a half crown each."

"Never mind the half crowns, Simon," said Victor, smiling. "I think my cousin and I are content to have the glory of the victory without the spoils. Is it not so, Catherine?"

Catherine gave him a speaking look. "To be sure it is," she said. "I should be greedy to desire more than I have already won today."

"A very pretty speech, my dear," said Mrs. Watt approvingly.

"Pretty good for a girl who lives in a cottage," muttered Lady Anne. She was standing impatiently by the door with her mother, waiting to go out to the carriage. The others began to get up, too, and to don coats, shawls, and scarves.

Victor signaled the footmen to pack up the picnic things and carry them out to the carriage. He then turned to the landlady. "I must thank you for your hospitality, ma'am," he said. "We would have been in great difficulties today if you had not been here to succor us. Here is the payment we agreed on for the use of your rooms—and please accept this also as a token of my gratitude."

The landlady looked down at the golden coins he had pressed in her hand. Her eyes widened. "But, my lord, I didn't do hardly anything!" she protested. "Just to iron the young lady's dress—and perhaps to fetch a bit of mustard for the ham. It don't seem right to take all this money for such a trifle as that."

"Indeed, you did a great deal more than that," said Victor, smiling. "You have provided us with towels, tables, and fires, waited on us all most indefatigably, and tied up your rooms from other trade for the best part of the afternoon."

"Aye, but there wasn't no other trade," protested the landlady. "The rain kept them all away."

"That is quite beside the point. As far as I am concerned, you have earned every penny of that sum. And if you like, I can put you in the way of earning a little more." Victor lowered his voice. "It has just occurred to me that one of our young ladies—the red-haired young lady whose dress you ironed—lost her hat on the way over here. Have you a hat or bonnet you might be willing to part with? I promise I would make it worth your while."

The landlady looked dubiously at Catherine. "A young lady like that couldn't wear just any old hat," she said. "If she has anything, she'll have to have my new bonnet. Very genteel it is, sir, and almost new—I just got it this last Tuesday week. It cost me half a pound and the ribbons tuppence extra. But I'd be willing to let the young lady have it, seeing as she's in such a fix. No, you needn't pay me anything for it, my lord," she added as Victor again opened his purse. "I'm sure you've been generous enough as it is."

Victor insisted on paying her for the bonnet, however, not forgetting the extra tuppence for the ribbons. He was a little nervous after making this transaction, fearing that his new purchase might prove gaudy, vulgar, or otherwise unsuitable for Catherine to wear. But it proved to be a simple cottage bonnet with blue ribbons, altogether modest and inoffensive.

"Here, Cousin," he said, handing it to Catherine with a bow. "Allow me to present you with a substitute for your lost hat." In a lower voice, he added, "It is not so pretty as your other one, I fear, but I thought it would be better than nothing."

"Much better than nothing," said Catherine, accepting the bonnet with a grateful smile. "I was debating whether I ought to tie my scarf over my head, in hopes of making myself less conspicuous on the drive home. But this will do splendidly." As she placed the bonnet on her head, she added, "You must tell me what you paid for this piece of millinery, Victor, so I may reimburse you when I get back home."

Victor hesitated. "Would you not allow me to make you a gift of it?" he asked. "After all, your other one was ruined because of me."

Catherine smiled but shook her head. "Thank you, but you

know my policy as regards such things, Victor," she said. "I prefer—"

"To keep things on a business footing," finished Victor with a wry smile. "Yes, I know you do, and I suppose I must bow to your preferences at present. But there is a time coming when I hope to be on a different footing altogether." He looked significantly at Catherine.

Catherine met his look steadily. "That may be, Victor, but for now I will take nothing for granted. When you have settled all this other business, there will be time enough to talk about it." She glanced at the Dowager and Lady Anne.

"This other business, as you call it, is already settled," returned Victor. "The lady has given me my congé—and given it me in no uncertain terms. Indeed, she has fired me off so publicly that I can bring a host of witnesses to testify to the issue if need be."

Catherine smiled, but there was a serious look in her eyes and a serious note in her voice when she spoke again. "I am sure it is as you say, Victor, but there is bound to be some further discussion between you and Lady Anne's family before you are free to speak of that other matter you allude to. And have you considered that you may not care to speak of it once you are free? You know that, when you have had time to reflect, you may feel rather differently about the situation."

"I shall feel exactly as I feel now," said Victor, with some heat. "A pretty character you give me, Cousin! If you think I go about the countryside throwing out marriage proposals right and left—"

"I don't think it, but I would rather you would prove it to me when the time comes," said Catherine, smiling. "Now we must go, Victor, for the others are waiting for us. Come to me when it is all settled, and we will talk—assuming you do not change your mind between now and then."

"Never fear," said Victor and kissed her hand. "You may look for me tomorrow morning, Catherine. And I shall hope to find you in a more yielding mood than I find you at present!"

Nineteen

Although the luncheon at the inn had proven surprisingly enjoyable, the drive back to Queen's Court was not without its awkward moments.

Politeness obliged Victor to ride once more beside the carriage of ladies. But since Lady Anne resolutely refused to speak to him or even look at him during the drive, this tended to put a damper on the party's spirits. The Dowager, too, was silent and wore a vexed look on her patrician features. Her vexation seemed to be directed more at her daughter than at Victor, however. The other ladies were clearly indignant toward Lady Anne and sympathetic toward Victor, but their sympathy was silent for the most part. Only Mrs. Watt dared to converse with her host despite the glares Lady Anne threw in her direction.

The gentlemen, too, appeared sympathetic to Victor's plight. Several of them made clumsy attempts to console him during the ride home. "I say, Caldwell, I wouldn't let it get you down too badly," whispered one. "Mean to say, if she's going to jaw at you like a Billingsgate fishwife every time you hand another gal a glass of wine, you wouldn't want to marry her anyway, what?"

Victor gravely assented to this proposition and to similar propositions made by the other gentlemen. In truth, his gravity was not altogether a pretense. It was a relief to be rid of Lady Anne, of course, but he was not presumptuous enough to suppose this automatically meant he would win Catherine. Indeed, he felt Catherine had been disturbingly noncommittal when he had spoken to her earlier. The fact that he could not speak to her now contributed to his insecurities. He recognized that etiquette obliged her to ride home with Sir Simon, her original escort, but he could not help wishing it was he rather than Sir Simon who might have the privilege of driving her home.

There were, moreover, grounds for disquiet in Catherine's and Sir Simon's behavior during the drive. Instead of dashing ahead of the others as they had done that morning, they lagged behind—often so far behind that they were out of sight of the rest of the cavalcade. On those occasions when they did come into sight, their heads were together in what seemed to be close and earnest conversation. Victor's neck grew sore with craning around to watch them. When the lane that led to Crossroads Cottage was reached, he watched moodily as the phaeton turned down it. Of course he trusted Catherine, and he had the memory of her kisses to comfort him, but he would have felt better if their love had been an open and published affair instead of the tentative and tacit agreement it was.

He was eager to shake free of the last shackles binding him to the Stoddards so that he might pursue Catherine in good earnest. He had hoped that Lady Anne's very public rejection would suffice to release him from those shackles, but he was not really surprised when, upon reaching Queen's Close, the Dowager summoned both her son and daughter to her rooms for an extended family conference. The upshot was that Victor himself was summoned not an hour later to Lady Stoddard's private sitting room.

Victor could not help feeling a little trepidation as he entered the room. His trepidation was not relieved to find the Dowager alone. Lady Anne and Lord Stoddard were so much the weaker vessels of the Stoddard armada that Victor would have considered their presence as strengthening rather than weakening his position. But the Dowager was a dreadnought, and though it was hard to see how she could make much of the present situation, Victor was not foolish enough to underestimate her. So he entered warily and seated himself in a chair in response to the Dowager's urgings.

"Well, Caldwell, I wonder what we shall do about this foolish child of mine?" she said, addressing him with a genial smile.

Victor cocked a surprised eyebrow. "We, ma'am?" he said. "I do not see that 'we' have anything further to do in the case. Your daughter made her position very clear this afternoon."

The Dowager smiled indulgently. "Ah, you are a great deal too hasty, Caldwell. Of course Anne behaved badly this afternoon, but I assure you that she now regrets her behavior very much. She has already begged my pardon and awaits only the opportunity to beg yours as well."

Victor shook his head. "That is not at all necessary, ma'am," he said. "At this juncture, an interview between Lady Anne and myself could only be painful for us both. If you will give her my assurances that I bear her no hard feelings—"

"But surely you do not mean to abandon your engagement only because of a few thoughtless words spoken in a fit of temper!" exclaimed the Dowager with feigned surprise. "I had thought you more of a man of the world than that, Caldwell."

"You do me too much credit, ma'am," returned Victor. "I am not man of the world enough to persevere in the face of an unequivocal rejection!"

"But it was not precisely a rejection, Caldwell. I admit it may have sounded like one—"

"Very much like one," agreed Victor, with an ironic smile.

"But of course that was only because Anne was out of temper, silly child," said the Dowager, ignoring the interruption. "You must know that she was jealous of your paying so much attention to your cousin, Miss Everhart."

"I am persuaded you are mistaken there, ma'am," said Victor gravely. "Lady Anne is not in the least jealous of my cousin. Why, Miss Everhart has not even a Grecian nose!"

The Dowager let this frivolity pass unremarked. "Of course Anne was very culpable in behaving as she did, but I assure you that she now regrets her behavior very much. If we can all simply forget what happened today and go on as before—"

"I hardly think that is possible, ma'am," said Victor dryly. "Counting the servants, there were more than a dozen witnesses who heard your daughter state that all was at an end between us."

"But surely you are not ungentlemanlike enough to take advantage of that!" exclaimed the Dowager, throwing off the gloves and proceeding to open brawling. "I shall think you an out-and-out villain if you do, Caldwell. To end the engagement after all that has passed would be very prejudicial to my daughter's reputation."

"She ought to have thought of that before she ended it then," said Victor. In a milder voice, he added, "But I am convinced you are mistaken on that score, ma'am. Engagements are ended every day, and I don't believe anyone will think the worse of Lady Anne for admitting she has made a mistake in this matter."

The Dowager merely sniffed. Victor went on, still endeavoring to be conciliating. "Indeed, if I may speak frankly, ma'am, it seems to me that what has happened may be for the best. For some weeks now I have suspected that Lady Anne and I were not really suited to each other. Far better to end things now than to go on with a marriage in which neither party loves nor respects the other."

"Fine words, my lord!" said the Dowager angrily. "But what of my daughter's prospects? The settlement you were to make upon her—"

"Ah, that is another matter that has been concerning me, ma'am. It happens that recently I have incurred some legal expenses that have served to reduce my fund of capital. As things stand at present, I am afraid it is out of my power to make any settlement on Lady Anne."

"Well!" said the Dowager in a voice like a hiss. "Then I must say that settles it, my lord. I could not possibly permit you to marry Anne unless you were prepared to make appropriate financial settlements."

"I was afraid that was the case, ma'am," said Victor meekly. "Give my respects to Lady Anne and tell her I wish her nothing but good for the future. Or if you prefer, I can tell her myself. I suppose I shall be seeing her at dinner this evening."

The Dowager gave him a look of acute dislike. "Under the circumstances, I think it best that Anne should keep to her room tonight," she said coldly. "Stoddard and I, too, shall keep to our rooms. We will, of course, be leaving Queen's Close first thing in the morning. I doubt I shall have opportunity to wait on your mother before I go. Give her my compliments, if you please, along with my gratitude and thanks for her hospitality."

"To be sure I shall," said Victor amiably. As he left the Dowager's rooms, he felt as though the weight of the world had just slipped from his shoulders.

As he passed along the windowed gallery facing the bedchamber doors, he observed that the sun was low in the west. A glance at his watch showed him it was almost dinnertime. Upon consideration, however, Victor thought it as well to fulfill his final promise to the Dowager and pass on her compliments to his mother before he went to change. There were one or two other matters he felt his mother ought to know about before she went down to dinner.

He found Lady Caldwell sitting quietly at her dressing table while her maid arranged a fresh cap atop her head. She turned a pleased but startled look on Victor as he came in. "Dearest, you are not changed yet!" she said. "You will be late for dinner if you don't hurry."

"Then dinner will have to wait," said Victor. "There is something I need to discuss with you immediately, Mama—yes, even before I change."

Lady Caldwell looked at him again, noted the familiar look of determination about his jaw, and gave a resigned sigh. "Very well, dearest," she said. "But do send a message to Marie-Claude and let him know you wish dinner put back. He always gets so upset when meals are delayed."

"Yes, I'll tell him. I must send a message to the kitchen anyway, as it happens." Summoning a footman to the door, Victor instructed him to tell the cook to set dinner back by a half hour. "Also, Lady Stoddard, Lord Stoddard, and Lady Anne will not be coming down this evening," he told the footman. "Please see that trays are sent to their rooms. You might as well send Lord Stoddard a bottle of the Malmsey Madeira while you're at it. It's the last wine of mine he'll ever drink, so I don't mind if he has the best."

Lady Caldwell listened with an expression of amazement as Victor gave these instructions. As soon as the footman had left on his errand, she dismissed her waiting woman with a gentle word of thanks, then turned to her son. "Victor, what in the world has happened? What do you mean by saying this is the last wine of yours Lord Stoddard will ever drink?"

"Exactly what I say, Mama. He's leaving tomorrow, and he'll never be coming back—at least, not if I have anything to say about it." Half smiling and half embarrassed, Victor looked into his mother's eyes. "Mama, would you be very much disappointed to learn Lady Anne has broken off our engagement?"

Lady Caldwell regarded him blankly a moment; then she threw her arms around him. "Oh, Victor!" she said. "Oh, Victor, I am so glad! Not but what I am very sorry, too, dearest, if this comes as a disappointment to you," she added with belated compunction. "But I really feel it is all for the best. Lady Anne is very lovely, of course, but—"

"But she has nothing apart from her loveliness to recommend her," finished Victor ruefully. "I know it well, Mama, and I can't conceive how I was fool enough to propose to her in the first place." He smiled a little, looking down at his mother. "That's what comes of trying to choose a wife in a rational and cold-blooded manner! I think next time I shall try the irrational and hot-blooded approach and see if I do any better."

His mother looked keenly into his face. "And have you a candidate in mind, dearest?" she asked.

"As a matter of fact, I have," said Victor, reddening under her gaze. "I don't know what you will say when I tell you, Mama.

But there, perhaps I won't have to tell you. Ever since I was a child, you have had an annoying way of guessing my thoughts, even before I was sure of them myself sometimes. Is it possible you can guess who the lady is to whom I have irrationally lost my heart?"

A delighted smile appeared on Lady Caldwell's face. "Victor, is it . . . ? Yes, I see that it is! Oh, Victor, I am so happy. Catherine is just the girl for you, and I knew all along you could not be quite indifferent to her. You were so very emphatic about her being plain and disagreeable, you know."

This speech made Victor laugh and shake his head at the same time. "What a pompous fool I was! It would serve me right if she refused me after the mess I have made of things."

"Do you think she *will* refuse you?" said Lady Caldwell anxiously.

Again Victor shook his head. "I hardly know, Mama. She has gone so far as to indicate she doesn't find me personally disagreeable, but it doesn't do to take things for granted with Catherine, I have found. Now that I am free, I intend to press ahead with my suit as quickly as possible, but I wish with all my heart that I had never complicated matters by embroiling myself in this business with the Stoddards."

"Well, I don't suppose Catherine will care for that," said Lady Caldwell. "She knows you are a nobleman and wealthy—a very desirable catch, as I believe it is vulgarly termed. It's only natural that people like the Stoddards should prey on you if they can. You were perhaps a little gullible not to see through them sooner, but I doubt not that Catherine will forgive you if you explain how it was."

"If you put it that way, Mama, I don't know that I want to explain," said Victor, laughing but also looking rather chagrined. "I would almost rather she thought me a knave than a fool!"

"Depend on it, dearest. She already knows you have been a fool," said Lady Caldwell cheerfully. "If you take my advice, you will admit the fact freely and so gain points for candor, at least. And if you like, I will write Catherine a little note, telling her how glad I should be to have her as my daughter-in-law. It is possible she might have some qualms on that account, too, you know."

"Yes, write your little note, Mama," said Victor, smiling. "And I will also take some flowers from the conservatory and any other ammunition I can scrape together. It may be a protracted siege, but I have hopes yet of winning the prize. At least the chief obstacle is out of the way." And he gave his mother an account of all that had happened on the trip to the abbey, suppressing only the mention of the kiss that had taken place between Catherine and him among the abbey ruins.

Lady Caldwell clucked her tongue a good deal on hearing of Lady Anne's behavior and agreed that Victor had been quite justified in taking her rejection as final. "Not that I necessarily blame her, poor child," she added, more leniently. "It is easy to see that she has had no upbringing worth the mentioning. Only look at her brother! Such a boorish man and quite bestial in his habits. I do not scruple to say that I will be glad to see the last of him."

"Yes, a pretty set of relatives I would have foisted upon you, Mama," said Victor with a grimace. "However, my next efforts in that direction should be more satisfactory, always assuming my suit is successful."

"I hope it will be, dearest," said his mother, kissing him. "I can think of nothing I would like better than to have Catherine living here at Queen's Close, unless it would be having Martha along with her."

"I'm one ahead of you there, Mama," said Victor, smiling down at her. "I intend to use all my eloquence to convince both of them to relocate here. But of course it is Catherine who has the deciding vote."

"Well, I wish you luck," said his mother and kissed him again. "Now you really must go and change for dinner, dearest. Much as I dislike giving dull domestic details precedence over a tale of romance, you know Marie-Claude will be most furiously angry if we keep him waiting any longer. You can come to me later tonight and tell me more if you like."

Victor shook his head. "With your permission, Mama, I would rather wait until I have something definite to tell," he said. "I intend to call at the cottage as early as I decently can tomorrow. And then we will see what Catherine will say."

Twenty

Twenty

That evening was a long one for Victor. But it proved not devoid of incident, even in spite of the absence of the Stoddards and in spite of Victor's own impatience to be off to Crossroads Cottage.

One of the most notable incidents was Sir Simon's behavior during dinner. He spoke scarcely at all and seemed not to notice what he ate and drank—an inattention that was out of character to say the least. When Victor saw him absentmindedly accept and drink off a glass of the rum punch that one of the gentlemen guests had insisted on making for the party, he knew something was seriously wrong. Sir Simon abominated punch drinking and had always loudly decried those guilty of spoiling their palates through such a barbaric practice. On this occasion, however, his prejudice seemed to have left him. As soon as the ladies and most of the gentlemen had left the dining room, Victor ventured to ask the reason for his change of heart.

"What?" Sir Simon looked down at his glass as though seeing it for the first time. "Oh, Lord, have I been drinking punch? Well, that just goes to show how upset I am. I didn't even notice." He pushed away his glass with a grimace, then looked at Victor. "I've had quite a shock, you see," he said soberly. "In fact, I don't know when I've been more put about."

"Indeed?" said Victor. Sir Simon nodded, sighed, and buried his face in his hands. It was an attitude of dejection; yet like all Sir Simon's attitudes, there was something a little studied and overblown about it. However genuine his sorrow might be—and it appeared to be genuine, to judge by the uncharacteristic punch drinking—Victor suspected Sir Simon was also obtaining a certain enjoyment from playing the role of a crushed man. He waited impatiently for Sir Simon to go on with his performance.

At last Sir Simon heaved another sigh and raised his face from his hands. "It's all over, Caldwell," he said in a broken voice. "I'm leaving tomorrow and never coming back."

"Indeed," said Victor, lifting his brows. "Well, I am very sorry to hear that, Simon. I had hoped we would be able to show you an enjoyable time, but of course the country is rather slow this time of year for anyone who doesn't hunt or shoot—"

"It's not *that*," said Sir Simon, his voice betraying a hint of irritation. "It's Catherine. It's all over between us, Caldwell. I don't know when I've been so broken up."

Victor gazed at him a moment, then took a drink of his own punch. "Indeed?" he said.

"Indeed, yes. And I wish you'd quit saying, 'Indeed?' as though you didn't believe a word I was saying! I tell you it's all over between Catherine and me. She told me so on the drive home this afternoon. Pretty ironic, isn't it? I mean, what with Lady Anne breaking your engagement at the inn—and then Catherine going and doing the same thing to me not three hours later."

Victor started to say, "Indeed?" once more, but caught himself. "Yes, very ironic," he remarked instead.

Sir Simon nodded morosely. "Well, *I* think it was. I know Catherine's your cousin, Caldwell, but I don't mind saying that I think she's treated me rather badly over this business. Not that she ever actually came out and said she'd marry me, but—well, dash it all. When a girl lets you hang about her for weeks on end and does nothing to discourage you, what *is* one to think? I'm sure she never said a word about *not* marrying me." He regarded Victor with an aggrieved face.

"Did she not?" said Victor. "Not even when you asked her to?"

Sir Simon started to speak, then stopped. "Well, now I come to think of it, I suppose I never did ask her in so many words," he said sheepishly. "I told her I was sorry for not standing by her after her father died—and then I asked her if she minded my coming to call on her now and then. And when she said she didn't mind, I took it for granted she was willing to marry me."

This speech greatly cheered Victor, making him feel he was not the only conceited fool in the world. He had certainly been foolish in his behavior toward Catherine at the beginning of their acquaintance, but he was pleased to think he had learned from his mistakes. Sir Simon, it appeared, had not learned—or perhaps it was merely that he had never understood Catherine in the first place. Victor became increasingly convinced that this was the case as Sir Simon went on speaking.

"Yes, it's been a leveler, to say the least. I never thought for a minute she'd turn me down like that. It happened on the drive home, just after we left the inn. I was talking about where we'd live when we were married, and whether we ought to buy a new traveling chaise or have new upholstery for the old one—just some little thing like that, you know. And she just came right out and said, 'I'm not going to marry you, Simon.' Just like that, out of the blue! I could hardly believe my ears."

"That she had rejected you?" said Victor. "Why not, Simon? You had done the same by her once upon a time, had you not?"

Sir Simon gave him an irritated look. "That was different. I did reject her in a way, I suppose, but that was only because of the money. She understood, or said she did, and so of course I assumed it was all settled between us."

"Obviously you did," said Victor. "But you know understanding and forgiving are not necessarily the same thing."

"I suppose not," said Sir Simon disconsolately. "Though she did say she forgave me, too. Indeed, she was perfectly pleasant about it all, but at the same time she made it clear that there wasn't a ghost of a chance for me. I tell you, Caldwell, it's been a real leveler. I had my heart set on marrying that girl."

"Catherine *is* rather special," said Victor carefully.

"Yes, she is. Though mind you, there're prettier girls out there. Richer ones, too." This thought seemed to give Sir Simon consolation. In a more cheerful voice, he added, "Indeed, if there's one thing that comforts me right now, it's knowing I won't be called on to marry a dowerless girl. I couldn't really like taking a bride who hadn't a sou to her name, though I was willing enough to do it if there wasn't any other way." He sighed. "But all the same, it's going to take me a while to get over this business. Catherine's a deuced attractive girl, Caldwell, though you may not know it."

"I do know it," said Victor.

He felt much better after this interview. It was clear from what Sir Simon had said that he was now out of the running as far as Catherine was concerned. This was a great weight off Victor's mind. Of course Catherine had already assured him that she did not intend to marry Sir Simon, but he could not help fearing that Sir Simon might somehow prevail upon her to change her mind.

By her own admission she had cared for him once, enough to accept a proposal of marriage from him. And though Sir Simon had since proved himself a presumptuous fool who was unworthy of her esteem, Victor felt he had been a fool only slightly less presumptuous than Sir Simon. It would merely be choosing among relative degrees of foolery if it came to an open competition between them, and Victor was not secure enough in his superiority to feel certain of victory.

Now, however, his prospects seemed favorable, if still not quite assured. This made him more than ever impatient for the morrow and his interview with Catherine. So impatient was he that he almost skipped going through the stack of letters and other correspondence that were waiting for him in his study upstairs. The sooner he went to bed, the sooner the morrow would come, and the sooner he would be seeing and talking to Catherine. But a latent sense of duty finally compelled him to walk into the study and flip through the letters, just to confirm that there was nothing urgent among them. When he saw a letter

bearing the direction of his London attorneys, he was glad that
he had.

Opening the letter, he read it through. In a few brief para-
graphs, Mr. Crabtree stated that the action his firm had under-
taken in regard to the estate of the late Matthew Everhart, Esq.,
had been brought to a satisfactory conclusion. Faced with ir-
refutable evidence of his wrongdoing, Mr. Carr had chosen not
to go to trial, as Mr. Crabtree had anticipated, but had agreed to
restore to Mrs. Everhart and her daughter those funds that had
been misappropriated upon the death of his partner.

> *These funds are to be paid over to the Everharts in a
> mixture of cash and securities, subject to your lordship's
> approval. The sum total is not so great as we had hoped,
> amounting to something in the region of thirty thousand
> pounds. But I do not believe we could obtain more from
> Mr. Carr even if we had taken the matter to trial. My
> investigations show that he has continued to dabble in
> speculations since his partner's death, and his financial
> affairs appear to be considerably involved. If we were to
> refuse Carr's offer in hopes of obtaining a better settle-
> ment via the courts, it might well prove that he would be
> unable to pay anything. Accordingly, I have thought it
> best to accept this arrangement on your lordship's behalf
> and proceed with all speed to restore the Everharts' prop-
> erty into their hands.*

The letter went on to detail the nature of the securities involved and the method by which they would be transferred to
the Everharts. Victor read the letter through several times. Of
course he must relay this information to Catherine and her
mother as soon as possible. He ought really to do so when he
visited Crossroads Cottage tomorrow.

But though he was glad to be the bearer of good tidings, Victor
almost wished these particular tidings had not come at this particular time. It was not that he grudged the Everharts their thirty

thousand pounds. Indeed, looking at the matter in a purely self-ish light, he ought to rejoice that the girl he wished to marry would no longer be "without a sou," as Sir Simon had basely described her.

But though Victor's mind revolted from this viewpoint, he could not help wondering uneasily how the improvement of the Everharts' fortunes might affect his courtship of Catherine. It might be that she would not feel obliged to marry at all now that she and her mother had enough money to support themselves comfortably.

Victor tried to put this idea away from him, but it haunted him throughout that night and was still with him the next morning when he awoke to a shining autumn day. Of course he had never suspected Catherine of wishing to marry for money. That idea would have been sufficiently scouted by her behavior in regard to Sir Simon, even had his own knowledge of her character not rendered it ridiculous. But so meanly did Victor now regard himself that he coveted everything that might possibly serve as an advantage in his pursuit of Catherine. He reasoned that his wealth might seem an enticement to a Catherine destitute, while a Catherine financially independent would naturally view it as much less tempting. Indeed, it was possible that a Catherine financially independent might decide she did not need him at all.

Still nervously dwelling on this idea, Victor rose and rang the bell for his valet. As he washed, shaved, and dressed, he played with the idea of withholding the news of the Everharts' windfall for a day or two. If he could obtain Catherine's consent to marry him first, he might afterward reveal to her the news of her improved fortunes without fear of its affecting her decision.

But as he put the finishing touches on his neckcloth in front of the glass, it suddenly came to him what he was doing. He dropped his hands and looked at himself with something approaching dismay. How could he think of asking Catherine to make a decision with such far-reaching consequences and then withhold a piece of information she needed to make her decision an informed one? Did he really wish to win her by means of such a stratagem as that?

"No, I suppose not," Victor told himself glumly. As soon as he had finished with his toilette, he went into his study, picked up the letter, and thrust it in his waistcoat pocket. He resolved that he would present the facts of the case honestly to Catherine, even if doing so should be fatal to his hopes. But it would not be dishonest to add what persuasions he could to his own side of the case. So he provided himself with a lavish bouquet of roses from his conservatory, a basket of grapes from his hot-houses, and a warm note from his mother expressing delight at the prospect of Catherine as a daughter-in-law. Armed with these few uncertain weapons, and feeling as nervous as though he were going into battle against a much better armed foe, Victor set off for Crossroads Cottage.

With so much to carry, he chose to drive his curricle instead of taking the footpath through the woods. Even had he not been so loaded with freight, he would have chosen to drive rather than walk that day, for he wanted to put his case before Catherine as soon as possible. He was eager to learn what might be his fate at her hands.

As he pulled up before the cottage, his eye instantly discerned Catherine's figure seated in one of the wicker chairs that lined the porch. Forgetting all about the fruit and flowers in his haste to get to her, Victor leaped down from the curricle, vaulted the fence, and hurried up the steps of the cottage. "Catherine!" he said.

Catherine looked up. She was wearing a dark green cambric dress with little frills about the neck and sleeves. A worsted shawl was bundled about her shoulders out of deference to the morning chill that still lingered in the air, but her head of ginger curls was bare and gleamed as brightly as the autumn foliage in the garden around her. She had evidently been doing the family mending, for a half-darned stocking reposed in her lap along with a needle, a reel of thread, and a pair of scissors. A basket of other garments lay on the floor beside her.

Something inside the basket moved as Victor came up. He halted halfway up the steps and stared at it, wondering if anxiety and excitement had rendered him delirious. Then a furry orange head reared itself above the basket's rim, and he realized it was merely Ginger, curled up amongst the mending. He smiled in relief, but his expression sobered again as he looked at Catherine.

Catherine had been smiling, too, but when she saw Victor's change of expression her own grew anxious. "What is it, Victor?" she asked.

Without a word, Victor produced the letter from his pocket and handed it to her. She opened it and began to read. "Oh," she said. "Thirty thousand pounds!" She said nothing more as she read through the rest of the letter. When at last she looked up, her eyes were unnaturally bright and her lips tightly compressed. Victor regarded her anxiously, wondering what this portended. She looked back at him a moment, then burst into tears.

This was the last reaction Victor had expected. Forgetting his anxiety, he dropped down on his knees beside her. "Oh, Catherine, what is it?" he said, taking her hand in his. "Why are you crying?"

Still weeping, Catherine gestured toward the letter. "This," she said. "I ought to have known. Oh, Victor, I am so happy." Her eyes, still wet with tears, glowed as she looked at Victor. "You can't think what a relief this is."

"Well, of course money is always useful," said Victor. He was puzzled and a trifle hurt by Catherine's attitude. If she intended to marry him, it did not seem to him that she would have been so elated by the gain of a few thousand pounds.

Catherine was looking down at the letter again. "Yes, of course the money will be useful," she said. "But it isn't really that, Victor. You know we were managing with what we had, and managing quite well on the whole." She paused to wipe her eyes. "But you see, this will mean so much to Mother. She has never said anything, but I know it has grieved her to think that Father made no provision for her as he had promised. This will vindicate him in her eyes—and in mine, too. I am afraid I have been quite angry at him sometimes, thinking he foolishly risked all we had without regard for our future. But I should have known— I should have known. And I have you to thank for it all." Laughing and crying at the same time, she threw her arms around Victor and kissed him soundly.

Victor received the kiss in stunned silence. It had never occurred to him that Catherine would look on the matter in this light. He had imagined her receiving the money as a pleasant boon, or as independence made concrete, but he had never supposed she would see it as an expression of love and concern on the part of her dead father. The revelation served to humble Victor even further in his own esteem. When he remembered that he had almost delayed granting Catherine this happiness for his own selfish purposes, he could not help wincing.

Catherine noticed the wince. She drew back at once, laughing but looking rather embarrassed. "I'm sorry, Victor," she said. "I didn't mean to fly at you like that. But I am so happy—"

"It's all right. I didn't mind at all," said Victor, holding out his arms in an encouraging manner. Catherine did not see fit to embrace him again, however. She merely reseated herself in her chair, her cheeks very pink and her eyes still a little dewy from the tears she had shed.

"Indeed, Victor, this is very good news," she said, picking up the letter from where it had fallen and smoothing it carefully. "I must tell Mother right away. If you will excuse me for a moment—"

"Wait!" said Victor. Catherine had half risen, but she paused to look at him inquiringly. Ginger was looking at him inquiringly, too, from his refuge within the basket. Victor drew a deep breath. "Wait, Catherine. Before you fetch your mother, there is something I must tell you. You know that letter was only one of the reasons I called today—and for me, at least, not the most important reason. Do you remember my telling you yesterday that I would wait upon you first thing this morning?"

Catherine's color grew deeper. "Yes, of course I remember,

Victor," she said. "When I saw you coming up the steps just now, I remembered it very well. But then this letter drove it all out of my mind."

"Well, put it back in your mind if you can," said Victor, taking hold of her hand. "It has never been out of my mind for a minute since I took leave of you yesterday. And if I do not make some of the speeches I have been composing in my head during these last twenty-four hours, I think I shall end up a bedlamite. Sit down, if you will, and compose yourself to listen."

Thus adjured, Catherine seated herself once more in her chair. Victor took the seat beside her, and Ginger emerged from the basket and settled himself on Catherine's lap. Victor reached out a hand to the cat, and after Ginger had sniffed it suspiciously, he consented to let Victor stroke his fur.

"I thought you did not like cats?" said Catherine, regarding these actions with surprise.

Victor smiled at her. "I didn't think I did. But my judgment has been at fault on so many subjects that I am prepared to change my opinion on that subject as well. The plain fact is that I had never had a close acquaintance with a cat before and so did not know exactly what to expect." There was mischief in Victor's eyes as he spoke these last words.

Catherine tried to look prim, but her own eyes were dancing. "Are you talking about me or Ginger, Victor?" she said. "That speech sounds suspiciously like an allegory."

"You are very quick," said Victor approvingly. "Yes, to be sure it is an allegory, Catherine. But I can, if you like, proceed in a more direct fashion. Here is another note for you to read, and while you read it I shall fetch you a few things I brought with me from Queen's Close." After giving Catherine the note from his mother, he went out to the curricle and returned with the basket of fruit and bouquet of flowers.

Catherine glanced at them, then down at the note. "Well," she said, "you seem to be doing this thing in a very thorough fashion, Victor."

"Yes, I flatter myself that I am," said Victor as he reseated himself beside her. "And in that regard, I must mention that I had a conversation with Lady Stoddard last night."

"Oh, yes?" said Catherine, looking up quickly.

"Yes, and the upshot was that all three of the Stoddards shook the dust of Queen's Close from their feet this morning and left, never to return I fervently hope. I am perfectly at liberty now to ask any woman I like to marry me, though I hardly dare hope any sensible woman would want to marry a man who has behaved like such a fool."

Victor looked at Catherine earnestly, but she glanced down at the note in her lap. "You have read my mother's note," he said. "You can see what her feelings are. And I think you know my feelings, Catherine. I love you, and I want nothing so much as to marry you and make you my wife. Can you see your way clear to accepting my proposal of marriage?"

Catherine was quiet a moment, still gazing down at the note in her lap. "Your mother writes very kindly," she said at last. "She, at least, seems to see no objection to our marrying—"

"Nor is there one," said Victor quickly. But Catherine shook her head.

"That is not quite true, Victor. I can think of several objections that might be offered to the idea of a marriage between us. And so, no doubt, can you if you are willing to be honest with yourself."

"Very well. By all means let us be honest with ourselves and each other," said Victor, settling himself to argue the case. "I suppose some people might object to my engaging myself again so soon after breaking off my engagement to Lady Anne."

He gave Catherine a challenging look. She returned it steadily. "Yes, that objection had occurred to me, I must confess," she said.

Victor nodded. "It would, of course. I have no one but myself to blame for having put myself into such a situation. If it would make you feel better, I would be willing to wait a month or two before our engagement was publicly announced." He took Catherine's hand and squeezed it. "But, Catherine, though some people might think it indecently soon even to declare myself, you must know I could not endure waiting a moment longer to tell you how I feel about you. Of course, if you choose to put me off or even refuse me, I must bear it. But if I do lose you, I am determined it shall not be because of any misunderstanding."

Catherine smiled. "Your honesty does you great credit, Victor. In return I shall say honestly that I have no wish to put you off or refuse you. I do think it would be better to delay any public announcement of our engagement, but I see no reason why we may not have a private understanding between ourselves and our families."

"Then you will marry me?" said Victor eagerly. "You have no other objection than that?"

"Well, there is the question of marriage portions," said Catherine. She slanted a rueful smile at him. "I confess that my pride has suffered a little to think that I must marry you without one and have it said that you took a pauper as a bride. But you seem to have effectually done away with that objection." Smiling, she held up the attorney's letter. "It seems I will now have a marriage portion again and cannot refuse you on that account, at least."

"And have you no other objections?" said Victor, pressing her hand.

Catherine was quiet a long moment. "You have spoken of having behaved badly in this business," she said. "But have you reflected that my own behavior has left something to be desired also?" Puzzled, Victor shook his head. "I am referring to Sir Simon, Victor. Surely you have not forgotten about him?"

"I could hardly do that," said Victor, smiling. "But I assure you that I am no longer jealous of Simon, Catherine. Not after last night, when he told me that you had finally put an end to his hopes."

"Yes, *finally*," said Catherine, making a wry face. "But in fact I ought to have done so weeks ago. I knew I ought to, and yet I kept him dangling, just to punish him for having jilted me before." She looked apologetically at Victor. "I'm no angel, Victor. I have a deal of pride and a hasty temper, and sometimes, together, they cause me to do things I later regret. They did on this occasion, and they might do it again. You ought to know that before you go making me proposals of marriage."

Victor laughed and leaned over to kiss her. "My dear Cousin Cat, I do know it," he said. "I got a taste of both your pride and your temper the first time we met—don't you remember?"

Catherine laughed and colored a little. "Yes, of course," she said. "I treated you very badly, didn't I?"

"No worse than I deserved. And I don't think you treated Simon any worse than he deserved either. I've talked with him enough to know what provocation he gave you, and I don't blame you a bit for what you did. In fact, if I'd been in your position, I daresay I'd have thought of a worse punishment for him than merely keeping him dangling for a few weeks."

"Truly, Victor?" said Catherine, giving him a searching look.

"Truly, Catherine," said Victor, smiling into her eyes. "You see we really are a great deal alike. So if you have no further objections . . . ?"

Catherine shook her head slowly. "I do have one more objection, Victor," she said. "And in some ways it is the most insurmountable objection of them all."

"I refuse to believe it," said Victor cheerfully. "The most insurmountable objection to our marrying, as I have already proved, is the clumsy, foolish, and pigheaded way I have conducted myself since the beginning of our acquaintance. And you've already said you don't hold that against me. As far as I'm concerned, any other objection must be a mere trifle."

Catherine smiled, but shook her head again. "No, indeed! I wish it were, but this is quite serious, Victor. I'm not sure I am free to marry anyone just now." Clasping her hands in her lap, she looked earnestly at Victor. "You see, Mother has come to depend on me a great deal since Father's death. She has no one else to look out for her and no one else whom she can really trust. I am afraid that if I were to marry and go off to Queen's Close, she would be very lonely and unhappy."

"Is that all?" said Victor. "My dear, I had already anticipated that difficulty—if difficulty it can be called when it poses no difficulty to anyone. Of course your mother will come to live with us at Queen's Close. There is plenty of room for her there, and my mother would be delighted to have the companion of her childhood where she could see and visit her every day. Already she is making plans to have the suite of rooms next to hers readied for your mother's reception. I mention that fact in hopes of shaming you into accepting my proposal, just in case you feel any qualms about accepting it on its own merits."

Catherine laughed shakily. "No, I have no qualms at all now," she said. Victor bent to kiss her, but his lips had barely touched hers when she drew back with a gasp. "Oh, but there *is* one more thing, Victor!" she said.

"What is it?" asked Victor, pausing in midkiss.

Catherine leaned down and gathered Ginger into her arms. The big cat purred sleepily and reached up to touch her cheek with his paw. With a smile half anxious and half defiant, Catherine regarded Victor. "You see Ginger depends on me, too, Victor. I've had him since he was a kitten, and now that he's getting old it would be heartless to abandon him. I know you don't like cats, but I could not go away and forget about Ginger any more than I could go away and forget about Mother."

Victor's lips twitched. "A case of 'love me, love my cat,' is it?" he said. "Well, why not? Queen's Close is a big place. Even if we do share a roof, I doubt our paths will cross very often."

He stopped. There was a peculiar expression on Catherine's face. "He sleeps on my bed every night," she said in a choked voice.

Victor looked at Ginger, then at Catherine. Finally an unwilling smile appeared on his face. "So be it," he said. "I would rather share you than not have you at all, Cousin Cat."

Ginger yawned as though signifying his uninterest in the negotiations just concluded. Victor laughed and reached down to stroke the cat's fur. Safe in his mistress's arms, he accepted the caress without any objection and even consented to emit a rumbling purr.

"I believe he's beginning to like you," said Catherine, regarding her pet with satisfaction. "I must say, I think it is very generous of you to behave this way, Victor."

"Not at all," said Victor. Smiling, he bent to kiss Catherine. "I have come to think I would quite like to have a cat around the house."

ABOUT THE AUTHOR

Joy Reed lives with her family in Michigan. She is the author of eight Zebra Regency romances, and she is currently working on her ninth, *Miss Chambers Takes Charge,* which will be published in April, 2000. Joy loves hearing from her readers and you may write to her c/o Zebra Books. Please include a self-addressed stamped envelope if you wish a response.

BOOK YOUR PLACE ON OUR WEBSITE AND MAKE THE READING CONNECTION!

We've created a customized website just for our very special readers, where you can get the inside scoop on everything that's going on with Zebra, Pinnacle and Kensington books.

When you come online, you'll have the exciting opportunity to:

- View covers of upcoming books
- Read sample chapters
- Learn about our future publishing schedule (listed by publication month *and author*)
- Find out when your favorite authors will be visiting a city near you
- Search for and order backlist books from our online catalog
- Check out author bios and background information
- Send e-mail to your favorite authors
- Meet the Kensington staff online
- Join us in weekly chats with authors, readers and other guests
- Get writing guidelines
- AND MUCH MORE!

**Visit our website at
http://www.zebrabooks.com**